WICKED DEVIL

Devils of Sun Valley High

DANIELA ROMERO

COFFEE
and
CHARACTERS

For the survivors

Before you Begin...

Wicked Devil is recommended for mature readers 17+

THIS IS YOUR TRIGGER WARNING. If you are easily triggered, Wicked Devil may not be for you. If you would still like to enjoy this book and perhaps gloss over the sensitive scenes, please skim/skip Chapter 25 and Chapter 35

**I do not say this lightly.
This trigger warning is very much necessary.
You have been warned. Now please fasten your seatbelts and enjoy the ride.**

update and get access to all the extra goodies like giveaways, exclusive bonus scenes, and updates on fun sh!t like alternative cover editions and where to grab signed copies.

ONE

Allie

"Alejandra, you're going to be late for school." Janessa calls out using my full name. I sigh and choose to ignore her. She won't think anything of it. She's done her job and informed me of the time, as I'm sure my father instructed her to do. *My father.* Thinking of Gerald Ulrich as anything aside from an absolute and total stranger just feels ... *weird.*

I worry my bottom lip and stare at my reflection in the floor-length mirror, bracing myself for what will be my first day at a new school, in a new town, with a new family. Because clearly, my life wasn't hard enough.

Tears prick my eyes but I blink hard to clear them. *Come on, Allie. Hold it together.* I refuse to allow myself to cry. Not today. Not tomorrow. Not again.

If I do, I'm not sure I'll ever stop.

Sucking in a shuddering breath, I take in my appearance. I look okay, I guess. Except the girl staring back at me is nothing like the Alejandra Ramirez I've been the past seventeen years. She looks preppier. Richer. Honestly, the girl staring back at me looks like a stuck-up bitch.

I look nothing like me. I'm wearing a pair of white skinny jeans that are all but painted onto my body and a soft pink floral top. It has sheer flowing sleeves and exposes a thin strip of my tanned midriff. It's beyond feminine. If my best friend Julio could see me now, he'd probably keel over laughing. This is not my look.

Not that anyone here cares.

Back home, I would have gone to school in ripped jeans, a vintage band tee with an oversized hoodie, and a pair of black K-Swiss sneakers. White if I felt like being fancy that day. It would have been okay to toss my hair into a messy bun and wear my gold hoop earrings with winged eyeliner and little else as far as makeup was concerned. Hell, most days I didn't bother with even the eyeliner. I'd always been a bit of a tomboy. I was still a tomboy.

Though looking at me now, you'd never know it.

But last week when I met my bio-dad, he took one look at me in his polished gray suit and disgust quickly curled his upper lip. Being a tomboy was unacceptable. I needed to look the part, as Janessa—his personal assistant—had reminded me on, so far, three separate occasions in the same number of days. I am Gerald Ulrich's daughter, not some *chola* from the wrong side of town. Gerald is a prominent member of his community. Gerald is a businessman. Gerald has a flashy car and money and probably only carries black credit cards in his wallet.

His daughter needs to hold herself to certain *standards*.

Bring on the eye roll and insert an insane amount of sarcasm here.

Until a week ago, I'd been his estranged and forgotten daughter.

Not anymore.

Not since my mom died.

I rub at the ache in my chest. *Why did you hide all of this from me, Mom? There had to be a reason.*

You'd think given everything I'd been through, the guy would cut me some slack. He'd ... I don't know, try and get to know me.

I huff out a breath and try to squelch the flicker of hurt inside my chest. Mom can't answer my questions. She's dead and I'm here.

Emotion clogs my throat.

Dammit. I refuse to let grief wash over me again. I shouldn't care if I'm not good enough for the guy. I'm here. That means something, right? I mean, he technically fought to get me here.

He could have left me back in Richland. I could have spent the remainder of my senior year as a foster kid. Though, if I'm being entirely honest with myself, I'm not sure I wouldn't have preferred that. At least then I'd be in my hometown. I'd have Julio and Gabe and Felix—my friends —people who actually care about me.

But minors don't get a say in these kinds of things.

If Mom were here, she'd tell me to be strong. To be brave. She should be here. But she isn't, so I need to be brave on my own.

Alrighty then. I can do that.

There's no other alternative.

Janessa had provided my first-day-of-school outfit, along with the rest of my new wardrobe, since mine had been destroyed in the fire. Technically, it isn't really the first day of school. I transferred to Sun Valley High near the end of the first trimester, but it would be *my* first day at this particular school.

Yay.

I hate the outfit. The wardrobe. The makeup and perfumes. But when I hinted that it isn't really my style, she'd scowled as if I'd offended her and then proceeded to remind me that I need to let go of my past.

She hadn't meant to hurt me with her words. At least, I don't think she did. Janessa doesn't strike me as a cruel person. But she thinks my life before the here and now is beneath me. Beneath the Ulrich name. And she's only my bio-dad's assistant.

After she told me how lucky I am to be reunited with my father, I decided it was easier to just go along and not rock the boat. It's my senior year. I'll be eighteen soon and after graduation, I can go back to my old life. I can leave this house. This town. These people.

Then I will grieve.

I leave my long, dark brown hair down, using the flat iron Janessa gave me to straighten it into sleek, glossy strands before applying a hint of makeup.

I need to make a great first impression.

A touch of concealer to hide the bags under my eyes from lack of sleep. A little blush and bronzer to mask my paleness. A touch of mascara and clear lip gloss to make me look a little more alive. Janessa would approve.

It isn't me, and while I hate that, I also know I don't really want to be me right now. I don't want to be the girl who lost her mom. The girl whose boyfriend dumped her the same night. Or the girl who lost her one female friend to that same boyfriend. The jerk had cheated on me. With her. And now, I get to start at a new school and live with a parent I barely know. The cherry on top of the sundae that is my life.

My shoulders slump. I grab my new, pale pink backpack—so not my color—and slide my feet into a pair of Chloe Lauren sneakers. They cost nearly five hundred dollars.

How ridiculous is that? Who spends five hundred dollars on shoes? That's like, rent. Well, maybe not. But it's enough to cover a utility bill and then some.

A sigh escapes me. I know I should be grateful. They're nice. But all the money and high-end stuff makes me a little uncomfortable. I didn't have stuff like this growing up. Mom was a single mom. She worked two jobs to make ends meet and I bought most of my stuff at Ross or Target. You should have seen the look on Janessa's face when I suggested shopping there to replace my things.

I head out of my room, jogging down the stairs and into the kitchen to grab a cup of coffee. Janessa stands by the marble island, a wide smile on her face and no Gerald in sight. She hands me a travel mug. "Here, darling. I made your coffee. We need to get going so you're not late for your first day."

I nod and follow her, quickly scanning the room as I take a sip of the sickly sweet coffee. *Yuck.* I drink my coffee black, not with whatever flavored concoction she's added to the mug. I'm tempted to pour it out and grab a fresh cup. But I don't. That would be *rude.*

Janessa sees my wandering gaze and answers my unspoken question. "Your father is at the office already. His schedule is pretty full and your arrival wasn't"—she pauses— "planned."

I press my lips into a thin line. No, it certainly wasn't. I bet he loved getting *that* particular phone call from social services. I'd stayed with Julio's parents the first week after Mom died while they confirmed my paternity. Dear old

Dad had to be sure. I had hoped to stay with my best friend through my senior year; Julio's parents had been on board with the idea. But as soon as the test came back confirming Gerald Ulrich is my father, that option was thrown out the window.

He wanted me. So, there's that, I remind myself. I am wanted. Though, he'd yet to act like it.

Outside, I climb into Janessa's white Porsche Taycan 4S. It sits ridiculously low to the ground and costs more than my old house did. I googled it. The cost of her car. I don't know how much Gerald pays her to be his personal assistant but it must be a lot if she can afford this. I wouldn't be surprised if she's more than his assistant, though, based on the few times I've seen them together. Office romance is more like it. What a cliché.

He's fifty-two and she's barely graduated college. Easily young enough to be my big sister. But who am I to judge?

Up until a week ago, I didn't even know I had a dad. I mean, obviously I knew someone contributed to me being born and all that, but I didn't know he was out there. That he knew about me. I kinda assumed he was dead if I'm being honest with myself. And I'd been okay with that.

Mom never talked about him and I wasn't one of those kids who felt like I was missing a piece of myself without a dad. She'd always been enough.

Tears sting the backs of my eyes and I push my old memories away.

It takes twenty minutes to get to Sun Valley High. Janessa rambles on about nonsense and I tune her out for most of the drive. Pulling into the school parking lot, her Porsche sticks out like a sore thumb and all eyes turn toward us as she parks. I swallow hard and rush to unbuckle. She puts the car in park as though she plans to come in with me. "I'll be fine," I assure her. "I'm a big girl." I grab my bag, purposefully leaving behind the coffee, and rush to open the door.

"But it's your first day. I can walk you in. I'm sure there's paperwork and—"

"It's okay. I got it." I don't miss the gazes of the students passing by. Some are curious but most look annoyed. I don't want that annoyance to morph into disdain. And I don't want to get labeled as a snob.

I'd had to beg Gerald to let me attend Sun Valley High. He wanted me to go to Suncrest Academy. The top private school in the area and the third most prestigious high school in the country. He didn't like the idea of me attending a public school with the *riffraff* of town. His words, not mine. But ever since winning that one, I hadn't fought him on anything else. Not the clothes. Not the living arrangements. Not the rules—only because I know a losing battle when I see one—but he'd conceded and given me this, and Janessa is about to ruin it.

"Are you sure? Your father wouldn't be happy if— "

"I'm good. Promise." I slam the door behind me, not giving her the chance to comment further, and rush across the parking lot to the school's front entrance. A large red devil mascot stares down at me.

Welcome to Sun Valley High, home of the Red Devils.

I pass through the open doors, a sense of foreboding washing over me, but I quash it.

I will be okay.

Mom was strong. I can be strong, too.

I just have to take things one day at a time.

TWO

Allie

The school was informed of my arrival late last week, so they had everything ready for me. I got my schedule from the school counselor—Mr. Kemp—along with a few forms he said I'd need to take home and bring back with Gerald's signature. I got my locker assignment and combination, though if Sun Valley High is anything like my old school, it would sit empty most of the year. I'll lug my books in my backpack between classes rather than dropping them off in my locker to save on time.

Since Sun Valley High is on a trimester system, I only have four classes. English, Calculus, Spanish 4, and Welding. Calculus will kick my butt. Math was never my strong suit. But the rest should be easy enough to get caught up on.

"Your, umm, Janessa informed me of your ... situation," Mr. Kemp says, a sympathetic frown tugging at his features. "If you need to talk to anyone, my office door is always open."

Always the diligent assistant. Janessa has taken care of everything, including airing my business. *Wonderful.*

"Thanks." I nod, not that I have any plans of taking him up on the offer. But Mr. Kemp seems nice enough. He's younger than most of the faculty I've seen so far. Late twenties, maybe early thirties. He has reddish brown hair and dark blue eyes. He's attractive enough and carries an easy smile. He seems to be one of the *cool* staff members, judging by the number of students shouting out hellos when they walk past his office door. A lot of "Yo, Mr. K." But I don't need a shoulder to cry on and I prefer not to build relationships with guidance counselors. They have the tendency to make things weird. I learned that my freshman year and I don't plan on having a repeat incident.

Besides, he's a stranger. I haven't bothered to confide in my new dad. Why on earth would I confide in *him?*

The warning bell rings signaling that first period is about to start. I stand up to leave, tucking my schedule into the front pocket of my pants. Before I can make it out of his office, a boy saunters in with a swagger and, what I'm sure, is his perpetual smirk. He tilts his head toward Mr. Kemp in greeting before plopping down in the chair I just vacated, not bothering to spare me a glance.

Rude. But, whatever. I'm the new girl. If Sun Valley High is anything like virtually every other high school in America, the students here won't be welcoming. But all of that is a-okay. I don't need to make friends here. I have Julio, Gabe, and Felix to get back to. I don't plan on sticking around long once I graduate.

"Mr. Valdez. To what do I owe the pleasure?" Mr. Kemp says with a stern tone, but I don't miss the slight curve to his mouth. I know right away that this guy, Valdez, is one of those kids who spends a lot of time in the office. There's an air of smug hostility about him, but Mr. Kemp doesn't seem bothered by it. He seems ... amused.

When the boy finally looks my way, he gives me a slow once-over before his upper lip curls in disgust. He mutters, "*Chiflada*," under his breath with a roll of his pretty brown eyes.

"Hey!" I snap. He doesn't know me and I don't care how cute he is, I am not a spoiled brat.

He sneers at me and turns back to Mr. Kemp without bothering to respond to my outburst, a bored look on his face.

"Roman." There was a warning in there, but the boy didn't seem to care.

Mr. Kemp waits.

My cheeks heat and I'm practically vibrating with irritation.

"What? Look at her." Roman shrugs. "Just calling it like I see it."

I bite my bottom lip to keep from snapping at him again before turning to leave. I don't need this.

"Ms. Ulrich," Mr. Kemp calls out.

I freeze. "That's not my name." There's a bite in my tone I hadn't intended but what I said is true. Ulrich isn't my name. Gerald wants me to take his last name. He's some hotshot in town and thinks his name will help open doors for me, but I don't want it. I've been Alejandra Ramirez—Allie for short—for the last seventeen years. I have zero plans of changing that in this life or the next.

Roman's brows lift, sudden interest sparking over our exchange.

"My apologies. *Alejandra.*"

"Allie," I correct again.

He grimaces and tilts his head toward the guy. "Allie, this is Roman. He's a senior, like you. And he happens to also have first period English." And I'm supposed to care why? "He'll show you to your first class and help you settle in. Think of him as your guide for the week."

My mouth drops open and I don't miss the look he directs at Roman. This isn't optional for him. I gape at Mr. Kemp before finding my words. "No, thanks. I'm fine." I try and wave him off.

He releases a sigh and leans back in his chair ignoring me completely. His eyes train on Roman who still has that bored expression on his face. "You here because you mouthed off again?"

Roman shrugs. "Maybe."

I roll my eyes. He's totally one of *those* guys. He's probably a jock too. He definitely looks like the athletic type. Broad shoulders, a muscular build. I can see the hint of a tattoo peeking out of the collar of his shirt too. He's a bad boy and he makes sure everyone knows it. Even his teachers.

I did not have time for a guy like him.

Mr. Kemp smiles. "Well then, rather than the usual detention, you'll have the pleasure of showing Allie around and helping her feel welcome. She's new to Sun Valley High and doesn't know anyone. Be a model student for once and help the girl out."

"I'm good," Roman says. "I'll take the detention."

Thank God.

Mr. Kemp folds his arms across his chest and raises a single brow. "You sure about that? This is your third visit to my office this trimester which means you'll get a full week of detention instead of the usual one day. You'll miss a week's worth of practice..." He trails off and levels Roman with a knowing look.

Roman curses. "That's bullshit." He shoots out of his chair. "You can't do that, Mr. K."

"It's out of my hands," he says, his hands lifted in a placating gesture. "You're the one incapable of keeping your mouth shut. Now, I'm not one to offer alternatives but I don't want to earn Coach Samson's wrath any more than you do. So, what'll it be Mr. Valdez? The girl or detention?"

Roman shoots me a withering glare.

"Wait, don't I get a say in this?" I do not need the kind of attention this will surely draw. I have every intention of blending in with the crowd. Being a nobody here at Sun Valley High. I have a feeling that anyone who associates with this Roman guy is not going to go by unnoticed. He's athletic, good-looking, and more arrogant than any other guy I've had the misfortune of crossing paths with, which can only mean one thing. He's popular. I don't do the popular crowd.

"No," both men say at the same time.

Urgh!

This is so unfair. Why am I being punished for this guy's attitude?

After several tense seconds, Roman mutters out a "fine" and storms past me. When I don't immediately move to follow, he glares back at me from the doorway. "You coming or what? I don't have all day, vanilla."

I bite the inside of my cheek but follow him.

Great. Looks like I'm already off to a great start.

THREE

Roman

Kemp did me a favor saving me from detention. Doesn't mean I have to like it. That girl is going to be a pain in my ass, I can already tell. She has fire. She'll buck against being put in line. And for some strange reason, just the idea of going to battle with her brings eager anticipation and a cruel smile to my face.

I almost feel sorry for the girl. *Almost*. It's her first day here and I don't plan on making it easy for her. Like every other student here at Sun Valley High, she'll need to learn her place. At the bottom.

I rule this school. Me and the other Devils—Dominique Price and Emilio Chavez. Which is how I know that despite his words, Kemp couldn't care less if I'm friendly to the girl. It works in my favor because when she decides she's had enough and goes crying to his office, he'll offer her words of comfort and little else. All he cares about—all any of the teachers at this school care about—is whether or not my friends and I will win the next game and what they need to do to keep us happy so we don't throw the next one to get back at them.

I like to think I'm above such petty bullshit. I have a full-ride scholarship lined up to attend Suncrest U and my performance on the field determines whether I'll keep it. Football is all that matters. I'd never jeopardize my future. But I'm not above holding that threat over the Sun Valley faculty. They need me on the field and they need me to win. It's how the school continues to rake in funding for all the shit they want to do.

I made varsity my freshman year and ever since then, we've gone on undefeated. Football might not seem like a big deal to some, but it opens doors, and not just for the players. It's why the Devils get preferential treatment and why, most of the time, teachers turn a blind eye when we mouth off or start a fight.

But Mrs. Jennings is the one and only teacher who doesn't seem to give a fuck about football. I don't know why she hasn't been fired yet. She's the only one to ever try and call me on my shit. I don't see her lasting long if I or Coach Samson have anything to say about it.

Allie's steps are nearly silent as she follows me down the hallway to first period English. She looks so fucking innocent as she hugs a textbook to her chest, looking around the hallway with wide doe eyes, and all I want to do is dirty her perfect image.

Underneath her first-class exterior is a spitfire just waiting to come out—and that's my job.

She's pretty, if you look past the preppy shit she's wearing. Long, dark hair. Brown eyes. Her white jeans hug her ass and highlight her hips. I wish she was walking in front of me instead of behind so I could watch that ass bounce with every step.

She's most definitely Latina but on the fairer side. Kemp called her Ms. Ulrich and there is only one Ulrich in these parts and he's an old white dude. Bet she's half on her mom's side.

I can already feel that familiar spark of interest. I want to play with her. Make her my shiny new toy. I don't usually bother with the chicks here. Most look at me as a status piece, a way to climb the social ladder. Or they see dollar signs because I'm a beast on the field and they think if they hook me early, they'll live the easy life when I finally go pro.

Allie doesn't seem like those girls. No. Those girls will do damn near anything for my attention. If I ask Allie to get on her knees and suck my dick in the janitor's closet, she'll blush and run the opposite direction. Or maybe I'll see some more of that fire of hers and she'll tell me off? No. Allie isn't the easy lay type. I wonder if I can change that...

My pulse quickens, morphing from a slow and steady thrum to a fast and hard clip just thinking about all the things I want to do to her. I don't care who she's related too. My pops would be pissed if he knew I plan on messing around with this girl. Gerald Ulrich is a big deal in this town. It might make some things difficult for my pops if word made it back to him that I'd sullied the man's daughter.

Good thing I don't care.

We reach the door to first period. The bell's already rung, and the door is closed. I make a big show of swinging it open, letting it slam against the wall so all heads turn in our direction. "After you, vanilla." I wave her in with a flourish.

She scowls and then freezes when she realizes we've grabbed the entire classes' attention.

I smirk. "You going to keep everyone waiting?"

Her cheeks turn an impressive shade of pink as she steps forward. I don't get out of her way, forcing her to brush against me as she passes. The room is quiet, all eyes on us.

She tries to slip into the first available seat. It's in the back row and closest to the door but the girl sitting beside it shakes her head. "You don't want to sit there," she says in a loud whisper.

"Why?"

I snort and the girl flicks her gaze toward me. "It's his seat."

Allie turns to look over her shoulder, giving me another frown.

I offer her a bored expression, wondering if she'll fight back on the seat or do the smart thing and move along. I'm almost disappointed when she huffs and walks toward the front of the class. She has to go around the entire room to reach the last remaining open seat clear on the other side, three rows from the front. By the time she sits, the class still dead silent, her cheeks are a brilliant scarlet. Like a rose. Can't wait to see her thorns.

"Alright class," our teacher begins. She makes Allie introduce herself, doing the whole bit of having her stand up. Asking her where she moved from, does she have any siblings? All the boring basic stuff.

I discover she moved from Richland. No siblings. No pets. She lives with her dad. *Interesting.* I never knew Gerald Ulrich had a daughter. I wonder where he's been hiding her all these years?

When she finally completes her interrogation, Mrs. Beck leaves her alone the rest of the period. I have the advantage of being able to watch her without her being able to watch me in return. She takes notes and actually pays attention. She's a goody-goody for sure which will make it all the more fun when I ruin her. This is just what I needed. Senior year was looking boring but now things are about to get interesting. I can hardly wait.

I get lost in my fantasies; my gaze glued to the back of her head as I imagine all the ways I want to hurt her. Fuck her. Ruin her. It's a sport, and one I just so happen to excel at. If she plays her part well, I might soothe some of the hurt I inflict. We'll see.

When the bell rings, I wait for her just outside the door. Her eyes are downcast as she stares at a piece of paper in her hands, not seeing me until she ends up crushing the paper between our bodies. Contact. *That's what I'm talking about.*

"Watch it, vanilla." I snatch the paper from her fingertips, scanning my eyes over her class schedule. I could have just asked what her next class was, but where's the fun in that?

"Hey!" She tries to grab for it but I lift my hand high above her head, tilting my gaze up to scan over the text. There's no way she can take it back unless I want her to. Or unless she decides to climb me like a tree. I would be okay with that.

She's five-two. Maybe five-three. Tiny in comparison to all six feet of me towering over her. Her hands clench into tiny fists at her sides. Her lips press together in a firm line. My dick twitches in the face of her anger but beyond that initial outburst, she stays silent.

Hmmm... I wonder what it would take for her to really get angry. To break out of this little mold of manners and contained ire?

English, Calculus, Spanish 4 ... hmmm. I eye her. Spanish 4 is for native speakers. I was right in my assumptions about her. "Mexican or Puerto Rican?" I ask, giving her another once-over. I'm betting Mexican but I've been wrong once or twice in my life.

"Mexican."

Right again.

I tuck her schedule into my back pocket and move down the hallway.

"Hey, I need that." She rushes to keep pace with me, her shorter legs having to work double time just to keep up. Students eye her with open interest and I decide to make things interesting.

Without missing a step, I toss an arm over her shoulder and pull her close to my body as I lead her through the halls. She stiffens. "Chill. I'm walking you to class. Just helping out the new girl."

Her mouth tightens but she nods, and I decide not to be a complete ass and slow my steps just a little. Not really for her benefit, but because I want to delay this little stroll and make sure as many students see the two of together as possible.

The guys in the hall eye her with a mix of fascination and confusion. The girls though, they're looking at her with open disdain. Perfect.

I spot one of my best friends—Emilio—further up the hallway waiting for me outside our next class. He lifts a single brow in question. The corner of my mouth lifts and I give him a knowing look. He doesn't bother to hide his annoyance. Emilio isn't one for games. He's one of those *you'll get more bees with honey* types, but he won't interfere. It's not his style to go against me.

I stop when we reach Allie's next class and once again I make a show of opening the door for her, only this time I shove her inside. "Yo, Silvia?" I holler.

Silvia Parish whips her head toward me. Her light brown eyes widen in surprise and the beginning of a smile curls her lips — until she spots Allie.

"Take care of my girl." I wink in Allie's direction and close the door.

Let the chips fall where they may. Silvia is going to have a field day with this one. The girl's been trying to get with me for as long as I can remember. She'll make Allie's life hell if she thinks she's a threat to her shot at the prize, and I just put a bright red bullseye on Allie's forehead.

A small group of students have formed behind me but as soon as I turn, they scatter, even though they'd been waiting to get into the class I just walked away from. I smirk. I'll never tire of being the reigning Devil here.

Emilio is waiting for me outside Economics and he doesn't look pleased. "That the new girl everyone's talking about?"

I shrug. "Might be."

His eyes darken.

"Why? You trying to call dibs or some shit?"

He shakes his head. "Do you always have to be a dick?"

Another shrug. "Don't act like you care."

He punches me in the shoulder. "We had a deal, remember? Football. That was what the three of us are supposed to be focusing on. No chicks. No more head games. We had an agreement, *cabrón*."

"My head is in the game. Stop stressing out over nothing. Kemp asked me to help her out this week as a way to avoid detention. I'm only doing what I was told."

Emilio doesn't look convinced but lets it drop with a shake of his head. "You don't ever do what you're told. Not unless you're getting something out of it. If this game of yours fucks up what we have going on the field, I'm coming for your ass and you know Dom will back me up."

Yeah. Yeah. Whatever.

FOUR

Allie

The looks I'm getting aren't friendly. I'm pretty sure that girl—Silvia—wants to murder me. I didn't miss the way she looked at Roman when he called for her. She all but preened under his attention. Until she saw me. She wants him. I can't really blame her. Before dating my ex—Ryker—I might have wanted him, too. The bad-boy type every girl thinks she can tame. But I learned my lesson going down that road once before and my heart's been through enough as it is.

I'm not some masochist, so she doesn't have anything to worry about from me.

He asked her to take care of me—*his girl*. Does he have any idea how much those two little words have royally screwed me? It's easy to tell Silvia is the one, if not the one and only, Queen B here at Sun Valley High. She's polished within an inch of her life and has a resting bitch face strong enough to peel paint. Following her lead, by the end of the day, every girl in this school is going to hate me.

Thankfully I don't have to sit by her and Calculus passes uneventfully with little more than hushed whispers and sneers aimed in my direction, but what can I do?

Nothing. That's what.

Sun Valley High is everything I expected it to be. Your typical public school. But I failed to take into account just how much of a stir I would cause as the new girl. It didn't help that I'd started school halfway through the first trimester. If I'd started on the very first day of school like everyone else, I might have had a chance of going by unnoticed. Maybe. Probably. Unless I'd run into Roman day one then, too.

I tug at the hem of my shirt, fighting off a wave of self-consciousness. No one here is dressed like me. Janessa made me believe they would be, going on and on about what popular things kids here liked, but she was way off base.

Most of the students are wearing ripped jeans, hoodies, and casual shirts. There's a small cluster of kids dressed to the nines—like Silvia—and I have a feeling they're the Sun Valley elite. The preppy jocks and spoiled rich kids. But their version of preppy is Rock Revival jeans and Free People tops.

Still over the top if you ask me but my shoes cost more than most of their outfits and it doesn't go by unnoticed. I get a lot of whispered "stuck up, bitch" comments directed my way, and by lunch I've picked up a new nickname, "Daddy's little princess."

I hate that one even more than when Roman calls me "vanilla."

He's waiting for me outside of class for lunch, taking me by surprise. I don't delude myself into thinking we'll become friends. Guys like him aren't friends with girls. I know the type. All I am is his punishment and it's evident he isn't happy about it, even if he is toying with me. Ryker used to do crap like this, too.

I follow Roman into the cafeteria and we each grab our lunches before heading to a table in the far-right corner. Two other boys are already seated at it. One is a tall black guy wearing charcoal gray sweatpants, a plain white t-shirt, and rocking a pair of Beast Mode sneakers.

Huh, a Marshawn Lynch fan. I can get behind that.

Well, Marshawn Lynch when he went to the Raiders. I was never one for the Seahawks.

He has full lips, and dark brown, wide-set eyes. His hair is braided tight against his head and he has two slashes through his left brow that I'm pretty sure were shaved into twin lines as opposed to being remnants of a scar. It gives him a more severe look and enhances his already good looks.

I take in the other guy beside him. He's shorter than the first but still around six feet tall. He's Hispanic like Roman and me but his eyes lift at the edges a bit more and his cheekbones are a little sharper. Not Mexican, I don't think. Maybe Honduran. He's the thinnest of the three but his arms are still wrapped in corded muscle. He just hasn't filled out as much.

He wears a white tank top, low slung jeans that expose the top two inches of his black boxers, and a silver chain around his neck.

He's gorgeous. All three of them are. And one look around the cafeteria shows me that these three are the cream of the crop. All of the girls stare at them with lust and hunger on their faces.

Can they be any more obvious?

The other Hispanic guy glances at me as I follow behind Roman, a question in his stare, but Roman doesn't seem inclined to answer.

"Por qué está ella aquí?" *Why is she here?* he asks when we finally reach the table.

Roman grunts, not offering a response. Wonderful.

I debate leaving. I can go to the library, have lunch there. Despite Roman dragging me over, the other two guys don't seem inclined to be all that welcoming, but I decide to introduce myself anyway.

"Me llamo, Alejandra. Allie." I decide to say in Spanish. I don't want to be a jerk, but I don't want him thinking he could use Spanish to talk about me without me realizing what he's saying, either.

He smirks and a surprised laugh escapes him. "Ooo, I love it when a girl speaks Spanish to me." I roll my eyes ignoring his attempt at flirting. He waggles his brows and asks. "What's your story, vanilla?"

Him too? I try not to glower. "It's Allie. Not vanilla," I say, working to keep the bite out of my tone. Neither of these guys did anything wrong to me and I don't want to alienate myself further. But I'm really not on board with the nicknames.

"Whatever you say, vanilla." *Urgh. I just might strangle him.* "I'm Emilio." He points to himself. "That silent fucker is Dom." He indicates the black guy beside him. Dom nods but doesn't seem all that interested in introductions. "There a reason you kicking it at our table? No offense, but we don't like to mix with the fairer sex these days."

Oh. *Oh.* "I'm just ... I mean ... No judgments here." I raise my hands in a placating gesture. "Really. If you're into other guys or each other—"

"We're not gay." Dom deadpans.

My cheeks heat. They're not? "Umm..."

I have no idea what to say.

Dom sighs and shifts to face me. "What Emilio meant to say— " he pauses and smacks him upside the head.

"Hey!"

Dom scowls at Emilio and continues, "...is that it's our senior year. We don't have time for chicks. We're focused on football. Only football. So, if you're trying to get with Ro— "

"I'm not. Oh, my god, I'm really not." My cheeks are flaming by this point but I don't want anyone here getting the wrong idea. "I'm his punishment. That is literally the only reason I'm here right now. Something about him having to show me around this week to avoid detention."

Emilio whistles. "No shit?" He eyes me up and down like I'm a piece of meat before turning to Roman with a wide grin on his face. "How'd you manage to get a hot piece of ass as punishment?" He says it like a joke but there's a certain level of concern in the question.

"It's not a big deal. Just Mrs. Jennings being Mrs. Jennings."

Both guys groan. I ignore what's said next and decide to check my cell.

I pull out my phone. It was buzzing on and off during first and second period but I didn't want to risk looking at it and having it confiscated. I don't know how strict the teachers are here.

I scroll through my text messages. I have three from my ex, Ryker.

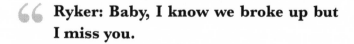

Ryker: Baby, I know we broke up but I miss you.

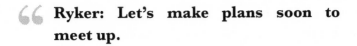

> **Ryker: Let's make plans soon to meet up.**

> **Ryker: I miss your kiss. The way you taste...**

Gross. The last includes a photograph. A dick pic. Wonderful. What an asshole. He broke up with me. The day my mom died. Who does that? And he cheated on me. With my only female friend. And none of these texts are an apology for that. Not that I'd forgive him even if they were. Instead he treats me like some booty call as if I asked for a stupid picture of his pencil dick.

I delete his messages, not bothering to respond and move on to the other two waiting for me.

> **Adriana: I know I messed up. I'm sorry. Talk to me? Please.**

Delete.

66 **Julio: If Adriana messages you, ignore her. She and Ryker are still fucking.**

I sigh. At least he doesn't sugarcoat it.

66 **Me: Thanks for the heads up.**

He responds almost instantly.

66 **Julio: I've always got your back. Miss you *Chica*.**

66 **Me: Miss you too J.**

Julio's been my best friend since grade school. Ever since Mimi Johnson stole my ice cream cone in the park and called me stupid. He told her she was fugly and that my stolen ice cream would make her fat. We've been thick as thieves ever since.

J knows me inside and out and I know he's always got my back. Only now he's got it from two hours away. I hate the distance between us, but I just need to make it through this year.

With a smile still on my face, I shove my phone back in my pocket. When I look up, Roman is staring at me. He doesn't say anything so neither do I. The other guys seem to consider me and then Emilio asks, "Hot boyfriend?"

I snort "No. Just some people from my old school." I tell him. There's no reason to lie.

He lifts a brow as if to say, *elaborate.*

When I don't, he says, "You get dick pics from people often?"

Oh, my god. He saw that?

"What? No." I hide my face behind my hands and all three chuckle. "It's not what you think. God. No." I shake my head and they laugh harder.

"Damn, vanilla. No judgment here. You can have all the dick pics you want. Tell you what, I can go in the bathroom right now and take one for you. Give me your digits and we'll make shit happen."

Mortification rolls through me. "It's not..." I shake my head in a definite no before exhaling an exasperated sigh. "My ex is trying to get me back. Sort of." I frown. "I'm pretty sure what he really wants is a booty call but that's not happening. So, no, I don't get dick pics often. He's just a moron and hasn't realized it's over. And no, I don't want pictures of your dick, either. Thanks."

"Holy shit, vanilla. Your life is the prequel to a telenovela. What else you got?"

I snort. "Nothing. My life is not exciting." A little tragic, maybe, but no one else needs to know those parts.

The guys talk football the rest of lunch. All three are on the varsity team which isn't surprising. There's a game on Friday but they don't seem concerned about it. The game two weeks from now has most of their attention. It's Sun Valley High's rival game against the Suncrest Academy Saints. Based on their expressions, it's a really big deal.

I try and track their conversation. Julio and I use to watch football together. Ryker plays for my old school but I never really went to his games. I'd just watch NFL with Julio and sometimes the high school recaps if the game was big enough that the news decided to cover it.

Adriana was always there, though. She was on the cheer squad. Maybe that was one of the reasons he never asked me to come?

As the guys talk, I learn that Dom is the school's quarterback. Roman plays wide receiver. And Emilio is a cornerback. All three seem to live and breathe football. Emilio makes a point of including me in their conversation, which is a little surprising since he didn't seem thrilled that I was here in the first place.

He peppers me with questions but I don't have much to contribute. I understand the game. I know how plays work and I thankfully don't get lost when Dom goes off on a tangent about a blitz the Saints made that worked out for them in last week's game against another school. The guys are intense and it's clear they do their homework on their opponents. I surprise them a few times when it becomes clear I know what they're talking about and I start to find my footing a bit.

These guys aren't that different from my crew back home. Roman is a lot like Julio. The leader of the pack, though more brooding and definitely more of a player. Emilio has a carefree attitude like Felix. He's quick with the jokes and always wears a comfortable smile. And Dom is the strong silent type like Gabe.

I start to feel like maybe today doesn't completely suck but I don't delude myself into thinking that once Roman's little punishment ends that any of these guys will want to still talk to me. Emilio already made it clear they don't mix with the girls of this school. They can't afford any distractions. Aside from that, it's evident we come from different social circles. They're the guys all the girls want and the guys all the other guys want to be. You can see it in the way everyone watches them. And me, I'm the girl who just wants to survive her senior year.

When the bell rings, Roman dumps his tray and presumably heads toward Spanish, not bothering to wait for me. I consider calling out for him but immediately decide against it. He seemed to grow more and more agitated as lunch progressed. I haven't done anything to him so I don't know why he has such a stick up his butt.

No one talks to me as I wander the halls trying to find my Spanish class. Roman still has my schedule and I don't really know where I'm going. I try and ask a few students but all I get are sneers and eye rolls. No words. No help.

Yes, I'm the new girl.

Yes, I sat at lunch with the cute guys who I've now learned are also the school's jocks.

And no. I didn't want to cause any waves in the stupid high school social hierarchy.

I didn't miss the fact that the guys don't sit with the rest of the football players, who are easy enough to spot based on their rowdy behavior and letterman jackets. But if you're the QB like Dom, you're practically high school royalty. So, if the guys always stuck to themselves, me being there isn't going to go over well with the rest of the school.

Which was made abundantly clear once I got a new copy of my schedule from the front office and stepped inside my next class.

The teacher doesn't make me stand and do the whole introductions thing, for which I'm grateful. I hate being the new girl and I hate being put on the spot even more. I already feel out of place and the extra attention and scrutiny makes my skin itch. The girl who sits behind me makes it a point to kick the back of my chair at least four times during class, and then when class ends, she calls me a slut and knocks my notebook off my desk as she walks past.

Wonderful.

Roman sees all of it and his only reaction is to smirk. This guy is some piece of work. One minute he's kind of nice and helps me and then the next he's openly hostile and encouraging this kind of behavior toward me. I start to wonder if maybe he called me "his girl" last period just to make things difficult for me. Like he somehow knew the reaction that would garner.

When she walks past him, he makes a show of throwing his arm around her and walking out of the class beside her.

So dumb.

I ignore it all, though, and head to my last class of the day. Welding.

After a quick trip to the restroom, I make it to class just after the bell rings. I'm greeted by a sea of confused expressions as I stand in the open doorway. There are maybe twenty kids in the class and all of them are boys. Not surprising. The class has already started and I don't want to interrupt, but when the teacher notices everyone's confused faces staring at something behind him, he turns and spots me.

"Are you lost?" he asks me with a frown.

I shake my head. "No. I have Welding fourth period," I tell him, stepping closer to hand him my schedule. "I'm a late transfer," I add sheepishly.

His frown deepens, his nearly white brows furrowing together like two fuzzy caterpillars.

"Were you dropped in here because of space issues?" he asks, seemingly still confused.

"No. I chose Welding as my elective."

That throws him off.

"Are you one of the boy-crazy ones?" There's annoyance in his tone.

I snort. At my old school, a lot of the girls would take weightlifting as their P.E. elective because all the jocks took it. It was a good way to bump elbows with the cool crowd, but I wasn't one of those girls. I actually liked this class.

"No, sir. I enjoy welding."

He raises a single brow. "You've welded before?"

I nod. "My old school offered it so this'll be my third year. I'm decent at MIG and Stick. My TIG welding is," I lift my hand and twist it side to side. "It's just okay."

His eyes widen but he nods his head and returns my schedule. "Alright then. Grab a seat. We're doing a bit of a refresher today, anyway."

I head to the only available chair. When I sit down, a boy leans over his desk toward me. "Hey, you're new here, right?"

I nod, bracing myself for whatever he says next.

"I'm Aaron. What's your name?"

"Allie," I say, surprised by the introduction.

"Cool. Nice to meet you, Allie." He flashes me a brilliant smile. He's cute. *Really cute.* He has shaggy blond hair that hangs down in his face and bright green eyes. Dressed in black Volcom pants and an O'Neill shirt he gives off a skater vibe, but it's cool and it definitely fits him. My assumption is confirmed when I spot the skateboard resting on the floor beside his desk.

I match his smile before turning my attention to our instructor.

Most of what he goes over I already know. He gives us a refresher on safety protocols. I guess they had an injury the day before.

Always wear your face shield. Always wear closed-toe shoes. Wear a long-sleeved nonflammable shirt when welding along with a welding jacket. Wear gloves.

He shows us where the eyewash station is and then goes over the equipment. Most of the kids ignore him but I pay attention just in case there's anything he might do differently from what I learned before.

"First trimester we cover MIG welding," Aaron tells me as we resume our seats. No surprise there since it's the easiest form of welding there is. It's like the hot glue gun of the welding world.

The teacher—Mr. Moyer—explains how the welder works and just as he starts diving into how to prep for your weld, the bell rings, signaling the end of class.

"We'll continue where we left off tomorrow," he says to the class. "Study your syllabus and get a parent signature on your safety waiver," he reminds me as I grab my things to head out.

I nod and pull my phone from my pocket, realizing I have a text.

It's from Janessa.

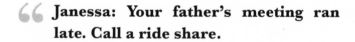

Janessa: Your father's meeting ran late. Call a ride share.

I frown but then decide it's probably good his meeting ran late. I wasn't exactly looking forward to the ride home with Gerald. I search the App Store on my phone for the Uber app and hit download. I haven't needed to Uber before, but it's not rocket science.

Aaron sidles up beside me and peaks over my shoulder at my phone.

"Something wrong?"

"No. Ger—my dad is just running late so I'm gonna catch an Uber."

"I can give you a ride."

"You don't even know me." I give him an incredulous look.

He shrugs and gives me back a boyish grin. "I know. But I'd like to get to know you."

Heat creeps up my face, but before I can respond, Roman is suddenly beside me. "Back off, Henderson." He shoves Aaron back into the lockers.

My mouth drops open and I grab for his arm. "What the heck, Roman?"

He raises a brow and the corners of his mouth lift in a devilish smirk. "Heck? Really?"

I glower at him. As Aaron shoves away from the locker, his face red and angry, I jump between them. With my back to Aaron, I scowl at Roman. "School's out. You don't need to babysit me anymore." Not that he was doing a great job of it to begin with.

Dom and Emilio walk up beside him and both level menacing gazes on the boy behind me.

"What is your deal?" I ask, not understanding where all of their hostility is coming from.

"You know him?" Emilio asks, tipping his chin toward Aaron.

I shrug. "Sort of. Yeah. We have Welding together." I can feel the anger radiating off Roman in front of me. His eyes are narrowed, his hands clenched into white fists at his sides, but he doesn't say anything. He just stares Aaron down behind me like he can kill him with just a look.

"He's bad news, vanilla. Make sure you don't ever get in a car with this one." Emilio says.

"Would you stop calling me that? I have a name." And why does he care if I maybe get a ride with Aaron? Is he some daredevil driver or something?

No one says anything for several seconds. I feel Aaron's hand on my hip a moment later and I turn to face him. "I'll catch you later," he grits out between clenched teeth. I give him a tight smile and a nod.

What else can I do? *So much for the lift.*

The three guys in front of me watch Aaron's retreating form with varying degrees of hostility. When I turn to head the same direction, Roman's hand shoots out, grasping me by my wrist.

"Henderson is bad news."

I pull away. "And I'm just supposed to take your word for it?"

He nods.

"Look. I don't know what your deal is but Aaron is the only person who's bothered being nice to me. I'm not going to stay away from him just because you say so."

"Hey! We've been nice," Emilio calls out.

I shrug. "You two have," I say, signaling to him and Dom. "But he," I point a finger in Roman's direction. "along with the rest of this school, have been complete jerks."

A tick forms on Roman's jaw but I'm not having it. I might look the part of a meek little wallflower but I'm not one.

I storm off toward the school's exit, ignoring him as he calls after me.

FIVE

Allie

The week goes by in a blur. After that first day, Roman stopped playing guide and I was fine with it. Sure, I missed the glimmer of camaraderie we shared at lunch that first day, but I wasn't looking for a replacement crew. Besides, he's a brooding jerk anyway.

I ignore him whenever I see him in first period or in the halls, and the rest of the school—aside from Aaron— thankfully decides to ignore me now that they've realized hanging out with Roman and his crew isn't going to be a repeat event.

Adjusting to life in Sun Valley is a new experience and it feels a lot like being trapped in purgatory. I see Gerald's assistant more than I see him. She's there every morning at half past seven, eager and willing to cart me off to school, though all week I've had to catch a ride share to get home.

It would be easier if I just took the bus but the look on Janessa's face when I'd made the suggestion made that an immediate no. The bus is beneath me. Seems fine for everyone else in this town but somehow an Uber is the classier, more refined choice.

Urgh.

I'm making my way out of my last class—eyes glued to my phone as I punch in the address of the school for a ride request—when Aaron calls out to me in the hallway.

"Hey."

I slow my steps and wait for him to catch up.

"Hey." I smile.

He tugs on the straps of his backpack, his skateboard strapped to the back of it, and a boyish smile on his face. "Got any plans this weekend?"

I shrug. "Not really. I'm still the new girl so I'll probably just hang out at home and get caught up on homework."

He nods and sucks on his upper lip. "Well, there's a party this weekend. It's sort of a pre-game tradition. A bunch of us go out in the woods and camp for the weekend before our big rival game against the Saints."

"You're into football?" I ask giving him a speculative look.

"Nah. But I'm into camping and partying so..." He shrugs.

"Oh. Cool," I say, not really sure where he's going with this.

He tilts his head, a question in his eyes, but I'm not sure what response he's looking for. He runs a hand through his hair and shakes his head. "So, uh, would you maybe want to come? With me, I mean? I can pick you up if you're cool with that..." He trails off and looks away, a slight blush on his cheeks.

Oh. *Oh!* "You're inviting me?" I squeak out. As soon as the words leave my lips, I want to smack myself.

The corners of his mouth twitch into the beginning of a smirk. "Yeah. I think it'd be fun. If you came, I mean. I think you would have a lot of fun."

I bite my bottom lip. I want to go. I could really use some fun in my life right now. And Aaron is the only person who talks to me, so I'm banking on him being my one and only friend while I'm stuck here. I don't want to disappoint him by turning him down, but would Gerald even let me go? How would I even go about asking him? I haven't seen him all week. Literally not once. He's always working and his meetings seem to run late every night.

"Um...." I glance around the hallway and I catch sight of Roman, Emilio, and Dom. All three of them are standing by the exit with matching scowls on their faces as they watch our exchange. I still don't know what their deal is with Aaron, but thankfully, this time they keep their distance.

Aaron follows my gaze and sees them, his grin quickly morphing into a grimace. "Are you into those guys?"

I'm a little thrown by his question. "What? No!" I rush to say.

He considers me for a moment like he isn't quite sure whether or not to believe me. "You sure? All the girls at Sun Valley High like the Devils."

"Definitely not this one."

He releases a relieved sigh. "That's good. They're assholes. I wouldn't want to see you hurt."

I don't argue because, well, they are, and the fact he's concerned about me is kinda nice.

I pull out my phone and shoot a text off to Janessa.

> **Me: Do you think my dad will let me go out with a friend this weekend?**

> **Janessa: Dates, Times, Location?**

I turn to Aaron. "My dad's assistant wants to know for how long and where we'd be going?"

He lifts a brow. "Assistant?"

"Yeah. I know it's weird but I'll get a faster response if I go through her rather than trying to track him down."

He nods like he understands. "Shadle Creek. Today until Sunday morning."

I shoot her the information and watch as the three little dots appear. Then they stop. Then they appear again. *Urgh.* Come on. Answer already.

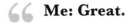 **Janessa: That's fine. Your father says to use the credit card he gave you if you need anything. He'll try and schedule a dinner with you when you get**

back.

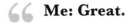 **Me: Great.**

I roll my eyes. I love the idea of having to schedule a dinner with my dad. I shove my phone back into my pocket and turn to meet Aaron's expectant gaze. "I'm in."

His eyes light up. "Really?"

I nod.

"Awesome!"

Aaron gives me a ride home and follows me inside. He sits on the edge of my bed, watching as I hastily pack a bag with the essentials. Underwear. Toothbrush. Hairbrush. Toothpaste. I'm not sure what all I'll need but it doesn't take long to realize none of the clothes Janessa got for me are going to work. Everything is white or blush and definitely not suitable for camping.

I dig through my dresser drawers and raid my closet looking for something passable. Aaron looks out of place in the space as he leans back against the pink floral bedspread covering the bed.

He's wearing his usual black Volcom pants, though today he's paired them with a Hurley long-sleeved thermal tee and a pair of checkered Vans. His shoulders are well defined, even beneath the fabric of his shirt, and his tee rides up, exposing an inch of smooth, tanned skin dusted with a light trail of blond hair.

I force myself to look away from the curve along his hips that I know leads to an Adonis belt I have no business admiring. How did guys get that? I've seen him eat. He's like a garbage disposal in the lunchroom, but looking at him now, you'd never know it.

"I can't believe you live here," he says, a touch of wonder in his tone.

"Yeah, well, only up until a week ago."

His head tilts in question and I sigh, not really wanting to explain but not really seeing a way around it either. "My mom died." I stuff down my emotions and force the words past my lips. "Dad's the only surviving relative I have, so I was shipped off here. I just moved in the week before last, so none of this," I wave at everything around me. "Is mine or even resembles the life I grew up with."

"No shit?" He shakes his head and his face pulls down into a frown. "Damn. I'm sorry."

I shrug. "It's okay. You didn't know."

Silence stretches between us, and after looking through the final drawer in my dresser, I give up in defeat. "I don't think this is going to work. I don't really have anything appropriate for camping," I say, resignation in my voice. I didn't realize just how badly I wanted to go until it became apparent I might not be able to.

Aaron considers me a moment before coming over to take my hands and pulling me from the floor where I'd been sitting. "It's cool. You can borrow some sweats of mine if you want. My bag is already packed in my trunk. Or we can always run by a store?"

"I don't think I'd fit in anything of yours," I say, eyeing his physique. Aaron is tall and thin, probably just shy of six feet. He's built like Chester Bennington from Linkin Park but with a young Ryan Sheckler hot skater-guy vibe.

"Is there, I don't know, a Target nearby or on the way?" I ask.

He chuckles. "I didn't take you for the Target type but yeah, there is."

My shoulders sag as I lean against the wall, relief sweeping through me. "I don't come from money. All of this, my dad's assistant bought it all for me when I moved in. I'm very much a Target kind of girl."

He grins this goofy lopsided smile. "I think I like you even more with that revelation. Come on. Let's get you some new kicks and go have some fun."

SIX

Allie

I've never been one for shopping but I absolutely raid Target as soon as we get to the women's section. I'm not the picky type so I grab the basics. Things I can mix and match with little effort. A few solid white shirts and a couple with band logo graphics. Some black ripped skinny jeans. A pair of shorts even though it's past fall and nearing winter. A swimsuit, just in case. And a few pairs of leggings along with a hoodie for good measure.

Aaron is a good sport, helping me carry the piles of clothes as I wander up and down the aisles without a single complaint. When I feel like I have enough, we make our way to the registers.

I feel bad when the cashier rings me up and gives me the total. Four hundred and thirteen dollars. I swallow hard as I hand over Gerald's credit card and guilt sweeps through me, reminding me I need to find a job so I don't have to rely on him. I'll be eighteen soon, and I need to be prepared for that.

It only takes a few minutes after she hands me my receipt to remember my mom just died and Gerald hasn't bothered to be around all week. What kind of father does that?

That helps sweep away any lingering guilt over how much I'm spending today. I'll still need to search for a job, though.

"Woah, Allie. You look good." Aaron says when I step out of the restroom.

As soon as I'd paid, I rushed to change into the ripped black jeans and a white V-neck shirt I'd just purchased. I even bought myself a pair of fake gold hoops. I was an idiot for thinking I wanted to be anyone other than myself. I hate all the expensive white and peach and pink clothes Janessa bought for me. And I really hate the way people judge me when I'm in them.

"Thanks." I tuck a strand of hair behind my ear and smile.

I was comfortable. I was me again.

I'd missed me this week.

With my arms full, Aaron helps me carry my load to his car and we toss everything in the back of his Subaru WRX. As I shopped, he told me about the cabin we'd be staying in. I was relieved when I learned I wouldn't need to worry about getting a tent or a sleeping bag. Camping with Aaron sounds more like staying in a hotel, so clothes and toiletries are all that is required.

I can tell Aaron comes from money. Not like Gerald does. That's an entirely different level. But Aaron's family is better off than just comfortable. It makes me wonder what he'd think if he'd seen my former home. If he'd still want to be my friend if he'd met the old me? The me before my mom died who lived in a one-bedroom, one-bathroom home on the wrong side of town with bars on the windows.

Then I shove that thought away because I realize I'm silently judging him the same way the students at Sun Valley High have been judging me. I'm not like that.

The drive to Shadle Creek takes a little over an hour. Aaron and I listen to The Red Jumpsuit Apparatus, All American Rejects, and Panic! At the Disco, and for the first time in over a week, I feel myself relaxing. The wind blows tendrils of my hair loose and I can't help but smile wide as Aaron navigates us down the winding roads, both of our windows rolled down and the sun shining through.

There's no pressure here. No hate-filled stares. Aaron is surprisingly funny and despite having a horrible singing voice, he has no problem belting out the lyrics to *I Write Sins Not Tragedies* right along with me.

Before I know it, the asphalt road turns to gravel and we're pulling into a clearing ringed with cabins. Dozens of teenagers—some I recognize from school and others I don't —are milling around, chatting, and drinking beer. Some are pitching tents and another group is getting a bonfire started in the center of the clearing.

As soon as we get out of the car, I close my eyes and breathe in the forest around me.

My shoulders relax, my breathing slows. I exhale and it's like all the tension from earlier this week melts away.

I catch Aaron ginning at me over the top of his car.

"Glad you came?"

I nod and grab my bags, following him as he leads the way to the first cabin on our right. "Yeah. This place is really cool," I say as he unlocks the door and we step inside. He drops his own bag just inside the doorway and I take in the rustic yet clean A-frame cabin. It's simple and screams teenager hangout with the mismatched sofas and already set up red Solo cups on the dining table. A game of beer pong is definitely in our future tonight, not that I'm complaining.

There's a surround sound system set up in every corner and an old school boombox with mini subwoofers built beneath the speakers resting on a cherrywood entertainment center. I spot the CD booklet sitting next to it and can hardly wait to rifle through it. MP3 players and streaming are so overrated. Mixed CDs are where it's all at.

"Thanks. My family owns this one and the cabin right next to us, but I'm letting a few buddies of mine use that one. We'll probably have some crashers here on the sofas later tonight. Usually, we leave our cabins open to whoever decides to stay, but there's a bedroom in the back so we'll have some privacy."

Oh.

We?

Crap.

I bite my lower lip as Aaron gives me the full tour. It's an open floorplan. There's a kitchen to our right. The fridge is already full of beer and not much else. When I ask Aaron about food he laughs and says they grill outside and most of the food is kept in coolers. I shrug and decide not to worry about it. It's not like I've been eating much as it is.

Next, he shows me through the living room area on our left and then down a wide hallway leading toward the back of the cabin.

"This here is the main bathroom. People will come in and out all night to use this one but in here," he opens another door that leads into the lone bedroom. "There's an attached bathroom that will be just ours. Everyone knows to stay out of bedrooms unless you know the cabin owner and have permission, so you won't have to worry about anyone barging in on you."

I nod, eyeing the single bed in the middle of the room. A queen-sized wooden sleigh bed. But there's just the one and I don't know Aaron all that well.

Sensing my apprehension, Aaron reaches out and places a hand on my shoulder. "You okay?" His brows pull down and a small crease appears on his forehead.

I nod. "Yeah. I was just wondering ... ummm ... where should I sleep?"

He clears his throat and shuffles his feet before saying, "I kinda figured you'd crash here, with me. I mean, If that's okay."

I flick a glance toward him and then back to the bed, twisting the teal corded bracelet around my wrist.

"I'm not expecting anything to happen between us," he rushes to add. "I probably didn't think this through but I figured you'd take one side and I'd take the other. Cool?"

I bite my lip. It makes sense. I'm mature enough to share a bed with a cute boy. I can do this. Right? No big deal.

Shoving my apprehension aside, I say, "Yeah. Cool."

He grins.

"Alright, then. Let's go out and grab a beer. I don't know about you, but after the drive, I could use one."

SEVEN

Roman

I pull up to the Shadle Creek campgrounds in Dominique's Escalade. I would have preferred to drive my old-as-shit El Camino but Dom's ride has more space, so here we are. Emilio sits passenger while Dominique is sprawled out in the backseat, snoring louder than a lawnmower. He doesn't usually let me drive. He's got control issues. But he's fucking beat. We all are.

We killed it in tonight's game winning twenty-four to three. It was a slaughter. But because of tonight's game, we're getting out to the campgrounds later that I would have liked. At least we still managed to make decent time.

"Wake up, *cabrón*. We're here."

Dominique groans but pushes himself into a sitting position before rubbing the sleep from his eyes. The three of us stare at the circle of cabins in front of us with varying expressions. Emilio is hyped as fuck and already has his door flung open. His hair is still wet. We all showered after the game in the locker rooms before heading out, so when he whips out of the car, water droplets smack me in the face.

Asshole.

Dom is his usual impassive self but side-eyes me as he grabs his shit from the back. It only takes a second for me to figure out why when all the blood inside me heats and anger spikes in my chest.

Allie is here, and just exited the first cabin with Aaron Henderson. *Fucking Henderson.* Just the sight of that wannabe asshole makes my blood boil. I told her to stay away from him.

I grit my teeth and tighten my hands on the steering wheel.

"Bro, come on," Emilio calls, slamming his door and grabbing his duffel from the back. Dom meets my eyes in the rearview mirror.

"You gonna eye-fuck the girl all weekend?" he asks.

"Fuck you." I flip him off.

He snorts and climbs out of the backseat, grabbing his bag before heading off to follow Emilio to our cabin. I watch them in my peripheral but I don't take my eyes off Allie. She looks good. Real good. She's changed her clothes since I last saw her at school, trading in her white jeans and flowing top for black, ripped jeans and a basic t-shirt. The top dips low in the front exposing a thin line of cleavage and I'm already envisioning her naked breasts.

I scrub a hand over my face. I need to stop checking her out. Emilio's been on my ass all week to focus on the field and yeah, we kicked ass tonight, but I didn't bring my A game and she's the cause of it.

I've stayed away from her all week, avoiding her in the hallways like a fucking coward. It was risky, especially if she decided to whine to Kemp about it, but she stayed quiet like I knew she would. Which makes her all the more intriguing. She didn't rat me out and land me in detention. She didn't beg for attention like other girls would have after being on the receiving end of my cold shoulder.

No. She kept her head down and acted like I didn't even exist. No chance glances my way. No longing looks.

I don't know what it is about her but I can't get her out of my head and it pisses me right the fuck off. I thought if I avoided her it would lessen my attraction to her, but seeing her now makes me realize that was a big fucking failure. If anything, I want her more. I want her as consumed with thoughts of me as I am with her.

It's becoming an obsession.

What am I doing to myself? I pull out a cigarette and light it up. I take one deep pull, holding the smoke in until my eyes burn before I release it. Fuck. I toss the cigarette out the window and then shove the smokes into the glove box before Dom sees. If either he or Emilio realize I still carry a pack on me, they'll both have my ass.

You can't be a star wide receiver and a smoker. The two don't go hand in hand. But damn if I don't want to smoke my way through the entire pack right now.

Dominique's parents own the cabin we're staying in. It's the nicest one out here. Two stories tall, it has four bedrooms and four bathrooms making it more of a vacation home than a cabin. Dom comes from money—enough to rival even Gerald Ulrich—and while the fucker may hate it, it does have its perks. We stay here at least once a month. It's nice to get away from things. Or it would have been if everyone else didn't have the same idea this weekend.

I glare at Henderson and Allie once more before slipping on a pair of mirrored aviators and following my boys. I don't care that it's late. No one is gonna say shit to me about the sunglasses.

The clearing is packed with people illuminated by firelight. Most hang out next to their cars, or in small clusters by the fire. No one speaks to me and everyone gives me and my boys a wide berth as we make our way toward our cabin.

A few guys I recognize from the football team are stupid enough to nod in my direction as if to say *sup?*

I don't reciprocate the gesture. I might talk to some of these assholes on the field when I have to, but I sure as shit am not going to tolerate them off the field. I am not one of them. Never will be and sure as shit don't want to be. They don't take the game seriously. It's all fun and games for them but for us, for me, Dom, and Emilio, football is life. We live, breathe, and sleep football.

All three of us have plans to go pro and we've all earned scholarships at division-one schools. It's a big part of why we don't hang out with the team. We can't afford to get sucked into their bullshit.

Football has to come first.

A group of bikini-clad juniors walk toward me. Emilio slows his steps a few paces ahead while Dom reaches the cabin porch and disappears inside. Beers in hand and wide grins on their faces, the girls sway their hips and offer flirtatious looks and stupid giggles.

I stifle a groan. At school, these chicks usually just give me googly eyes but leave me be unless I approach them, but I can tell they've already had some booze.

One of them is particularly brave. "Hey, Rome. You gonna party with us tonight?" she calls out.

At the mention of my name, I see Allie's head jerk in my direction. *That's right, pretty girl. I'm here.* I don't bother hiding my smirk. "Maybe." I holler back to the girl, wanting to gauge Allie's reaction. She scowls and turns away while the bikini chick giggles. Fucking giggles. I swear these girls get stupider each year, but I eye her rack anyway. Stupid or not, she's got a good one.

Maybe a quick fuck will get Allie out of my head?

"Come find me later," she says and I give her a noncommittal grunt.

I need to get laid, but the idea of fucking her doesn't pique my interest. Allie on the other hand... *Fuck*.

Inside the cabin, Dom flicks on all the lights and we each throw our stuff in our respective rooms. Our cabin is off limits to everyone outside of our group. We've been known to bring a few girls back for the night but our cabin isn't one of the open ones for partiers.

"I see your girl is here," Emilio comments with a shit-eating grin when I make my way back to the porch. I accept the beer he offers me and my eyes track Allie as she follows Henderson over to a group of his skater friends.

My hand clenches around my beer and I clench my jaw. The fucker smiles at her as he leans down to whisper something in her ear.

"I don't have a girl," I say.

That earns me a grunt from Dom. "Then why are you eye-fucking her?" he asks.

I flip him off with my free hand. "You can't see my eyes, asshole. I'm not even looking in her direction."

"Liar," Emilio adds. "Just fuck her and get it out of your system already."

I roll my eyes, not that he can see it. "I'm not interested in fucking her. I— "

"Right. You want to be a dick and toy with her, that it? You need a new pet project to focus on?"

"What the hell is your problem, man?" I flick up my aviators and glare at him.

Emilio laughs but there's an edge to his voice. "Nothing. You do you. Fuck her. Don't fuck her. I don't care. Just make up your mind already so we can enjoy the damn weekend. I'm too tired for your games so whatever you have planned, leave me out of it."

"Count me out, too," Dom adds. He leans back in one of the wooden porch seats, his legs wide and a beer in hand, pretending like he doesn't have a care in the world. "We agreed we'd focus on our futures. You don't have time to be chasing tail. Get laid. Don't get laid." He shrugs. "I don't really care. But you were off today and you know it. She's in your head, so do what you need to do to get her out. If that means playing one of your mind games with her, so be it. But we're not backing you this time around." He tips back his beer.

I grind my teeth together. "Fine." Assholes. We've always messed around with the same girls in the past. It made things fucking convenient, but whatever. I didn't need them to get what I wanted out of Allie.

Emilio downs his beer before reaching for a new one. "I'm going to go find myself a piece of ass. I earned it after tonight's game. I'll catch up with you two later."

He jogs down the steps and heads straight for the bikini girls, throwing his arms around two of them. I won't be surprised if both end up in his bed tonight. Emilio's been known to enjoy his fair share of threesomes and even the occasional foursome.

"I'm surprised his dick hasn't fallen off yet with how many holes he sticks it in," Dom says.

I lift a brow. "Like you're one to talk."

He shrugs. "I'm taking this year easy. Focusing on what's important." I follow his gaze and catch him staring at Kasey Henderson. He tracks her movements like a lion hunting its prey.

"You want Henderson's little sister?"

He shrugs but doesn't take his eyes off her.

"Dude. She's a freshman."

Another shrug.

"Whatever. If you want jailbait, go for it. You've got two months before she's off limits so I suggest you work fast."

He grins. "I'm always up for a challenge."

EIGHT

Allie

He's here. I don't know why I assumed he wouldn't be. Maybe because of the game? He doesn't seem the social type apart from the two guys I met earlier this week. He sticks to Dom and Emilio and they have a bit of a fearsome threesome going on. No wonder everyone calls them the Devils. They're always together, and I haven't missed the fact that everyone else seems to give them a wide berth. They're popular, sure, but it's almost like they're unwilling participants in the game that is high school social hierarchy.

Rulers who don't really want to rule.

I haven't made friends at Sun Valley High—at least none aside from Aaron, but I've heard the whispers in the halls when those three walk by. Everyone seems to want to get their hands on one of the Devils. I don't even think the girls have a preference between the three.

Aaron hands me another beer and I gratefully accept it before noticing Emilio heading my way with a lopsided grin on his face. His arms are wrapped around two girls. One a leggy blonde with a bright red bikini top, the other a brunette with a black bikini and a pair of cut-off shorts. Don't these two realize it's cold? It can't be more than fifty degrees outside. Fall is upon us and winter is fast approaching but these two don't seem to have gotten the memo.

"Yo, vanilla. How's it going?" Emilio calls out across the fire. I hate that nickname and I'm almost positive he and Roman use it just to get a rise out of me.

I force a tight smile and lift my beer in greeting. "It's going," I say, hoping he'll turn his attention back to the two girls beside him. They're running their hands all over him and one is actively trying to suck on his neck but she's just a few inches too short to reach and he doesn't seem inclined to accommodate her.

"Tonight, stop by our place." He turns and points with his beer to the monstrosity of a cabin behind him. "Alright?"

"Why does he want you to go to his cabin later?" Aaron whispers beside me. "I thought you weren't into any of the Devils?"

"I'm not. And who knows. I don't get these guys."

Before I can answer Emilio, Aaron decides to do it for me. "She's got plans tonight," he says, throwing an arm around my shoulders. There's a possessiveness to his touch and I'm not sure how to feel about it. I like Aaron. He's nice and he's cute, but I just got out of a relationship. I'm not looking to dive into another one, and Aaron seems the relationship type.

Emilio's eyes narrow and laser in on the contact.

I cringe.

"Maybe later, then?" he says.

I can hear the bite in his tone, but I don't know if it's directed at me or Aaron. "Sur—"

"Nah. Sorry, man. She's busy *all* weekend." He drags out the word "all," and without saying anything else he's sunk a heavy amount of innuendo into that one sentence.

I turn to him with a confused expression, but he doesn't seem to be paying me any attention. His eyes are narrowed and there's a triumphant look on his face as he and Emilio glower at one another. Like he's won something. Like he's won me.

I'm not some prize in these guys' pissing contest. Whatever issue they have with one another, I don't want any part of it.

As unassuming as I can, I shrug out from under Aaron's arm and stand up. "I'm going to explore a bit. I'll catch up with you later." He scowls but nods, and I turn to head in the opposite direction from him and Emilio.

I make it twenty feet when my phone buzzes in my pocket. I'm surprised I even have cell reception out here. I check the screen and release an audible groan when I see who the message is from.

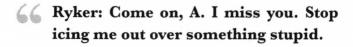 **Ryker: Come on, A. I miss you. Stop icing me out over something stupid.**

Anger bubbles up inside of me and before I can talk myself out of it, I message him back.

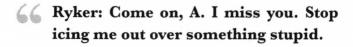 **Me: You broke up with me the day my mom died!**

Those three little dots appear and I stare at them as I wait for his response. But instead of another text, my phone rings in my hand.

Ryker.

"Chingada madre!"

Do I really want to talk to deal with him right now? As I stare at the illuminated screen trying to decide, the ringing stops, saving me from having to make a decision. But then it starts right back up again. I must be a glutton for punishment because on the fourth ring, I answer.

"What do you want, Ry?" I ask.

I walk toward the back of Aaron's cabin and step onto the back patio. Thankfully, no one else is out here so I claim a spot on a wooden bench and lean back, waiting for Ryker to respond.

He's quiet for a second and it's as if I can hear the gears turning in his head. Ryker was always good at that. Finding the right words to say to calm me down. Looking back, I can think of at least a dozen instances when he manipulated me into forgiving him for one thing or another. He was never a good boyfriend. I don't know why it took me so long to realize that.

I finish the beer in my hand and since Ryker still hasn't said anything, I dip inside the cabin through the rear entrance in search of something stronger. I'm going to need it for the conversation I'm about to have.

"Baby," he breathes out, longing in his voice. I roll my eyes and spot a stray bottle of tequila. I swipe it and pour a shot into a red cup before adding in some Sprite as a mixer.

"Don't 'baby' me," I tell him, taking a healthy swallow of my new drink. "I can't believe what you did, Ry. I can't..." I choke on my words, unable to force them out as the tequila burns down my esophagus, making me cough. I probably should have taken a smaller sip. I give myself a few seconds, take another drink because, yes, I am a glutton for punishment. "You hurt me." I don't know why I'm saying this. Maybe a part of me wants him to understand just what he did to me. Maybe then he'll finally leave me the heck alone. "You hurt me when I was already hurting."

"Fuck," he mutters. "I know, baby. I know. I'm sorry. Okay? I fucked up. I was drinking and I wasn't thinking straight. *Fuck.*"

I can hear him pacing on the other end as I step back outside and reclaim my spot on the bench.

"What do you want me to say?"

"The truth. For once in your life, Ry. Can you just be honest with me?" I still don't know the full story. I know he cheated on me with Adriana but I don't know any of the details and I don't know why he broke things off between us the way he did. Ryker was an asshole, but until then, he'd never been cruel.

Another curse. "Baby, it's not that simple. Adriana, she came on to me and at first I thought she was you." His words are rushed. "You've got to believe that. I would never—"

"You expect me to believe that?" Is he kidding? Does he really think I'm *that* stupid? I seethe. "Ry, I'm not an idiot."

He groans. "I know. I know. But it's the truth. I was wasted, babe. And I didn't mean to break up with you."

I snort. "Oh really? Then what did you mean when you texted me—the same day my mom died I might add— saying, 'I think we should see other people'. Huh? How is that anything other than breaking up with me?"

There's a loud bang on the other end of the line like maybe he hit something.

"Look, I'm not proud of this, okay. And I didn't know your mom had died when I sent it. Adriana told me you found out about us. That you were going to dump me. I just"—he sighs—"I was stupid and I wanted to break things off with you first before you turned around and ended things with me."

Wow. Just wow.

What an asshole.

He's quiet for a beat and I take another drink from my cup. The alcohol burns and I relish the pain. My throat tightens so I take another drink, eager to chase away the ache forming in my chest because it still hurts and I hate that. I hate that he still has any sort of hold over me.

"I loved you," I tell him, my voice cold.

"Baby, I love you, too. So much."

I shake my head even though he can't see the movement. "No, Ry. Loved. I *loved* you. I don't anymore. Not after what you did."

"Allie, baby. Please. Don't be like this. We can fix this. I know we can."

"Nope." The 'p' makes a popping sound to emphasize my decision. Another drink and my cup is empty. I set it aside and lean back, relishing the slight spinning my head is doing right now. "I might have been able to get past the

cheating if you'd been honest with me. I was that invested."
He'd been my first kiss. My first love. The guy I lost my
virginity to. Maybe that was why I'd put up with so much
for so long. Not anymore. I deserved better. I knew that.
"But Ry, you dropped me when I needed you the most.
There's no coming back from that. Stop texting me. Stop
calling. I'm not going to forgive you. Not for that."

A movement to my left draws my attention and I spot
Roman leaning against a tree, staring at me. His face is
blank, but he's removed his aviators, giving me a glimpse of
his dark brown eyes. There's fire in his gaze, and I shiver.
When he sees I've spotted him he steps forward and sits
beside me.

He puts a hand out, silently asking for my phone. I frown,
but what the heck? I hand it to him.

He lifts the phone to his ear and says in a gruff voice,
"Listen to her. Stop calling. Stop texting. You two are done.
Got it?"

"Who the fuck are you?" I hear Ryker bite out.

"Your replacement." Roman deadpans. He hands me back
my phone after he ends the call. It starts ringing almost
right away but I silence it and shove it in my back pocket.
He offers me his beer and I take it. I tilt the bottle back to
my lips, letting the cool liquid slide down my suddenly dry
throat.

My vision blurs for a second but I blink fast to clear it and
hand the beer back to him. Heat rushes up my neck and I

can feel the effects of the alcohol kicking in even more now. Good.

I don't want to be sober. Not tonight.

Neither of us say anything after that. Both content to gaze up at the starless night sky. Roman takes a few pulls from his beer bottle and I watch as his Adam's apple bobs with each swallow.

When the seconds turn to minutes, I feel my cheeks go numb and my head begins to swim. I've always been a lightweight. Drinking and partying was never really my thing. I hadn't expected the liquor to hit me this quickly, though I can't say I regret that it has and I'm already wishing I had more.

Roman nudges me with his shoulder and I meet his gaze. The mask is still in place. His expression unreadable. A tendril of dark brown hair has fallen forward and I reach out, brushing it back.

His hand shoots up to grab my wrist and I gasp, but rather than tightening his hold on me, his thumb rubs small circles along my pulse as he lowers my hand between us. He doesn't release me. He continues to rub lazy circles across my skin and goosebumps break out on my arms. He tugs at the teal bracelet on my wrist drawing my attention.

His eyes meet mine again and this time, I see him. I see the want and the need there. The desire.

I swallow hard and a bout of nerves has my stomach tightening.

"That the ex?" he asks. His voice is smooth and he's still rubbing those darn circles along my skin. I can't think with him touching me.

"Yeah." My voice is more breathless than I'd intended, but all of a sudden, it's like I can't get enough air inside my lungs. Walk away, Allie. You don't need to fall for another asshole.

"He cheated?"

I nod.

"And your mom's dead?"

Another nod.

He seems to ponder my words. "So, who are you living with now? Your pops?"

I nod. "Yeah. Bio-dad."

He tilts his head in question and he shifts so our bodies are closer to one another. One arm curls around my shoulder, the other still on my wrist, but I can feel the heat from his body so close to mine now.

"I, uh... don't really want to talk about it." I stutter my words. Being so close to Roman has me on edge. I'd done so well avoiding him this past week that I'd almost tricked myself into believing he's forgotten about me. Clearly, that was a stupid thought because here he is, in the flesh. A gut feeling has me believing he's planned this meeting. Why else would he have followed me to the back of Aaron's cabin? What other reason did he have for being here?

"Allie?" His voice is flat yet somehow filled with so much suppressed emotion.

I swallow hard and tug my hand free from his hold.

Silence hangs between us again and I push up from my seat. "I'm going to get another drink," I say, needing a reason to escape his presence. There's something about Roman that has me convinced he's dangerous, yet I'm drawn to him all the same.

He doesn't say anything and he doesn't try to follow me. He brushes a hand through his thick, dark hair, his nostrils flaring, but no sound escapes him. I pause by the door, giving myself one last second to drink him in before I escape inside, cursing myself for being stupid. Roman is trouble, and I'm not going to make the same bad decisions again.

NINE

Allie

"Allie!" Aaron shouts as soon as I step into the living room. He must have come inside after I left the bonfire. "Come play with me." He's standing in front of the dining table. Red cups set up to form triangles on either end.

I smile but it's forced. "I was wondering when the beer pong games would begin," I say and head toward him.

The cabin is packed and I have to weave my way through the sea of bodies to get to Aaron. No one bothers to get out of my way but when I finally reach him, he tugs me closer, an arm wrapping around my shoulder as he lifts a beer high in the air. "I've got my partner. Who's brave enough to be our challengers?" Cheers go up and I can smell the beer radiating off him as though it's seeping through his pores.

How many has he had?

I pull away from his hold and shake my head. "I'm not really in the mood to play tonight. But I'll watch."

His bottom lip juts out. "Aw, come on, Allie."

I shake my head. "N— "

The leggy blonde from earlier steps up beside Aaron. "Hey, Henderson. I'll be your partner," she purrs.

He looks at her and I track his gaze as he takes in her barely covered body. His lips press into a tight line but his eyes don't leave her. I can tell he's tempted so I decide to give him a nudge in the right direction.

"Cool. Thanks," I tell her. "I appreciate you taking my place."

She sneers at me. "I'm not doing you any favors. Why are you even here?"

I suck in a breath, taken aback by the open hostility. I open my mouth and then close it. Unsure how to respond. A few other girls beside her start laughing and I stumble back a step.

"Good one, Sarah," a girl remarks.

The blonde, Sarah, beams at her friends and then turns back to me with an obvious look of contempt. "Really, though. No one wants you here. Why don't you slink back to whatever stuffy prep school you were expelled from? I'm sure Daddy Warbucks can help you out."

"Hey. Not cool." Aaron finally comes to my defense.

The girl rolls her eyes. "Come on, Aaron. You know she doesn't belong here." She wraps her arms around his neck and mashes her breasts against his chest. "Send her away already so you and I can have some fun," she whines. The sound grates on my ears. Does she think guys like that?

Aaron's gaze flicks between us with uncertainty.

Seriously? He invited *me*.

Anger ignites in my chest.

Seeing my expression, he pulls her arms away from his neck and takes a step back. "Sorry, Sarah. Allie's my friend. I'm not cool with you talking to her like that."

Her eyes widen and her mouth hangs open for a second before she snaps it closed. "Excuse me?"

He shrugs and runs a hand over the back of his neck. "Look. I know— "

"Screw you! Your loss, Henderson. Don't expect to get a second chance." She brushes past me to leave the room, shoulder checking me along the way. I bite the inside of my cheek to keep from lashing out at her and turn grateful eyes toward Aaron.

"Thanks. You didn't have to do that," I mutter.

He shrugs. "Yeah. I did. I invited you. And Sarah can be a real bitch when she wants to be. She doesn't usually seek me out at parties like this. She's younger but she's with the 'elite' crowd." He makes air quotes for the word elite and sighs. "We don't run in the same circles. But she's my neighbor. We sort of grew up together and sometimes she can be a decent human being." He pauses as though choosing his words carefully. "She's used to being the center of attention. Honestly, I wouldn't be surprised if she only came on to me right now because you showed up."

Oh.

"I'm sorry. That's a crappy thing to do. Are you into her?" I ask, not wanting to cock block him because, yes, he did invite me and I'm grateful he came to my defense, but if he wants to *carpe diem* and all that, I won't stop him. I know how guys can be sometimes. If he were Felix, he'd have gone with her, had his fun, and then apologized to me later.

But Aaron only shakes his head. "No. Not really. I know the kind of girl she is and that's not what I'm after. I think between the beer and her boobs, I got a little confused."

I can't help but grin. Aaron has a sheepish expression on his face as he says, "So, any chance I can change your mind and convince you to be my partner after all?"

I start to shake my head but then I spot Emilio, Dom, and Roman as they crowd into the space. Emilio's smile is wicked as he looks at me and says, "Come on, vanilla. Let's play. We can make things interesting."

Great. Vanilla again. I scowl, but I'm curious now. "What sort of interesting?"

"If we win," He points to the three of them. "You wear a bikini the rest of the weekend. Day and night. No exceptions."

I snort. Typical. "And if I win?"

He shrugs. "What do you want?"

I consider this. I don't know if they're any good and I don't know if Aaron is either but I do know that I am. As long as Aaron isn't god-awful, there's a decent chance we can win. I've always been one of the guys and beer pong is a party go-to. Julio and I use to make off at parties like thieves. We'd make things interesting with cash on the table, but this is my first party with this crowd, and I don't know what the expectations are here. They don't really seem like the gambling type.

I'm still riding a decent buzz so I decide to focus on that and turn tonight around despite my ex's call and Roman's strange behavior.

"If I win, you three wear bikinis all weekend. Day and night. No exceptions, either."

The crowd cheers on the idea and Emilio's grin widens while Dom and Roman's matching scowls deepen. I don't even bother trying to hold back my laugh.

"Alright. Alright. I can get behind that."

"No," Dom says. "You fuckers have at it. My black ass is not wearing a bikini."

Emilio chuckles. "But Dom, you'd look fine as fuck in one and you know it."

His scowl deepens even more and I clutch my stomach, laughing, as I picture Dominique in a bikini. "Alright. You get a pass," I say when I can catch my breath again. "But only because teams need to be equal. Two on two."

I turn to Aaron and he gives me a reassuring smile. He's in, even though I'm pretty sure if we lose, the guys only care if I'm the one in a bikini. Good thing I bought one today.

Then I turn to Roman and lift a single brow. I'm almost positive he'll bow out like Dominique did but he surprises me when he grabs a ping pong ball and says, "Rack them up."

TEN

Roman

I'm going to murder my best friend for getting me into this. Allie and Henderson are kicking our asses. They're two cups away from handing me my ass and a fucking bikini is not going to be enough to cover it.

Allie's eyes are glassy. The booze is hitting her hard, but with a grin on her face she raises her hand, shoots, and lands the damn thing in my cup.

Fuck.

She jumps up and down, her tits bouncing with the motion, and Henderson high-fives her.

Emilio grabs the cup. Downs it in one swallow and then takes aim.

The fucker misses and I bite back a groan.

Shit.

"I'm going to kill you," I tell him, low enough that only he should hear but I don't miss Dominique's dark chuckles behind us. He's enjoying this shit. He's probably hoping we lose, too.

"Nah, man. You won't," Emilio tells me. "Because I'm helping a brother out by putting you front and center for her. You might hate losing but you want that girl's attention."

"No. I don't," I mutter. "She's no one to me."

Emilio ignores my comment and now it's Henderson's shot. He takes aim for the last cup on our side and at the last second, his eyes flick up to mine and I stare him down. He falters and I let a murderous grin wash over my face. My vision tunnels and all I can see is him. His green eyes darken and I know his surroundings are fading away from him. The crowd around us cheers him on.

"Shoot."

"Shoot."

"Shoot."

I narrow my eyes further. His jaw tightens and he shoots but the fucker isn't looking at the cups. He's still looking at me like he's two seconds away from pissing himself.

He misses.

I grin and blink, breaking the stare off between us and he curses.

That's right, fucker.

It's my turn so I grab the ball and without any fanfare, I shoot it into one of their three remaining cups. Henderson swears again, downs the cup, and hands the ball to Allie.

She smirks at me, completely in her element, and lands the ball in our final cup. Emilio moans beside me but I know it's all for show. He couldn't care less whether we win or lose. It's all a game for him. He lives for this kind of shit even if he tries to claim otherwise.

Slowly, making sure to keep my eyes locked on hers, I lift the cup and down the remaining beer.

"You lose," she says and her satisfaction is clear.

"I did. Guess you better go grab me that bikini of yours," I tell her.

"Mine?"

I nod and suck in my bottom lip with a nod. "Yeah, vanilla. I want yours."

"You can have mine," one of the chicks beside me says.

I lift a brow. "And you are?"

She looks surprised I don't know who she is, but why would I?

"Silvia. Silvia Parish. I have second period with her." She reminds me, angling her head toward Allie. Recognition clicks back to when I told her to watch out for *my girl.* Guess I do know her name after all.

I shrug. "Well, Silvia Parish," I say, "Thanks. But no thanks. I want Allie's. Only hers will do."

Silvia pouts and Allie rolls her eyes. Her annoyance is sexy as hell. "Whatever. *Andale pues.*"

I don't think she realizes she told me to hurry up in Spanish, but I like it. I like that it rolls off her tongue like it's natural. It probably is. And I really fucking like that Henderson has no idea what the fuck she just said. It wasn't anything sexy. There was no hidden meaning there. But he doesn't know that.

I make sure to shoulder check him as I shove past to follow Allie.

"Watch it, Henderson," I say so low only he can hear. "I wouldn't get in my way."

His jaw locks and I wait, making sure he gets my meaning.

It takes longer than I like, but eventually, he nods. *Good.*

I follow Allie through the crowd of people, shoving against bodies when they get too close. This is why we don't open up our cabin. I don't like people in my space.

She leads me back to a bedroom and as soon as I step inside the dimly lit room, I shut the door. I exhale in relief and Allie laughs. "Not one for crowds?" she asks.

"Not one for idiots," I retort.

She smiles and digs through a bag until she retrieves a black two-piece swimsuit. The bottoms are taller, like they'd go past her hips, and the top is a thick band that ties in the back. Hmmm. Interesting. "No slutty string bikini?"

She shakes her head. "Not really my style." She holds her hands out, but before I accept it, I pull off my shirt and let the fabric fall to the floor before unbuckling my jeans.

She sucks in a breath. "What are you doing?"

I can't help my grin at her freaked-out tone. When I look up and see her eyes locked on my abs, heat simmers in my chest and my dick twitches. Her gaze rolls over me with blatant interest and my smile widens. I shove my jeans down, leaving my black boxer briefs on and then step out of the jeans, discarding my socks and shoes along with them.

"Like what you see?" I ask, holding my hands out wide with a cocky smirk on my face. I know I look good. Her expression confirms in.

A delicate hand reaches out as if to touch my tattoos and I wait, eager to feel her hands on me though I can't explain why. *What is it about this girl that draws me to her?*

Hands pressed together in prayer are inked on my right side, a strand of rosary beads between their fingers. My right arm sports a half sleeve filled with an intricate Aztec falcon totem. And on my left collarbone, climbing up my neck and down over the top of my bicep and pectoral, is an Aztec devil mask.

My gaze heats as I watch her eyes drink me in but instead of trailing her fingers over the designs, she hovers over the left side of my rib cage. She has her bottom lip trapped between her teeth and a hint of concern flickers across her face. *Concern for me?* I'm surprised when I spot the emotion.

I look down and realize her eyes are glued to a purplish yellow bruise that's formed across my left side.

I remember the hit I took in the fourth quarter. I'd been running for a touchdown and the guy had come out of nowhere, tackling me in the end zone even though I'd already dropped the ball. Ref threw a flag but it didn't matter. The game was over by then.

Her fingers brush over the damaged skin and she whispers, "Does it hurt?"

I bite back the groan I want to release at her featherlight touch. "Nah. It looks worse than it is."

She steps back and her eyes widen, as though realizing that she'd just been intimately close. A pretty blush spreads across her cheeks. I step closer to her before she can retreat further, and I wrap my hand around her delicate wrist. "You gonna give me the suit?" I ask.

She's maybe five-two to my six-one. A tiny little thing so she's forced to tilt her head back to meet my gaze. All it would take is me dipping my head a few inches to catch her lips with my own, but I don't. Her eyes glaze over as she stares back at me. She licks her lips and I trail the movement.

"Ww...What?"

I quirk a brow. "The suit," I say again, tugging on the material that's clutched in her hands.

"Oh. Oh!" She drops the fabric like it's hot to the touch and steps back, her face even redder than it had been before. Taking the swimsuit, I stretch the top over my chest, the fabric barely able to tie in the back over my broad chest. Then I hold up the bottoms and meet her gaze. "I'm not sure these will fit over my legs, but if you want me to try, I will. Or..." I trail off and wait.

She swallows hard, licking her lips again. "Or what?"

I toss her swim bottoms back to her. "Or I can go like this. My boxer briefs don't cover much more than those would." I point to the swim bottoms. "More leg but less abs." I lift my shoulders in a shrug. "It's your call."

"Oh. Yeah. Sure. That's fine."

ELEVEN

Allie

I don't know why I care that Roman is wearing my swimsuit top. It's just a stupid top. But he's wearing it and it's mine. My stomach flip-flops and I toy with the teal bracelet on my wrist. Following him out of Aaron's room, I try to slow my racing heart. The crowd presses in on us, forcing us to take a few steps back until Roman shoves one of the football players out of his way with a two-handed shove. He's wearing his jersey as are a bunch of other guys, making them easy to spot.

The guy whirls on Roman with a fist raised as if to swing, but suddenly halts before dropping his hand back to his side. "Hey, Rome. My man, uh..." He rubs the back of his neck. "Sorry, man. I didn't realize it was you."

Roman doesn't say anything. He just stares, his eyes narrowed into slits and the guy backs up, hands lifted in surrender. "Yeah. Sorry. Let me get out of your way." He gives Roman a nervous chuckle as he moves.

I expect Roman to shove past him leaving me behind but instead, he turns back, grabs my wrist, and hauls me after him. I squeak and stumble, my body brushing up against a few of the players, but as soon as I come into contact with them, they step back. What is it about him and grabbing me by the wrist? "I'm perfectly capable of walking," I say, but he either doesn't hear me or chooses to ignore me.

We exit the house and find Emilio wearing a neon pink bikini top over his bare chest and string bikini bottoms over his dark blue boxer briefs. I have no idea how he manages to make it look good. But he does.

Emilio has tattoos as well and his chest piece is on full display. A gothic portrait of a woman with her hair flying back and a mix of sparrows and ravens flying around her with strands of her hair lifted in their beaks.

It's surprisingly beautiful. When he catches me staring he rubs his chest and bites his bottom lip. His eyes become hooded and he lifts his brows in a suggestive manner. Roman steps in front of me with a growl and Emilio explodes into a fit of laughter.

I spot Dominique beside him, his shoulders shaking. His lips are pressed together and I can tell he's fighting to contain his own laugh but in the end, he fails.

"Rome, if you could see your face right now."

I move forward to gauge his expression but the mask he usually wears is firmly in place. "Well, uh, I'll let you guys do your thing." I inch around Roman and head back toward the fire, my eyes scanning around for Aaron. When I spot him, there's a girl in his lap kissing at his neck. I can't make out her face but...

My steps falter.

I look again and yep, it's Sarah. The bitchy girl from earlier. Awesome.

Warm breath on my neck catches me off guard and then I hear his voice. "Looks like your boy is busy tonight." His voice is low, his tone suggestive. "Fool. Going for that when he could have had this instead." His fingers brush up my spine and I release an involuntary shiver.

"No one is having *this*," I snap, hating what he's implying. "Besides, we're just friends. He can go after whoever he wants."

Another caress, this one along the back of my hip. "Yeah?"

"Yeah."

Roman's fingers tighten on my hip into an almost bruising grip as he draws me tight against his body. "What if I decided I want you?"

My breath hitches and he's still behind me, trailing his lips up the column of my exposed neck. It's not a kiss. The touch is featherlight but it feels like he's marking me, branding me as his. "I'd tell you to screw off."

"Liar."

I step away from his body, instantly missing his warmth.

"Come with me." He twines his fingers with mine and despite knowing better, I allow him to lead me toward one of the larger cabins.

I stumble after him, but he doesn't pause or slow his steps. He just tugs my hand harder, forcing me to quicken my pace. "Where are you taking me?" I ask, finding my voice.

He smirks over his shoulder. "You scared, vanilla?"

I scoff but continue to follow him, my steps hurried as I try to keep up with his longer strides. "Hardly."

The cabin is empty aside from the two of us and I take everything in. Much like the outside, it looks more like a regular home than a cabin. A large leather sectional takes up most of the room in front of a wood-burning fireplace. And the kitchen and dining area look like they came straight out of a magazine.

Roman watches me as I soak everything in, gauging my reaction though I'm not sure what he's hoping for. Everything inside screams expensive, but it's tasteful and you can tell that each piece in the space was carefully thought out.

Looking at it makes me think of movies in front of the fire huddled up with friends. Julio and Adriana and I would do that sometimes. Sometimes Gabe or Felix would join us. Before she did what she did. Before my mom died.

We'd watch stupid movies and eat popcorn. Julio always poured a bag of Swedish fish in my bowl so I could find sweet surprises. We'd fight over who got to eat the last one and the night almost always ended with Adriana sprawled out on our only sofa, Julio and I on the floor. He'd lean against the sofa with me lying beside him, my head in his lap.

I think of what it would be like being huddled up next to Roman in front of that fire and warmth spreads inside my chest. It wouldn't be like when I watched movies with Julio. There would be no easy carefree affection.

"What are you thinking?" he asks, stepping closer to me.

"Nothing."

"Mentirosa," *Liar*, he says.

Maybe I am, but I know better than to share my true thoughts with him, so I say, "I was just thinking this place is nice. Homey. I know it probably cost a fortune but it doesn't feel cold." *Like my new living arrangements.* But I don't say that out loud. "I like it."

He nods and heads toward the kitchen, leaving me to follow him. He opens the refrigerator and starts pulling out ingredients. Carrots, celery, a package of ground beef. Then he opens up cupboards and pulls out onions, garlic, potatoes, spices, a few cans—corn and tomatoes from the looks of them—followed by a bag of rice.

"What are you doing?"

"I'm cooking."

A laugh escapes me. "I can see that but what are you making, and why?"

"I didn't eat after the game." A shrug, his broad shoulders flexing with the movement, and I fight the urge to trace every contour of his body with my gaze. He should look ridiculous in my swim top. But he doesn't. It's unnerving.

I still haven't decided if he's the enemy or not. He runs hot one minute. Cold the next. I can't get a solid read on him.

"I'm making *albóndigas*."

My heart seizes in my chest and memories of my mom and me cooking at the stove wash over me. "Yo...you are?" I turn to hide the sudden tears pricking the corners of my eyes, barely catching his nod.

Thankfully, he doesn't look up from what he's doing. He peels the onion and with quick efficiency, dices it into small neat squares. "Here." He hands me a second cutting board and a sharp knife. "Dice these." Then he hands me the celery, potatoes, and carrots.

I take them and do as instructed, ignoring the sudden emotion clogging my throat. "You know albóndigas take at least two hours to make, right?" And even then the flavors aren't completely melded. My mom would make the soup and let it simmer on low on our stove for several hours, making sure everything married nicely together. There's no way the soup will be done in time to eat tonight.

He nods. "I know. I'm cheating."

I look up from my task and spot him pointing to an Instant Pot, of all things, on the back counter. I can't help the laugh that bubbles out of me.

"My mother would be mortified."

He gives me a devilish smile. "Mine, too. And my grandmother would probably disown me, so this is top secret. No sharing trade secrets, vanilla." He winks. "I don't want burgers or hot dogs. I want real food. Food I'd eat at home." Another shrug. "This will cut back on time. Once we get everything in there, we'll have fresh soup that tastes like it's been cooking all day within fifteen minutes."

I smile to myself. "You're not what I expected you to be."

He eyes me up and down and I almost miss the hunger in his eyes before it disappears. "Neither are you."

TWELVE

Roman

She's smiling. A real smile, not one of the forced, fake ones she gives everyone else at school. This one is genuine, and I don't miss the glimmer of tears in her eyes before she banishes them away. The girl has demons. Hell, hers might even be worse than mine.

I've got an overbearing pops whose expectations I never seem to measure up to. She's got a dead mom and a cheating ex. What other damage is she hiding behind that smile?

Maybe that's what draws me to her. I want to hurt her. Bite her delectable lips until they bleed. Caress her body until it bruises. I'm not a gentle lover. I kiss hard and fuck even harder. But I also want to protect her. Something in me wants to hold her. Mark her as mine and shield her from the world even as I strip her bare of all her protections and expose her to me and me alone.

The anticipation of having her builds inside me.

I never should have brought her here.

I put everything in the pot and set the time on the pressure cooker before making quick work of cleaning up the mess we made getting everything together.

"I'll wash that," Allie says, taking the cutting board from my hands as she moves to the sink. She then puts it back in the drawer I'd pulled it out of earlier. With her back to me, I step into her space and place my hands low on her hips. I dip my head down, drawing in her woodsy vanilla scent as my nose drags along her neck.

She sucks in a breath but doesn't move. I draw her back until our bodies are flush with one another before trailing my lips down the column of her neck. She tilts her head to the side, granting me better access and fuck, her skin is so smooth. I nip and bite at the tender flesh. She hisses from the sting of pain but doesn't pull away, surprising me, so I do it again. This time biting hard enough to leave a small bruise behind. I chase away the sting with a kiss and suck on her sensitive skin ensuring that she'll carry my mark after the weekend is over.

One of my hands slides over her hip to trail up her stomach until I'm cupping one of her breasts.

"Roman...?" Her voice is quiet, hesitant.

There's a question there but I can't answer her. I don't have the words for it, because I have no fucking idea what I'm doing, and I sure as hell am not going to admit that.

She cranes her neck to look at me and I see the same want and need inside of me reflected in her gaze. I've never cared what a girl is thinking about or what she might be feeling, but with Allie, I can't help myself from wanting to figure her out. Does she miss her old school? Her old life? What is she planning to do once she graduates?

She's become my obsession and even as I tell myself she's nothing, no one, I dip my head down and capture her lips with mine, desperate to taste her. She gasps and I take full advantage, sweeping my tongue inside her mouth and drinking down her soft moans.

My other hand moves up to cup the back of her neck, angling her head more so I can deepen the kiss while I squeeze her breast, and fuck, does she have nice ones. Full and round. Just enough to fill my hand. I grip the plump flesh, satisfaction flaring within me when she arches her back, pushing her breast further into my grasp before twisting in my arms.

She's so responsive. So fucking hot. Her arms come up to wrap around my neck. Her breasts press against my chest and I'm two seconds away from stripping her out of her clothes and fucking her right here on the kitchen counter when voices outside grow nearer.

She tears her mouth from mine. "Roman." Her breathing is heavy. Her chest heaves up and down and I realize mine is, too. I want this girl, and I have no fucking idea why. I steel myself and mask the need to sink myself inside her, fitting a bored expression on my face as our eyes connect.

"I..." Her brows furrow as she takes in my expression. Confusion flashes over her features.

The voices grow louder and she takes a step back, trying to put distance between us, but I'm not ready to let her go. I grip her hips with bruising force, refusing to let her back away. She's not the one in control here. I am.

The door to the cabin opens and Emilio strides in, Dom hot on his heels.

"I told him you'd be busy," Dominique says in way of greeting. I lift a single brow as if to say the interruption is of little consequence.

Emilio's still got two girls, one under either arm beside him. He's got that junior chick from earlier on his right and Silvia on his left. I can tell he's drunk. His eyes are glazed over and he has a stupid happy smile on his face as he takes in the scene in front of him. "Hey, vanilla. You going to bang my bro, Rome, tonight?" It's all I can do not to punch him in the face. Silvia's eyes shoot to Allie and she visibly stiffens. I step forward, blocking Allie from view and Dominique smacks Emilio upside the head, muttering "stupid fucker," under his breath.

"Hey!" Emilio cries out, rubbing his head as if Dominique actually hurt him. We both know it's all an act. "Not cool, man. What the hell?"

Dominique points down the hallway. "Take your women to your room or send them on their way." He takes a deep inhale before a grin spreads across his face. He's had a few, too, because Dom isn't usually one for smiles. "Roman's cooking tonight."

Emilio perks up like a five-year-old about to get an ice cream cone or some shit and his gaze snaps toward me. "You cooked?"

I nod.

"What'd you make?" He's all but forgotten about the two girls with him. Silvia and the other chick whose name I don't know and have no interest in learning stand just behind him with worried expressions on their faces. Looks like things aren't going as they'd hoped.

"Albóndigas," I tell him.

His smile widens and he turns. "Ladies, it's been real." He ushers them back to the front door despite their protests. Silvia is clearly digging her heels in, not liking that she's being shown the door.

"But, Emilio. I thought we were gonna party," she whines.

"Sorry, uhhh..." He pauses and gives her an apologetic look.

Her mouth drops open and her eyes narrow before she responds with a drawn out, "Silvia."

He snaps his fingers together. "Right. Silvia. Sorry. Something came up. I'll call you later, okay?"

Her cheeks heat and she pushes out her bottom lip. "You haven't even asked for my number yet."

He grins at her. "I'll get it. I have my ways. Don't worry that pretty little head of yours."

Before she can respond, he gives her and her friend one last little push and closes the door behind them. Then he turns back to me. "I just gave up some prime pussy so you better feed me, fucker."

We all laugh. "You've got ten more minutes. Go find something to watch and I'll get tortillas going."

He nods and then moves toward Allie.

I growl.

"Hey, man. I was just gonna show your girl around. Chill."

I glower at him. He doesn't need to show her around anything. Knowing Emilio, the first place he plans to show her is his bedroom. Dominique knows this too, and interrupts before things have a chance to get heated. I might claim disinterest when it comes to Allie but I am anything but disinterested in her and I do not share my toys with others. I want to know everything about her. To own all her secrets and learn all her desires. I need ammunition against this girl. She already has too strong a hold over me.

"Wanna help pick the movie for tonight?" Dom asks her.

Her brows pinch together and she gives us all an assessing look. I can tell what she's thinking. It's written all over her face. We're the grade-A assholes of Sun Valley High. The Devils. So why are we holed up in our cabin when it's barely midnight instead of partying it up outside with everyone else? And what she probably wants to know even more than that is why the hell we're being nice to her when all week we've pretended she doesn't exist.

Dominique answers her first unspoken question. "We're beat from the game today. And that out there," He throws a thumb toward the direction of the front door. "Isn't our scene."

Her lips purse. "You guys don't party?"

"Oh, we party." Emilio chuckles and gives her a suggestive look. "But we do it on our terms and we don't need wannabe assholes around to do it. Besides, today was a game day. That means tonight is a recovery night and Roman is a greedy bastard who doesn't cook for us often. We gotta enjoy it while we can."

"Oh. Okay." She follows Dom towards the sofa and he gives me a quick nod before showing her to our DVD stash. We don't have WiFi out here, so streaming something isn't an option.

As they dig through the movie selection, Emilio heads to his room and comes back in a pair of sweatpants. He's still got his ridiculous bikini on over them but he walks in like he's the hottest shit there ever was. I chuckle under my breath. The guy's got no shame.

Allie hides her smile behind her hand when she spots him. "You don't have to keep that on." She's taken the corner spot on the sectional and has the throw blanket tucked tight around her body. Is she cold? Do I care? I frown, not wanting to examine my feelings where her well-being is concerned.

Emilio looks down at himself, a smug expression on his face as he says, "I mean, I'm all for rocking my birthday suit, but I don't think these two would appreciate it."

"I was talking about the swimsuit," she says. I watch as heat creeps up her cheeks. She has the prettiest blush.

"What? I look damn fine in this thing." He cups his junk over the ridiculously bright fabric. "Pink is my color. Besides, a bet is a bet."

She rolls her eyes and turns to me. "It's just the four of us. You don't have to wear it either. But I'm holding you to wearing it anytime you step outside this cabin this weekend. Fair is fair." Her lip curls into a satisfied smirk giving away that she's a hint competitive. I'll have to file that bit of information away for later use.

"I can get behind that." I untie the black top and toss it on the counter just as the Instant Pot beeps letting me know it's finished. I turn on the *comal*—a cast iron griddle of sorts —and warm up tortillas before portioning out the soup. Normally I'd make them serve themselves but I don't want Dominique eating all of it in one go. Emilio and I are used to home cooking. Dom's not, and every time it's offered the man wolfs it down as though he's been starved.

My mom practically lives in the kitchen and there is always something hot and ready as soon as I or my pops walk in the door. But Dom's parents are rarely home and dinner is almost always some catered solitary affair. It's why Emilio and I try and have him over to our houses for dinner throughout the week. No one should eat alone. Food is meant to be enjoyed with family and those two fuckers are as family as it gets for me.

"Grab your food," I tell the guys as I grab two bowls, handing one to Allie. Then I go back for the tortillas and place a few on a napkin on the empty seat beside her. I sit down and tug some of the blanket from her lap. I don't actually want it, but I want an excuse to be close to her. I haven't had the chance to catalog her features. To memorize her expressions so I know exactly what she's feeling when she's feeling it.

"Hey!" Her eyes narrow and there's visible tension in her shoulders.

"I'm in my underwear. It's cold." I lie because I'm definitely not cold, but I really want under the blanket now.

She rolls her eyes but doesn't object again. *Score one for this Devil.*

Dominique gets the movie going and credits begin rolling as we all dig into the meal.

Allie moans and I fight back a smirk. There's something satisfying about knowing she likes it. That she's enjoying something I made for her. "This is so good. I haven't had albóndigas since—"

She cuts herself off and I turn to look at her. She blinks rapidly then stares down at her bowl like she's fighting back tears. I take in her bottom lip as it wobbles. The red splotches that appear beneath her eyes as if she's already cried her eyes out.

An unfamiliar jolt of something I don't want to realize hits me in the chest. *Fuck.* She hasn't had albóndigas since her mom died. That's what she'd been about to say.

Emilio sees her reaction and meets my gaze with a concerned look of his own. I lift my shoulders just enough as if to say *I have no fucking clue what's set her off,* because I sure as shit am not about to share her secrets with him. They're mine, and mine alone. But in typical Emilio fashion, he saves the night with a wise ass joke.

"Damn, Allie. You can't moan like that over soup. My head's going all sorts of directions after hearing that sexy noise out of you."

She laughs but there's a hiccup in there. "You're such a guy." She throws a tortilla at him before swiping one of mine to replace the one she just lost. I pretend not to notice.

"Don't hate. I can't help I was born with one of these." He grabs himself underneath the bright pink bikini bottoms covering his sweats and then takes a big bite out of the tortilla she hit him with.

She groans again, this time in feigned annoyance. "I don't even know what to do with that statement." This time, her voice isn't as tight, and some of the redness has receded from her face.

"Yo. Pipe down. Movie's starting," Dominique cuts in, and all of our attention goes back to the screen just as Norman Reedus and Sean Patrick Flanery appear on-screen and walk past the priest to kiss Jesus's feet.

Emilio groans, cocking his head to one side before shaking it. "Boondock Saints. Again?"

To which Dom replies, "Don't gripe at me. Allie picked it. Girl's got good taste. Not our fault you don't."

Emilio harrumphs but leaves it be and focuses on the albóndigas as we all turn our attention to the screen.

As soon as Allie finishes her food, I whisk the bowls back to the kitchen. The movie is almost halfway through and it's just now getting to the good stuff.

I reclaim my seat and tug at her blanket once more. She scowls at me and tugs some of it back so I jerk at it again. This time I'm met with a glare. "What are you doing?" she whispers.

"Shhh—" Emilio snaps, engrossed in the show. He might complain about how often we watch this movie when we come out here but he loves it just as much as we do.

Ignoring Allie's question, I lift the blanket and shift closer until our sides are pressed up against one another. I wrap one arm around her shoulders and pull her closer to my chest while adjusting the blanket until it comfortably covers the two of us.

Her body stiffens for just a moment before she relaxes against me and a small thread of satisfaction filters through me. One of her hands presses to my chest right over my heart and I wonder if she can feel it pounding. This girl makes me feel things I'm not entirely sure I want to feel.

My eyes stray to the teal bracelet on her wrist. She's worn it every time I've seen her. Is it sentimental or something? The urge to ask her about it is strong but I hold myself back, unwilling to expose just how much she intrigues me.

Allie definitely isn't like other girls. Those girls want to get with me or my boys because we can do something for them. If they're connected to one of us, their social status goes up. Even if all we do is sleep with them, more guys after that will want them. They want what the Devils have had.

Allie doesn't seem to care about any of that. She doesn't seem to care about status or power.

And knowing that draws me to her even more.

THIRTEEN

Allie

I don't know what is going on between us. It's like something has shifted, the air is charged and the tension thick. Roman's muscular bronze chest is warm beneath my cheek and I find myself absently trailing the devil mask tattoo on his collarbone.

He sighs in contentment and pulls me closer. I'm certain it's a subconscious reaction, because there's nothing sexual about the touch at all. And despite the warning bells in my head, I'm not uncomfortable in his arms. In fact, I'm very comfortable. Like, this is where I belong. Right here in his embrace.

It's not the platonic feeling with him the way it's always been with Julio, however. I have stupid butterflies in my stomach and an ache in my core that has me clenching my thighs together. I don't remember being this drawn to Ryker, as though I want to sink into his skin, share the air he breathes.

Maybe it is sexual.

It's all so confusing. I barely know Roman Valdez, and what I do know paints him as an arrogant jerk. I shouldn't be here with him. I shouldn't let him hold me like this. But I am and no matter how many times I tell myself I need to leave, I stay.

The movie ends and Dominique quietly slips away to his room. Emilio hesitates like he wants to hang out some more but a single death glare from Roman sends him on his way.

Alrighty then. So much for having a buffer.

I stand up once they leave, feeling awkward and out of place. I have no idea what time it is but the commotion outside has quieted. It's safe to assume most of my classmates have gone to bed or are in the process of doing so.

I fold the blanket we'd been using and place it on the back of the sectional before slipping my feet into my sneakers.

"What are you doing?" Roman asks, his arms folded over his chest and his legs spread wide.

Well, someone sure has a self-assured look on his face. I wish I knew what he was thinking. I feel like I'm about to do the walk of shame when I step outside the cabin door, yet we haven't even done anything. Well, unless that kiss earlier counts.

"I was, uh, just getting ready to head out." I shrug.

Roman clasps my hand and tugs me toward him. "Why?"

I bite my bottom lip. He tugs at my hand again, this time harder, and I stumble forward. He catches me and adjusts my weight so I'm straddling his lap, his face now only inches from mine.

I'm drawn into his dark brown gaze and heat pools between my legs. My core tightens and I feel his cock harden beneath me. I'm tempted to shift and rock against him but I don't. I shouldn't. I can't.

"Why are you planning to leave, vanilla?"

With that one word, it's like a bucket of water is dumped over me. "Why do you keep calling me that? What is your deal?" My voice is heated. I hate that he keeps making digs at me. I thought... I don't know what I thought. But I don't like him making fun of me.

He chuckles and my annoyance spikes. "I call you vanilla because..." he trails off with a grin.

I smack his chest lightly. "Come on."

His smile widens into the devilish smirk I've quickly grown accustomed to seeing on his face. He leans forward to whisper in my ear, "It's my favorite flavor."

His breath heats the shell of my ear and I can't fight the tingles that race up and down my spine. "Your favorite flavor?" I ask, confused.

He nuzzles me and murmurs, "Mmm.... Mexican vanilla. The sweetest taste there is."

Oh. My. God.

He trails kisses along my neck, his hands digging into my hips before he pulls back.

"I..." I swallow hard. "It's late. I'm supposed to stay in Aaron's cabin." At the mention of his name Roman growls, a deep throaty sound that leaves more liquid heat pooling between my thighs.

His eyes lock on mine for the briefest of moments before his lips come crashing down on my mouth, and then I'm drowning in him. His touch. His taste. I can't seem to figure out up from down. All I know is that I want him. No. I need him.

My hips thrust forward and I grind against him. He groans and I want to hear that sound again, so, so bad. I press my core against him harder and swivel my hips. His fingers dig into me hard enough to bruise as he clutches me tight to his chest.

"What are you doing to me?" His voice is husky.

I have no answer for him so I kiss him again. I continue rocking against him, swallowing his groans as he greedily drinks down mine. The reality that one of the other guys can walk in on us at any moment doesn't matter. All I can think of is how good he feels.

One calloused palm rises beneath my shirt and tugs down the cup of my bra. He pinches one hard peak and I cry out. It's as if my nipple and clit are connected and I feel my release move closer, hovering just out of reach.

"Oh, God," I gasp and try to move away. This is too much, too fast but Roman chases after me with his lips and I give in to him, too weak to shove him away. I trail my fingers over his bare chest, reveling in the feel of every dip and valley. He tugs my shirt up and I raise my arms, allowing him to pull it from me.

A quick motion at my back and the clasp on my bra comes free. It slips down my shoulders before Roman tugs it forward, discarding it somewhere to the side.

He drinks me in. His hungry gaze locks on my breasts. "So... fucking... beautiful," he murmurs right before his mouth is on me. His lips wrap around my nipple and his tongue lashes at me as his other hand kneads my tender flesh.

I can't take it. I writhe on top of him, pressing myself closer. Wishing there was nothing between us. I need to feel him inside of me. I need to feel something good. Something that can take all the pain and grief away. I know what I'm doing now and for a moment, guilt slams into me before I shove it aside.

I'm using him. But isn't he using me, too?

With me still in his lap, Roman cups my rear and stands. I wrap my legs around his waist and allow him to carry me down the darkened hallway. I kiss his neck. His shoulder. I can't stop touching him.

When we reach a closed door, he fumbles to open it and then steps inside and carries me to the large bed in the center of the room. He lays me down with surprising care and just stands there, looking down at me with wonder on his face.

The emotion worries me. I need whatever we're doing right now to have boundaries.

"Roman?" I push up to my elbows and he cocks his head to the side, his eyes boring into mine. I lick my lips. "This ... whatever this is ... it's just fun. Okay?"

Anger flashes for a split second and then it's gone as though it'd never been there. An easy smile tugs at the corner of his mouth and he reaches for me, his hand trailing up my side to my face before gripping my jaw as he brushes his thumb along my lower lip. "I want you." There's an edge to his voice. It's all I can do not to reach out for him, draw him closer. His hands move to the button on my jeans. "I want to fuck you. I want you to scream my name. And I want you to come on my cock."

I suck in a shuddering breath.

"But I don't do relationships, vanilla, so don't get this twisted. I'm not a nice guy. Right now, I only want one thing from you and that's access to your pussy." As soon as my jeans are undone he slips a hand inside, sinking two fingers deep inside me.

I hiss.

The rational side of me knows this is a bad idea. He'll hurt me. He'll use me and toss me aside and no matter how many times I tell myself I'll use him too, that this is a fair exchange, I know it isn't. But I refuse to worry about that now.

Roman Valdez is like a drug and I'm desperate to get my fix, all the while praying I don't develop an addiction after just one hit.

He slides out of me before hooking his finger in my jeans and panties and in one smooth motion, he whisks both of them off, and then I'm bare to him.

He groans again, his eyes hooded as he drinks in my naked form.

A hand runs up my thigh before pushing my legs apart, exposing my most intimate flesh to his hungry gaze. Instead of climbing onto the bed like I expect him to, he kneels down at the edge of the mattress, bringing his face eye level with my core.

Instinctively, I try and close my legs but his hands on either side keep me spread and open to him. "I'm going to kiss you," he tells me and then begins trailing hot wet kisses along the inside of my leg. He bites the sensitive skin of my inner thigh, forcing me to stiffen and cry out from the unexpected sting. But then he's laving his tongue over the small wound, kissing the slight pain away, and I relax in his hold again. When he gets close to my core he repeats the movements on my other thigh, taking his time. His teeth scrape against my skin and I'm panting now. A complete puddle as my limbs tighten in eager anticipation.

When his face finally comes back to my center, his eyes darken, drunk with need. He takes a deep breath, inhaling me before his tongue darts out and licks me back to front. My hips buck off the bed and I cry out at the sensations. *Holy... wow.*

After that one lick, Roman buries his face between my thighs. Licking, sucking, biting. Sensations tumble through me, too many to count and the next thing I know my release is thundering toward me. I'm so close. I can feel my release *right* there. And then, like breaking through a damn, it crashes through me. It's like a tsunami I can't escape, the fastest, hardest orgasm I've ever experienced, and I cry out with my release, screaming his name. "Roman."

Then he's on top of me. He's removed his boxer briefs and his hard length is pressed against my lower stomach as he pulls my legs up on either side of him, nestling himself between me. He slides against my wet center and I tilt my hips back, widening my legs to grant him a better angle.

He rears back and curses. "Fuck."

I startle and my eyes go wide. "What?"

He climbs off of me and runs a hand through his dark brown hair.

Humiliation sweeps through me and I jerk into a seated position, wrapping my arms around my chest to cover myself.

"Condom," he bites out. Then he looks at me and his eyes narrow. "What are you doing?"

"I..." A blush warms my cheeks as he stands there in all his naked glory without a care in the world. "I... Ah..." I have no words.

He steps closer and leans down, kissing me hard and deep before biting my bottom lip and giving it a tug. My hands fall away from my breasts and I moan into his mouth.

He pulls back with a devilish smirk, "I'm getting a condom and then I'm fucking that tight little pussy of yours."

I swallow hard. "O-okay," I whisper, hating how unsure I sound. I brush loose strands of hair from my face and then his words slam into me. *Condom*. Oh my god. I almost had sex with him without one. What was I thinking?

He strides out of the room completely naked, only to come back seconds later with a square foil packet in his hands. He tears it open with his teeth, rolls it on his thick, hard length, and then is right back in front of me. He kisses me again and leans forward, pressing me back against the mattress.

"Ready for me?" he asks as he lines his cock up with my center. His eyes are hooded, his expression now serious.

"Yes," I say, because right now the idea of him anywhere but inside of me gives me a panicky feeling. When the head of his erection nudges against my core, he locks his eyes with mine and he holds my gaze.

"I won't be gentle."

I nod in consent and with that one small motion, he's slamming into me in a single hard, smooth trust. Stars explode behind my eyelids and I push my hips up to meet his, gasping at how full I feel. He lets out a string of curses. One hand tightens on my hip, pressing me down into the mattress as the other rests beside my head, bracing his body above mine.

"So fucking good, vanilla."

I whimper his name and kiss the strong column of his neck, nipping playfully.

He slides out of me, slow and smooth before thrusting back inside, this time even harder. Deeper. I grab hold of his biceps, holding onto him like my life depends on it. His groans undo me.

He grips my jaw and slams his mouth down on mine, devouring me like he's starved for my mouth. He kisses my lips, my neck, my shoulder, and then he's thrusting hard and fast, not giving me a chance to catch my breath. His kisses grow more aggressive as he all but punishes my body. His hold on me is so tight I know I'll have bruises in the morning and I don't even care.

I'm on fire. Every cell in my body humming with greedy need and expectation. I can feel another orgasm building inside me and I offer no resistance.

A needy moan climbs up my throat, my body winding tighter and tighter. *Oh my god.* "I'm going to come again," I pant.

Roman pulls out of me and I cry out at the loss of contact but then he's flipping me over onto my stomach, pulling at my hips until my ass is raised high up in the air. Then he slams his cock back inside of me. This angle has him thrusting deeper almost to the point of pain. But it's the best pain.

"Come for me, Allie. Come hard." He tangles one hand in my hair, pulling my head back as far as it will go, my spine arches and my breasts thrust forward. My inner walls clench tight around him and my orgasm shatters around me. Colors explode like fireworks behind my eyelids. He feels that good. So, freaking good.

He begins driving himself harder into me, grinding his teeth with each savage stroke. "Mine," he snarls, biting my shoulder like a wild animal. He fucks me raw and angry, pounding into me without mercy as though he's exorcising his demons. My hands itch to touch him. To roam his muscular body. But I can't in this position. All I can do is barely manage to hold on to my sanity as he fucks me like I've never been fucked before, effectively ruining me for anyone else who might come after him.

I scream his name again as my body locks up for the third time, my inner walls gripping him tight as I shatter, drowning in the waves of yet another release. I collapse face first onto the mattress, the sensations too much for my body to bear. His hands hold my hips back and he stiffens behind me, his body shuddering against mine with his own release before he pulls out, leaving me empty and aching.

His lips find my ear and he says, "My pussy. Got that? For as long as I want it."

I want to deny him. To tell him to fuck off because he doesn't own me, but at the moment, all I can manage is a grunt and I don't even know if it's in agreement or denial.

He tugs me into his arms, nestling me beneath his chin as we both struggle to catch our breath, and when I finally do manage to get my breathing under control, I decide not to address his statement. I can't form the words let alone digest the meaning behind what he just said.

It's possessive in the extreme.

After a few minutes pass, he gets up, leaves the room still gloriously naked, and disposes of the condom. He comes back with a warm washcloth and with surprising care he wipes away the remnants of my release from my thighs before tossing the washcloth in a dark corner of the room.

I consider getting up and leaving. Finding my clothes and heading for Aaron's cabin. I shouldn't stay here. It would send the wrong message. This is just fun. No strings. No emotions.

But when he tugs me toward the head of the bed and helps me slip beneath the covers, I resign myself to the fact that I don't have it in me to fight him.

Neither of us says a word. Roman reels me in until I'm resting splayed across his chest, my ear pressed against his beating heart and the night melts away. My body slips into the first restful sleep I've had since my mom passed away.

FOURTEEN

Roman

I wake up to a loud banging at the front door. What the fuck?

Allie is asleep beside me. Her hair is a tangled mess of brown waves and her expression is relaxed. I watch her for a moment as her chest rises and falls, the sheet barely covering her pert breasts.

Just as I'm about to lean down and suck on her beautiful tits before rolling her over and sliding into her wet heat, the knocking that woke me up in the first place sounds again, though this time louder, closer.

Someone better be dying because Dom and Emilio know not to come knocking this early in the fucking morning.

I groan and throw my legs over the edge of the bed, rubbing my eyes to clear the sleep from them. Finding my boxers, I slip them on and then open my bedroom door with a scowl on my face.

"What?"

Dominique stands on the other side, an amused expression on his face as his eyes wander past me, spotting Allie in my bed. I step to the side, blocking his view of her as I cross my arms over my chest and raise a brow. "*Cabrón*, there better be a good fucking reason you're waking me up right now."

He tilts his head back toward the front of the cabin. "Henderson's looking for her. Figured you'd want to deal with that."

Any good mood I woke up with instantly sours at the sound of his name. "What the fuck does he want?"

Dom shrugs. "What you've got in that bed of yours would be my guess."

I flip him off. "Keep your voice down. You're going to wake her up." He nods and I throw on a pair of sweats and a Sun Valley High hoodie.

Dressed, I head toward the front of the cabin and find Henderson pacing on the front porch. His brows are furrowed and he runs his hands through his shaggy blond hair. Asshole looks like a Bieber wannabe.

When he spots me, his eyes narrow into slits and his fists clench at his sides. He looks me up and down, hate evident in his glare. I wait. As if this fucker can scare me. He'll need to do a hell of a lot better than that.

He takes in my outfit as though searching for evidence of what happened last night. I snort. Is he expecting to find me with the condom still wrapped around my dick?

"Where is she?" he bites out.

"Sleeping," I tell him, enjoying the anger I see bubbling up inside of him. He wants to hit me. I can tell by the tick in his jaw and the way he keeps clenching then unclenching his fists, but Aaron Henderson isn't a complete idiot. He knows he can't take me. He may hit the gym and ride that stupid board of his but I dominate on the field and take hit after hit day in and day out. Doling out some of my own in return both on and off the field.

Henderson wouldn't stand a chance against me and he knows it.

"What did you do to her?"

I roll my eyes, not even bothering to pretend I didn't fuck her brains out. Better for this asshole to learn now that she's mine. Mine to use. Mine to fuck. He lost the game before he even had a chance to play. "Nothing she didn't want." I let my words sink in.

He takes a menacing step forward. "I want to see her," he snarls, inches away from my face.

I lean against the doorway giving him a bored expression. "Why? So you can apologize for fucking the girl who was a bitch to her? You think that will get you inside her tight little pussy?"

He draws back in surprise and flicks his eyes up toward me. "She saw that?"

I fold my arms over my chest. It's not my job to explain shit to him. I don't want him thinking Allie's only here with me because he fucked up. I'm not her second choice. She came eager and willing. It had nothing to do with this asshole.

He looks away, nodding his head and muttering to himself, but I don't bother listening. "What do you want, Henderson? It's early and I haven't had any coffee so get to the point of this little visit and then get off my fucking porch."

He tugs at his blond hair, making it stick out in all directions. "I just wanted to check on her. Make sure she was okay. She didn't come back to the cabin last—"

I cut him off. "If you were that concerned, you would have been looking for her last night. Not this morning after your piece of ass slinked out of your bed."

Guilt flashes across his face confirming what I'd suspected. Henderson got his dick wet and didn't once think about Allie until after he'd gotten what he wanted. "Good thing for you, I took *real good* care of her. Fucked her all night long." I push off the porch and step toward him, using my height to tower over him. "And fuck, Henderson. You don't know what you're missing. She's so tight and when she begs for it"—I grab my crotch in a suggestive manner—"music to my fucking ears."

I have no fucking idea why I'm saying any of this. Why I want—no need—Henderson and every other asshole at our school to know that Allie Ramirez is off limits until I deem otherwise.

We agreed to fun. No strings. No commitments. I'm not the relationship type, so hearing that from her last night should have made me happy. Instead, it made my blood run hot. It filled my ears with a roar and I took my anger out on her hot little body. I was the one in charge. I decided whatever this was or wasn't between us.

I should wake her up and send her on her way as soon as this fucker leaves. It's what I would do with any other girl. But that idea has me gritting my teeth.

If I do that, Henderson will just make another play at her. I'll keep her this weekend to stick it to the asshole. Remind him that I can take any girl I want when I want. Yeah, sounds like a great fucking idea.

I step back inside and slam the door in Henderson's face, not giving him a chance to respond. I can't stand guys like him. He's such a fucking tool.

Back inside, Dom waves toward the fresh pot of coffee. I wave him off. "Later," I say. Because right now there is a naked woman in my bed and I have plans to do wicked, wicked things to her body.

FIFTEEN

Allie

I wake to unfamiliar surroundings. Bright light filters in through the window. I close my eyes against the early morning rays as the scent of chorizo and eggs assails my senses. Mmmm. Stretching my arms above my head, my face still pressed against the mattress, I work out some of the lingering aches in my body.

Who's cooking? Mom? I wonder with a frown, face still buried in my pillow.

That can't be right. What day is it today ... Saturday? She'd be working at ...

Then I remember she wouldn't be working anywhere because she's gone.

I'm immediately hit with a crushing wave of sadness. I choke on a gasp but before my grief can consume me, I feel fingers skim lightly down my back. A roughened jaw scrapes against my skin. Memories of last night and who I shared them with come rushing to the forefront of my mind. And when Roman rolls me over to my back, splaying my legs wide and teasing my body with skilled fingers, I arch toward him, immersing myself in the sensations of his touch as I push away the ache in my chest.

He worships my body and I drown in him. His taste. His touch. Breathing in the scent of sun, coriander, and musk that is uniquely him, it's as if I'll die without him in my lungs.

When emotions threaten to bubble up inside of me, I urge him to go faster. Harder. And he's all too happy to comply. Fucking me to the edge of orgasm again and again without letting me dive off that particular cliff as I cling to him, almost afraid for when I fall.

Each time I get close to the edge, he shuts it down until I'm a writhing ball of desire, unable to think beyond the need coursing inside of me.

He's just as rough with me this morning as he'd been the night before only this time, he doesn't mask his hunger. His bone-deep desire to consume me. It should scare me. But it doesn't. I need this just as much as he does.

My orgasm is right there, so close yet so far away, when Roman slows down his thrusts.

I cry out in frustration, desperate for my release.

"You wanna come, vanilla?"

I nod, unable to form coherent words and I clench around him, chasing what I know waits just around the corner.

"Beg. Beg for it and maybe, just maybe, I'll let you come."
His words are harsh, his tone mocking.

I bare my teeth at him, hating that he has this power over
me. I shake my head, refusing to voice the words he's asking
for. I need to come but not like this. Not at his mercy.

His eyes narrow, a tick forming in his jaw as he slows his
thrusts once again.

"Beg, baby girl." He nuzzles my neck, nips my jaw. "Or I'll
leave you wanting."

"No."

Something deep inside makes me rebel against his
command. To show him he isn't the only one in control
here. I know he wants me. This. Whatever it is. Just as
much as I do. I can feel his need. He's shaking with it.

With a snarl he slams his mouth to mine, our lips meeting
in a furious kiss of tongue and teeth before he bites my
bottom lip hard enough to make me gasp. "Don't say I
didn't warn you."

I open my mouth to smart off but before I can speak a single
word, he flips our position until I'm on top of him, forcing
me to ride his cock. For a split second, I'm relieved. I can set
the pace I want, and I do. I grind my hips against his pelvis
and he thrusts up into me, driving himself deeper until, in
three harsh strokes, he's shuddering beneath me. I curse,
knowing he came and not being able to do a damn thing to
stop it. I grind up and down on his now softening dick and
he folds his arms up behind his head to watch the show.

But nothing is going to happen because his dick is getting soft and dammit, I still haven't come. Fury thrums through me. I tighten my jaw and dig my fingernails into his chest as I push myself off of him.

He almost manages to hide his flinch. "Should have begged for it," he says.

"You're an ass."

"Never pretended not to be," he calls to my back as I gather my clothes to get dressed. *Un-fucking-believable.*

"Oh, and by the way, Henderson came looking for you this morning." I pause but before I can ask what he said, he continues, "Don't worry though. I told him I took *real good* care of you."

Emilio offers me a breakfast burrito as I head out the door but I decline. Not the least bit hungry. I haven't been eating much since Mom died, and after what just happened with Roman, I have absolutely zero appetite. I'm fuming over the fact he took his pleasure and then denied me mine. Who the hell does he think he is? *Stupid devil.*

I go searching for Aaron uncertain of what sort of reception I'll get. I can't believe Roman said that.

Asshole.

I march across the clearing in search of Aaron, pissed at myself for allowing Roman to get under my skin and determined to smooth things over with Aaron in person. I can't afford to screw up one of the few friendships I have in this town.

I find him easy enough. He's sitting on the back of someone's tailgate, drinking a beer, and joking with a group of guys similarly dressed. They all look like they just walked out of a Zumiez so I figure they're boarders like Aaron.

When he spots me walking toward him, he sets down his beer and leans back against the bed of the truck. I can't see his eyes masked behind a pair of blue mirrored Ray Bans but I can tell by the downward curve of his lip that I'm not going to get a warm reception.

"Hey," I say and offer a small wave. *Really Allie? A wave? Because that wasn't awkward.*

"Hey."

I stand there, shifting from one foot to the other. He doesn't say anything else and the other three guys with him are now staring at me like I've grown three heads while wearing a tutu.

"Can we talk?" I ask.

He shrugs. "Sure. Talk."

Okay then. I guess I should have expected that. I lick my lips wishing I could see his eyes, gauge just how mad he is with me right now.

"*Aaron,*" I drag out his name.

He huffs out an exasperated sigh. "Whatever. Fine." Jumping down from the tailgate he walks toward his cabin and stops just in front of the porch to lean against the railing. "What can I do for you?" He waves his beer with an over exaggerated flourish.

"You don't have to be a jerk," I mutter, folding my arms across my chest.

He's silent for a beat and I realize he's not going to say anything. Awesome. Now it's my turn to sigh. "Look, I just wanted to apologize for bailing on you last night. I saw that girl on your lap by the fire and figured you'd want the room to yourself." I shrug and do my best to adopt an apologetic look. "I wasn't trying to ghost you."

Silence.

"If you don't want me here anymore, I'll grab my things and get a ride back to town."

Nothing.

Wonderful.

"Whatever." I turn to head inside his cabin to grab my stuff, praying I can catch an Uber out here in the middle of boom-freaking-nowhere when his hand on my elbow stops me.

I pause, but don't turn back to him.

Gravel crunches beneath his feet as he steps closer, moving around me until we're facing one another. He rubs the back of his neck in an almost nervous gesture, but I must be reading that wrong.

"I'm sorry. I was a dick." The corner of his mouth curls up in an apologetic smile.

Really? "I'm sorry too. I really wasn't trying to be a B and ghost you." It's true. Granted, I also wasn't trying to steer clear so I wasn't a cock-block either. But he doesn't need to know that. He also doesn't need to know I was swept away by good looks and hot tattoos. Wouldn't be the first time I'd made poor decisions while intoxicated. First Ryker. Now Roman. *Urgh.* And if I'm being honest with myself, it probably wasn't my last. And if I was really, really honest, booze had nothing to do with it. "Are we cool?" I ask, shoving away my inner monologue. I could berate myself and my poor decision-making skills later. "Because I like hanging out with you. I don't have many friends here and it'd be nice not to lose that with you."

He exhales sharply. "Yeah. I know I'm overreacting, it's just," he pauses. "I have bad history with the Devils, ya know?"

I quirk a brow in question because no, I don't know. I have no idea what issues lie between them. Only that it appears to be mutual.

"They're all assholes. Especially Roman. I don't want to see you get hurt. Those three can be cruel to girls after they get what they want from them." He gives me a knowing look.

I can't stop the heat I know is spreading across my cheeks, so I look away. Is that what's going to happen? Is Roman going to move on now that he's had his fun? If he does, it's not like I should be surprised.

But I'm not looking for a relationship. I have too much baggage for something like that right now. I wanted fun, and last night I got that. Sure, this morning sucked and Roman is a complete asshole, but it's not the end of the world either.

Aaron reaches out and tucks a strand of hair that escaped my braid behind my ear.

I still can't see his eyes and have no idea what he's thinking, so I go with my gut. "You don't have to worry. We came here to have fun, right? You got laid. I got laid. Neither of us needs to make a big deal of it. Is what's-her-name you hooked up with the love of your life?"

He snorts.

"That's what I thought. Let's not make mountains out of molehills. How about we hang today? Just you and me and whatever friends you have here that you actually like? No Devils allowed."

His smile widens, giving me a glimpse of dimples I hadn't noticed before. "Yeah?"

"Yeah."

SIXTEEN

Roman

She doesn't look at me the rest of the weekend. I should have expected this. Calculated the risk. I know she's not some meek little wallflower, no matter that she sometimes pretends to be. She's punishing me for leaving her hanging and it's fucking working. What was supposed to be a punishment for *her*, a reminder of who the fuck was in charge here, ended up backfiring on me and now I'm watching her like some lovesick dog without his bone.

I keep forgetting she isn't like the rest of the girls here at Sun Valley High. She doesn't give two shits who I am and she's making that abundantly clear. She sticks close to Henderson all day Saturday, leaving me little room to swoop in and take her. Not unless I want to make a big show of it, and yeah, that's not happening. So, I'm left to stew as she laughs with the motherfucker, drinks with him, lets him touch her. It's not romantic. At least I don't think it is for her. But every time that asshole throws an arm around her shoulders, I want to pummel his face in.

Allie Ramirez is mine. Mine to fuck. Mine to hurt. Mine to soothe, should I decide to. I'm itching to touch her and it's doing things to my head I don't like.

"Ro, what's your deal, man?" Dom asks as I brood on the cabin porch sipping on a glass of water, nursing back a bit of a hangover from the night before. I don't drink often. None of us do. Football is too important. But the few beers and the game of beer pong are leaving their mark today. "I figured you'd fuck the girl out of your system and walk away. What gives?"

I grunt. "Maybe I just want a few more fucks before I move along."

Before I finish the sentence, he's already shaking his head. "Nah. I've seen you with girls. This one is different. I get the whole mind-games shit you like to pull with chicks, but even that's different with her. You cooked last night, and don't try and bullshit me into believing that was for me or Emilio. You did that for her. Why?"

Emilio interrupts, stepping outside, still rocking that stupid bright ass bikini over his sweat pants. "I like Allie. Can we keep her?"

Dom and I both jerk our heads toward him. "What?" I ask, surprise coloring my voice.

"I said, can we keep her?"

"She's not a puppy," Dom chides, but his brows furrow like he's wondering the same thing.

"Why?" I ask again.

Emilio rolls his eyes. "Hello, I just said because I like her. Are you even paying attention? What is up with you today, man?"

I turn to Dom but all he does is shrug and raise a brow as if to say, *don't ask me*. Some help he is. I don't get this side of Emilio. Sure, the guy's nice to pretty much everyone, but only at face value. He doesn't actually like people. I don't even think he cares for Dom or I all that much and we're his best fucking friends.

"What happened to you two fuckers saying I needed to focus on the field?"

"I changed my mind. I wanna keep her. If you're not into her anymore now that you've had your fun just say the word. I don't mind sloppy seconds. Based on the sounds I heard coming from your room last night, that girl is well worth the trouble."

I stand and take a menacing step toward my best friend, ready to nail the asshole in the face with my fist when Dom steps between us. "What are you planning here?"

"To wipe that smug look off his face." I point my water bottle right at Emilio and the fucker smiles at me.

Dom shakes his head. "Not with numb nuts over there. What are you planning with Allie?"

My jaw tightens and I glare at him. "I don't have any plans," I bite out, "Why the fuck are you two down my throat about her all of a sudden?"

"She's not like other girls," he says.

"I'm aware. If she was, she'd be over here kissing my boots instead of playing around with Henderson all goddamn day. What do you want from me?"

Emilio shoves himself between the two of us and flicks his gaze back and forth. "He wants you to lay out your intentions, Rome. We both do." And for once the dude has a serious expression on his face.

I glower. "Why the hell are you two so goddamn interested in who I fuck all of a sudden?"

Dom grunts. "Because Emilio is right. We like her. Neither of us wants you to fuck things up for us."

My mouth drops open. "For *us*?"

Emilio nods and smacks me in the chest light-heartedly. "Yeah, fucker. For us. Like I said, we like her. She fits in with our crew. She doesn't see dollar signs when she looks at any of us like every other chick in this town. We could use a feminine touch up in here. Too much testosterone with you two jackasses all the time if you ask me, and your dick is going to fuck that up so this is us telling you not to do that. Lo entiendes?" *Do you understand?* Was he fucking with me right now? "Say whatever you need to say to her. You fucked something up this morning or she wouldn't be hanging with that ass wipe and you wouldn't be over here brooding."

My jaw clenches. "This isn't how things roll with us." There's a bite in my tone I usually reserve for everyone but the two people beside me. Dominique and Emilio are like my brothers. They're family. But I don't take orders from anyone and I don't have to explain myself to them.

Emilio meets my stare and his eyes narrow, sparking with something I'm not used to seeing in his gaze. "She's the relationship type."

I work my jaw harder. "And this matters to you because..."

"You're not."

"Never tried to claim I was," I remind him. And then I add in for good measure, "She laid her cards out first. She wants fun. No strings. Don't jump down my throat for giving the girl exactly what she asked for."

Both their expressions consider me for a moment, searching for any deception. Then Dom asks, "She really said that?" He doesn't sound convinced.

"Yeah, fucker. She did. So calm down."

"Fine, let's assume we buy that. What'd you do to piss her off?"

My shoulders sag and I grit my teeth.

"Come on, fucker. Spill." Emilio says, all but bouncing beside me. The guy is wired this morning. I need to remember to hide the coffee from him.

"I fucked her."

"And...?"

I huff out a breath. "And I withheld her orgasm when she refused to beg for it."

Dominique whistles and Emilio whoops, then says, "I always knew you were a shady asshole with control issues but fuck, man, that's cold. And let me guess, you still got yours?"

I nod.

Emilio cackles, covering his mouth as he folds over at the waist before he straightens. There are tears of laughter shining in his eyes. "Damn. If you want inside that pussy anytime soon, expect to do some groveling."

Not. Fucking. Happening.

SEVENTEEN

Allie

The hallway is teeming with activity as I walk toward my first class Monday morning. I ignore the looks directed my way as I have been since I transferred here, but something about a few of them make the hairs on the back of my neck stand on edge.

There's more hostility in them now. Not just the usual indifference I'd grown used to last week.

I'm not winning any popularity contests this year, not that I expected to being the new girl, but I have a feeling the camping trip is why I've suddenly earned the extra attention, in particular from the girls of this school. If looks could kill, let me tell you, it's like I just walked onto the set of *Mean Girls* and every girl walking past is another Regina George with their eyes locked on me, marking me as prey.

I shiver and cast a quick glance over my shoulder as I head to my English class. Spotting Silvia and a group of her friends, I step to the side, hugging close to the lockers to avoid her, but of course she sees me, and before I can slip into my first period, she's shoving her way through the crowded halls right toward me.

I cringe. This isn't going to end well.

I'd kind of expected a confrontation up at Shadle Creek and was relieved when one never happened, but it looks like she's been biding her time and now this seems to be her golden opportunity to put the new girl in her place.

Her upper lip curls into a sneer and four more girls close in beside her. I brace myself for whatever verbal lashing she has to offer, knowing it likely has to do with her being kicked out of the Devil's cabin that first night, when the next thing I know, an open palm slaps me across the face. My head snaps to the side, my mouth dropping open as my hand jerks up to clutch my cheek. I barely register the sting and all I'm thinking is, *WHAT. THE. HELL?*

The blow had come out of nowhere. I'm so startled by the violence that I don't react other than to clutch at my face, my eyes wide and my body immobile.

"You're such a stupid whore," she snarls, spittle flying toward me coupled with her vile words. All eyes turn toward us, the silence in the previously boisterous hallway deafening.

Goddammit. I can't hit her back. Her friends have stepped forward, forming a half circle around me. If I hit her, they'll step in and help. I don't have friends here and I don't feel like being jumped, but the urge to fight back has me clenching my hands beside me into tight fists as I take a deep breath, my nostrils flaring.

I step forward determined to force my way past her but she shoves me back into the lockers. My back slams into the cool metal surface and a single manicured finger lifts and points arrogantly in my face.

I grit my teeth together, refusing to rise to the bait. The shove was hard. The slap harder. But she isn't that strong. Neither have done more than surprise me and I refuse to stand here and cower to the school's resident mean girl.

I tilt my chin up, meeting her emerald gaze head on.

Silvia's one of the it girls. In the eyes of the students here, she's at the top. And I'm at the bottom. I don't expect anyone to come to my aid, which is why I'm surprised when the crowd parts and Emilio swaggers toward me, an easy grin on his face—but I don't miss the bright hot fury in his eyes.

He assesses the situation before him, a tick forming along his jaw and between one second and the next, I can tell he's come to some sort of conclusion about what's going on here.

A flash of concern crosses over Silvia's face when she spots him before she tries to mask it with cool indifference. Hands propped on her hips she purses her lips while she continues to stare down her nose at me.

Emilio makes a noise to catch her attention before snapping his fingers like he's just realized something interesting.

"You were at the campout this weekend, right?" he asks, moving closer toward us.

When he's only a foot away, he leans next to the lockers beside me, lifts one hand and rubs his bottom lip with his thumb as he gives Silvia a considering look as though he's trying to place her.

She mistakes it for interest and turns her full attention toward him. Her scowl is now a seductive smile, and at this point I'm all but forgotten. "I was." Her words are breathy. She pushes her shoulders back, ensuring her breasts are thrust out toward him before lowering her head so she can look up at him through her lashes.

I roll my eyes, at her come-hither expression. It's so blatantly obvious I can't imagine guys actually fall for this crap.

Emilio pushes off from the locker, his eyes darkening as he closes the distance between them. I guess her little seduction tactics really do work.

"Yeah, I remember you. I almost fucked you." His words are husky, shot full of arrogance.

When he's a scant few inches away, he raises his hand to cup the side of her neck, his thumb resting in the center of her throat. "MmmHmm. We can rectify that anytime you'd like." She leans toward him as he dips his head to whisper just loud enough for our ears to hear.

"Pass. You must either be blind or stupid then, because if you were paying attention, you'd know Allie's with us.

She's Devil property and we don't take kindly to people fucking with what's ours."

His thumb presses firmly against her throat and she gasps. The skin around his grip whitens and her eyes are wide, suddenly filled with fear.

Then he releases her and steps back as if nothing happened. An easy smile slips into place and he tosses an arm around my shoulder, drawing me in to his side.

"We gonna have problems, Silvia?"

Her lips tighten, heat now coloring her face and neck.

"She's an outsider," one of the girls beside Silvia spits out.

It's the wrong answer to Emilio's question. His fists clench at his sides and he looks around the hallway, all eyes still glued to the scene in front of us.

"Ice them out," he says to no one in particular, but heads all around us nod.

Silvia sucks in a breath as her four friends all take quick steps back, putting distance between themselves and her. "You can't do that."

He chuckles, but it's a dark, dangerous sound. "I can do whatever the fuck I want. You made a mistake. I suggest you learn from it."

She opens her mouth to respond just as another voice calls out over the sea of students.

"What's going on over here?" A man's voice booms through the hallway. "Break it up. Everyone get to class." The hall empties just as the first bell rings and everyone heads to their first period.

Silvia waits for a beat before she, too, leaves, but not before I see the hate-filled look in her eyes telling me things between us are far from over. If anything, Emilio stepping in only added fuel to the fire. If she didn't hate me before, she certainly does now.

Mr. Alvarez—the school principal—comes into view, eyeing Emilio and me warily. "Mr. Chavez, Ms. Ramirez, get to class." He claps his hands and I jump and move to do as I've been told but Emilio's grip on my wrist stops me from making my escape.

"That shit happens again, you find me. Got it?" His dark brown eyes meet mine.

"Why?" I'm so confused as to why he'd help me in the first place. Is this because I slept with his friend? Emilio comes off like the nice guy, sure. He reminds me a lot of my friend Felix back home. Which is how I know Emilio never makes a move that isn't calculated and he had no reason to step in just now and help me.

He frowns at me. "That's a dumb-ass question, vanilla. What do you mean, why?"

I shrug my shoulders and rather than answering him, I say, "Fine. I'll find you."

"See that you do." Satisfied, he releases me and we both head off to our first class. I spot Roman waiting for me outside the door leading into English. He doesn't say anything. His dark brown eyes meet mine but I can't get a read on him. I know he saw what just happened but whether he cares or not is a complete mystery to me. I wish I could crack his hard exterior shell. I'm still pissed at him. He was a complete ass Saturday morning and never bothered apologizing for it afterward, not that I'd expected him to. However, I did expect him to talk to me again, but I got nothing. Not even a goodbye on Sunday as everyone drove out heading back into town.

Without a word he turns and heads into class. I sigh. I do not have the energy to deal with both Silvia and Roman today.

By lunch, the entire school is buzzing with news that the Devils have claimed me. And not just one Devil. No, though that would have been more than enough, but Emilio made sure to say *ours* as if he speaks for all of them, making me the property of not one asshole but three. I'm not entirely sure what being *claimed* by them means, but the stares and whispers have definitely increased tenfold. If I thought this morning was bad, the afternoon is even worse.

So much for flying under the radar till graduation.

I grab my lunch as quickly as possible, intending to take it and hide out in the library, but Dominique puts an end to that idea when he lifts my tray from my hands and with his own, carries them both over to the table in the corner forcing me to follow if I want to eat. I almost consider letting him just have my food. It's not like I plan on eating much of it anyway.

I've lost six pounds since mom died. I should eat more but I just can't seem to stomach it. Though I had no problems eating the *albóndigas* Roman made for us.

Dom sets my tray down on the table beside Roman before rounding to the other side and taking a seat next to Emilio. No one says anything about my arrival, they just dive into conversation about an upcoming game like nothing is weird about me sitting with them.

Alrighty then.

I poke at my lunch—a chicken patty with mashed potatoes and gravy on the side. The lunch lady said it was chicken fried steak day but nothing about this looks like chicken fried steak. Still, I make an effort to swallow a bite before using my fork to move things around so it at least looks like I ate something.

I spot Aaron a few tables away, his gaze trained on me. When he realizes I'm looking at him, he flicks on his mirrored shades and turns back to the guys he was talking to.

I deflate and look away only to see Roman's gaze lasered in on me. His mouth is set in a hard line as dark brown eyes search mine. "Something going on between you and Henderson?" he asks.

I roll my eyes. "He's my friend and he doesn't seem all that fond of you three. That answer your question?"

Roman nods and sucks his bottom lip into his mouth before throwing an arm over my shoulder and giving Aaron a fuck-you grin. God. Guys can be such assholes sometimes.

I shrug out from under his hold. "Stop trying to stir up trouble," I tell him, smacking his arm.

He grips my chin and turns my face toward him. I lick my lips and his eyes track the movement, hunger in his gaze. "Allie, haven't you learned I'm nothing but trouble?"

His head dips and he presses his lips to mine. At first, it's a soft press but then his teeth are tugging on my bottom lip, urging me to open for him. I do and his tongue darts in for a quick taste that leaves me reeling in my seat.

He pulls back, cocky arrogance stamped on his face before I catch him looking over my shoulder. I don't need to turn to know he and Aaron are locked in a stare down. My cheeks heat and anger unfurls inside of me.

"When you decide to stop being a jerk, let me know." I stand to leave the table but his hand around the back of my thigh stops me.

"Sit down."

I snort and take a step but his grip only tightens. "Allie—" there's a warning in his voice, one I choose to one hundred percent ignore.

"I'll catch up with you guys later."

I pull away and make my way over to Aaron's table, knowing Roman would never follow me. Guys like him can't be seen chasing after a girl, let alone a no one like me. When I reach Aaron, his glasses are still on so I reach down and push them up over the top of his head.

"Hey." I pause, suddenly unsure of what to say to him. The drive back from Shadle Creek had been fine. I thought we had things sorted but judging by the look on his face, he's still pissed.

He tilts his chin toward Roman and the guys. "You looked cozy."

I fold my arms over my chest. "And you look mad."

He shakes his head. "Nah. Not mad. Disappointed. But why should I be, right?"

"Excuse me?"

He stands and moves closer to me, his mouth so close his lips brush along the shell of my ear. "Every girl in this school wants to spread their legs for Roman Valdez. I just assumed you wouldn't be one of them. My bad. From what I hear, it sounds like you're screwing all three."

EIGHTEEN

Allie

I'm still reeling from Aaron's words when I get home from school. I have nothing but time on my hands so, of course, I stew. I can't believe his nerve. I'm not some whore. I don't sleep around. Roman is literally the second person I've slept with and I sure as hell don't allow myself to get passed around like some hood rat. I am not one of *those* girls.

I pace my room, leaving a worn path in the pale beige carpet, and I finally decide enough is enough. I can't let his opinion consume me. I know who I am. If he wants to be an ass, let him. I don't need him.

Powering up my laptop, I catch up on some homework before touching up my resume and sending it off to at least a dozen local businesses. I need a job. All this downtime is driving me insane. I need to find a way to stay busy. I spot the sneakers I bought at Target and an idea forms in my head.

Stripping out of the white skinny jeans and lavender blouse I wore today, I throw on a pair of leggings, a band shirt, and my new Target sneakers. I curse when I realize I don't own a sports bra but figure what I'm wearing will do. Throwing my hair up in a messy bun, I tuck my phone into the hidden zipper pouch on the side of my leggings and grab my wireless earbuds and a water bottle.

Janessa sent me a calendar notification earlier letting me know Gerald has requested my presence at dinner this evening. I confirmed that I'd be there, though I'm still not sure where *there* is exactly, since under location it said TBD, but I do know the time. She scheduled dinner for six, so I have a little over an hour before I need to be back in order to have enough time to shower and get ready.

Jogging down the stairs, I tuck in my headphones, blaring some old-school Linkin Park. *Numb* drowns out my thoughts as I head outside and let myself get sucked into the heavy thrum of music. It's still fairly warm, despite it being November, and a thin sheen of sweat coats my body within the first fifteen minutes of my run. My breathing is heavy, my legs already cramping, but I push myself to keep going. I need this. I've never been much of a runner but already I can tell I'll be doing this again.

Fifteen minutes turns to thirty before I stumble to a stop. Bracing my hands on my knees I suck in lungfuls of air. The sun is setting, suburban streetlights illuminate the streets. A car rumbles in the distance, growing closer, but I don't bother looking up until I realize it's slowed to a stop and is now idling beside me.

I stand to my full height, propping my hands on the back of my hips as I try and catch my breath, while at the same time, I'm ready to run hard and fast should I need to. But then I see it's Aaron in his WRX.

Mouth pressed into a tight line, he looks me up and down. "You look like shit."

I flip him off, not even bothering with civility at this point.

He leans over and opens the passenger side door. "Come on. I'll give you a lift home."

"I'm only a few blocks away."

He lifts a single brow as if to say, *so?*

"Fine." I climb in, immediately sinking into the cool leather seats. Cold AC fans my face and I sigh, closing my eyes.

"I didn't realize you were a runner."

"I'm not. Just ... needed to clear my head."

He's quiet so I open my eyes and glance at him through my peripheral. He pulls up to the mansion that is Gerald's elaborate home and I move to open the door. "Thanks for the lift."

Before I can step out, he halts me with a hand on my arm. "Wait."

I stop and turn to face him, leaving the door open.

He scrubs both hands down his face before dragging his gaze back to me. "I hate the Devils."

My anger flares and I suddenly remember what he said to me earlier and why I should still be pissed off with him. "Noted." I get out and step away from the car, slamming the door behind me.

The engine shuts off and Aaron's door opens and closes, but I'm already heading for the front door. "Allie, wait," he calls out, but I don't bother stopping. I'm almost to the door when it swings open and Gerald's stern face greets me, bringing me to a hard stop.

"Alejandra, is that you shouting out here?"

His pale eyes flick from me to the boy I know is standing a few paces behind me. "Sorry." I wilt under his scrutiny. "We didn't mean to disturb you."

"Have some decorum. We have neighbors."

My face falls and I nod. "Sorry," I mutter, hating that this man I barely know has the power to make me feel two inches small. I'm just about to slip in past him when I feel Aaron step in beside me.

"I'm Aaron Henderson, sir. I go to school with Allie. It's nice to meet you." Aaron thrusts out his hand and surprisingly, Gerald takes it, giving it a firm shake and giving Aaron an assessing look.

"You're Allen's boy?" he asks.

Aaron nods. "Yes, sir."

Okay, hold up. What is going on right now?

"I'm happy to see my daughter making respectable friends. I was worried when I agreed to send her to Sun Valley Public instead of Prep, but it was your father who reminded me he'd made a similar decision with you. Thank you for looking after her."

Aaron nods. I shoot him a questioning look but he either doesn't see it or chooses to ignore it.

"Well uh, thanks for the ride." I give Aaron a small wave, cringing at the awkwardness of it when Gerald does the unthinkable and invites him in.

"Allie, why don't you run along and get ready for dinner. Aaron and I will be in my study when you're done."

What?

Aaron's expression brightens at the invitation, and when Gerald steps back, opening the door wider to grant us both entrance, Aaron sweeps right on in as though he's been here a dozen times.

"Uh..."

Aaron meets my gaze giving me a small nod.

Alright then. "I guess I'll go take a shower."

Neither one of them respond. Gerald grips Aaron's shoulder in an almost fatherly embrace as he leads him away from me and toward his study.

I jog up the stairs, stripping my sweat-soaked clothes off as soon as the door to my bedroom is firmly closed behind me.

Why would Gerald want to talk with Aaron in his study?
Clearly, he knows his parents but ...

I rush through washing my hair and body, taking the fastest
shower of my life. Something about leaving Aaron and
Gerald alone together is setting off alarm bells in my head.
And what was all that about looking after his daughter?
Why didn't Aaron mention that our dads knew each other?

I dry off at record speed before pulling my hair into a wet
and tangled messy bun. I'm assuming dinner will be here
since Gerald invited Aaron to join us. I throw on a knee-
length, long-sleeved dress in a soft blue, cinching a belt
around the waist and slipping my feet into a pair of strappy
sandals.

I don't bother putting on any makeup before heading
toward Gerald's office. Murmured words greet my ears as I
approach but I can't make them out. I haven't been in
Gerald's office before. He's always given the impression
that it was off limits and I never wanted to impose. After
knocking three times, I reach for the handle and let
myself in.

Gerald is sitting at his desk, a cigar in one hand and a glass
of amber liquid in the other. He's smiling. I've never seen
him smile, but whatever Aaron must have just said clearly
amused him.

Aaron is sitting in a leather lounge chair opposite Gerald, a
matching glass of liquor in his hand, though his glass looks
untouched.

"Umm..."

"Alejandra, come in." Gerald says in a booming baritone. "Aaron was just telling me all about the camping trip the two of you went on together."

I frown, worried Gerald will get the wrong impression and I'll wind up in trouble. He'd given me his permission to go but I'd intentionally left out the fact that I was going away with a boy, assuming he'd think I'd made girlfriends. But he seems pleased anyway, not shocked or upset as I would have expected. Mom would have murdered me. I wasn't even allowed to have Julio over without leaving my bedroom door wide open. "Oh," is all I manage to say before taking a seat in the chair beside Aaron. He gives me a reassuring smile. I'm not sure what to think of that.

Aaron certainly looks comfortable. Like this is an everyday occurrence for him. He's dressed in his usual Volcom black jeans and a charcoal Hurley t-shirt, ever the skater boy and at complete odds with Gerald who's wearing a custom-tailored suit, crisp white dress shirt, and burgundy tie. Yet the two are chatting as though they're old friends. Aaron's even holding himself taller. Like he's not just your average high-school kid.

My head is spinning. I take my seat and fold my hands in my lap. Gerald's eyes zero in on the movement before his scrutinizing gaze takes in my appearance. "I see Janessa's provided you with adequate clothing."

I nod.

"Though it seems a trip to the salon may still be in order."

My head snaps up toward him. "Excuse me?"

He turns to Aaron. "Women often need help making themselves presentable. Don't judge my daughter too harshly. She didn't have the upbringing she should have. But a project can be rewarding. Alejandra here is our diamond in the rough."

My cheeks are flaming. I can't believe he's criticizing me right now. In front of Aaron.

Aaron laughs but I can hear the strain in his voice. "It's one of the things I like about your daughter, sir. She isn't like the girls I've grown up with. She's comfortable in her own skin."

Gerald looks like he's just bitten into a lemon. "Hmm. Yes, well, she could still use some lessons in behaving like a proper young lady. Really, Alejandra. You look like you have a bird's nest on top of your head."

I force my hands to remain in my lap instead of adjusting the bun on my head. I don't care what he thinks. He's not anyone to me. A sperm donor who decided to show up too late in the game. I clench my jaw and tilt my chin up. "I didn't realize I needed to impress my own father when I'm in my own ... *home*." I keep my tone even, but this isn't my home. It's a halfway house until I get to wherever it is I'll be going after graduation.

"You need to be presentable at all times, even in your own home. You never know who may be stopping by. Just look at yourself. And you have a guest here, one you were well aware of before you came downstairs." He shakes his head, his upper lip curling in disgust. "If I'd known about you sooner, we could have gotten a handle on this, but at the rate you're going, you're going to end up just like your mother."

He may as well have just slapped me the way he spoke of her, as if being anything like my mother is an insult. It's not. My mother was a proud, hard-working woman. She was compassionate and loving and she always, *always*, made time for me, despite working two jobs. Which is more than I can say for the man sitting in front of me. He missed out on seventeen years of my life, yet I can count the number of times I've seen him on one hand since moving to Sun Valley.

I'm not ashamed of my mother. I aspire to be like her.

I bite the inside of my cheek until the tangy bite of copper hits my taste buds. My anger rises and with it comes a crashing wave of emotion. Blinking rapidly to keep my vision clear, I push myself out of my seat. "You'll have to excuse me. I forgot I have homework I need to catch up on."

Gerald doesn't even acknowledge my departure, too engrossed in whatever subject he's moved onto with Aaron. I storm up to my bedroom, opening my laptop to send off another dozen resumes. I need a job. I won't allow myself to be trapped here any longer than I have to be.

Twenty minutes later there's a knock on my door. But before I can tell whoever it is to go away, it opens and

Aaron steps inside. The chagrined look on his face is the only thing that keeps me from snapping at him.

He pads over toward me, claiming the seat beside me on the bed as I roll onto my back and stare at the ceiling. He's quiet for a moment before heaving a long-suffering sigh. "I'm sorry about that," he says.

I keep my eyes pinned on the light fixture above me. A stupidly feminine bedroom chandelier with wrought-iron roses and dangling crystals. "Why? Are you worried I'll end up like my dead mother too? Am I doomed to become a commoner?" I sneer.

He scrubs a hand over his face. "That's not what I meant and you know it."

I flick my gaze toward him. "Do I? You seemed pretty chummy with Gerald there."

He sighs. "My dad works with yours. They golf together. He's been to my house for holidays." A shrug. "I've never been here before we went to Shadle Creek. I didn't put two and two together until he opened the door or I would have said something. I... I don't really know what else to say. Gerald is an ass. He shouldn't have said what he did and"—another sigh—"I should have come to your defense. I'm sorry. That was a dick move."

I push myself into a sitting position. He sounds genuine, but... "Then why didn't you?"

Green eyes search mine, no doubt trying to understand what's going on inside my head. "Because I'm an idiot. Our parents have certain expectations. I guess I just fell into the comfortable role of not wanting to rock the boat."

I nod because, yeah, it sucks, but I get it.

"You hungry?" he suddenly asks just as my stomach rumbles. We both laugh.

"Yeah. You could say that. I was supposed to have dinner with my dad, but I think I'll go back to avoiding him after today."

He pushes to his feet and holds out a hand for me. "Come on, I know the perfect spot. A hole-in-the-wall diner with the best burgers in town."

I hesitate. "Aaron I—"

"Allie," he cuts me off. "I was an ass. I'm sorry. Not just for now but for earlier too. At school. I shouldn't have said what I did. I was being an asshole because I was jealous. It won't happen again. I promise. Give me another shot at being your friend. I won't fuck up this time."

I worry my lower lip, indecision sweeping through me. Then again, it's not like people were knocking down my front door begging to be my friend. "Alright. But can we not talk about my dad? Or the Devils. Or anything that will upset either one of us?"

He chuckles. "Deal."

NINETEEN

Allie

I ride with Aaron to the Sun Valley Diner, a local twenty-four-hour restaurant on the edge of town. The bell above the door jingles, announcing our arrival, and one of the waitresses waves at Aaron with familiar recognition before returning her attention to her customer.

Stepping inside, I'm immediately taken in by the old-fashioned vibe of the place. Black and white checkered floors are paired with red and white vinyl booths, and the bar counter boasts black, Formica countertops.

Aaron heads straight for the counter, claiming one of the red barstools as I climb onto the one beside him. A boy I don't recognize heads toward us and says something to Aaron, but I don't hear what it is as I'm too busy taking everything in. The diner almost reminds me of a Johnny Rockets, though maybe not as polished. I turn in time to see Aaron slap something into the boy's hand in a discreet gesture. I miss whatever it is before the boy shoves his hand into his pocket and makes a hasty retreat after a quick nod in thanks.

"Who was that?" I ask, my curiosity getting the better of me. I'm pretty sure I know what just went down, and I'd be lying if I said I wasn't surprised. I never would have pegged Aaron as the dealer type.

"Just a guy from class." He shrugs, but when I don't say anything else, he continues. "I borrowed twenty bucks from him last week after losing my wallet. It was stupid." He offers me a sheepish grin. "I barely know the guy but he helped me out. I was just paying him back."

Oh. I guess that makes sense. All of a sudden I feel like a complete jerk for assuming the worst of him. What is wrong with me? Obviously he's not some low-life drug dealer. What had I been thinking?

A waitress bounces toward us, her perky ponytail bobbing behind her. "Hey, little Henderson, you off tonight?"

Aaron smiles up at her, his dimples making a sudden appearance. "Yep. I've got the rest of the week to myself."

Her eyes sparkle with mischief. "Lucky. Who's the hot date?"

I cough, thrown off by her assumption. I'm just about to correct her when a group of familiar male voices enters the diner. "Ro, Dom, grab the booth in the back. I'm gonna take a leak." It's Emilio's voice. I see him out of the corner of my eye stalking toward a small hallway to my right. I hunch my shoulders and angle my head away from the walkway, but perky waitress over here decides to draw his attention.

"Hey, handsome. Can I put in a drink order for you?"

Emilio lifts a hand to wave her off, but he catches sight of me and who I'm sitting next to. He comes to an abrupt stop and quirks a brow. "Well, well, well. What do we have here?" He comes closer and a knot forms in the pit of my stomach just as he calls out, "Yo, Rome. Your girl's here."

My cheeks heat and I wish more than anything I could disappear beneath the counter. It's almost comical how quickly I go from relaxed and at ease to epically uncomfortable and Aaron sees it. His jaw tightens, a vein in his neck popping out.

The waitress's eyes narrow in confusion as she flicks her gaze between Aaron and a now standing-and-heading-in-our-direction Roman who, I might add, looks royally pissed. This isn't going to end well.

"I'll leave you three love birds to your squabble," Emilio chuckles and heads to the bathroom.

I grit my teeth. *Bastard.*

Roman crowds in beside Aaron, propping his forearm on the counter as he drinks me in. I don't miss the hunger in his gaze or the fury rising in it. I flick a glance toward Dominique who's settled back in the booth with an amused smirk on his face as if he's settling in to watch the show. Roman clears his throat, drawing my attention back toward him.

"Care to explain?" His lips press into a thin line. I don't know why I'm looking at his lips. Scratch that. I absolutely do know and it's because he kissed me in the lunchroom today. I'm still pissed at him for it, too. Why does he continue being the asshole showing off that he's got the girl when he doesn't even want me?

"She doesn't have to explain anything to you, man." Aaron pushes up from his barstool, but a firm hand on his shoulder shoves him back down into his seat. Roman doesn't even look at him. His eyes stay locked on mine, a tick now forming along his jaw.

"Alejandra..." He draws my name out, the sound low and seductive, sending fire through my veins. He's using his bedroom voice, and God does it do things to me that it shouldn't.

I take a deep breath. *Come on, Allie. Be strong.* I square my shoulders. "I'm having dinner with a friend," I say, proud when my voice comes out even. "Is there a problem with that?"

His eyes darken as he straightens. "Yeah," he says, "there is."

"Umm..." Our waitress opens and closes her mouth. She looks like a goldfish, and I almost laugh.

"We're good, Heather. Thanks." Aaron waves her off, and we all watch as she scurries away to help other customers before Aaron turns to face Roman head on. "Look, man. I get you don't like me or trust me—the feeling is mutual, by the way—but Allie's my friend. I don't care what you two have going on, that's your business, but stop being an asshole for no reason. Why don't you try being a normal guy and, I don't know, call her or ask her out sometime?"

The urge to say "Yeah," in a snarky *told you so* voice is strong, but I hold myself back and wait for Roman's reaction. With exaggerated slowness, he swivels his head to give Aaron his undivided attention. I swallow hard at the look in his eyes. White. Hot. Rage. Had I been standing I would have taken several steps back—and I'm not even the one on the receiving end of that look.

Aaron's Adam's apple bobs up and down, but he manages to meet Roman's glare and hold it. *Impressive.* Whatever issues lie between them, Aaron's no coward.

Hostility radiates off both boys as Roman stares at him, unmoving, never saying a single word. Tension builds in the air. It's suffocating. I rub my palms over the tops of my knees debating whether or not to intervene when Emilio finally pops out of the hallway, oblivious to the tension in the air.

"Hey, fuckers. We still chatting?"

Like a bubble being popped, the pressure releases and I noisily exhale. "Nope." I turn to Emilio, a fake smile plastered across my face. "Roman's just being Roman. You guys should probably get back to Dom, though. He's looking lonely over there."

Emilio looks over my shoulder and his grin widens. "Yeah, he doesn't look so lonely." I turn and spot our waitress— Heather—leaning toward him, her breasts intimately close to his face. Dom licks his lips.

I sigh. And then my stomach does the unthinkable and growls like a rumbling bear. How *em-barr-essing*. "Come on, vanilla. We need to put some meat on those bones." Emilio tugs me from my seat angling me toward the booth Dom is still sitting in but I dig in my heels.

He stops and scowls over his shoulder at me. "What?"

I tilt my head toward Aaron and Emilio snorts. "You're going to pick Henderson over us?" he asks as if the very idea of doing exactly that is unfathomable.

"Uh, yeah. I came here with him. I'm not going to just bail because you three showed up."

He frowns like he never thought of it like that and I have to smother a laugh. The Devils really are used to always getting whatever they want. I tug my hand free from his grip and reclaim my seat, but rather than heading to the booth as I'd expected, Emilio grabs the stool beside me and Roman takes the empty seat beside Aaron, who looks anything but thrilled to be seated beside him. As soon as he reaches for a menu, Dom rises and heads toward us, taking the last empty seat next to Roman.

Aaron's jaw ticks and he clenches his hands into fists on the counter. I rest a hand on his knee and mouth one word

—*Sorry*. Roman sees the touch and his eyes narrow so I quickly snatch it away.

"We can head out," I mutter. "Grab something on the way back to—"

"Nah. Don't be like that." Emilio moves to squeeze between Aaron and me, throwing his arms around both our shoulders and pulling us toward him in a weird side-hug embrace. "Stay. You want us to get along, right?" he says to me. "Be friendly and shit?"

I nod.

"Alright then. We're doing our part. Henderson,"—he meets Aaron's frustrated green gaze—"you don't mind, do you? It'll be just like old times."

Aaron shoves out of his seat, forcing Emilio to stumble back a few steps. "I'm not fucking doing this." His chest rises and falls with each heavy breath and he bares his teeth. Roman and Dom also stand, folding their arms over their chests.

I jump to my feet, eyes wide. "Hey, it's fine. We can—"

"No. It's not fucking fine."

I flinch at Aaron's tone.

"Don't talk to her like that." Roman comes to my defense, taking a menacing step forward. All of this is escalating way too fast.

"Hey. *Hey!*" I draw everyone's attention back to me. "What am I missing here?"

"Nothing," Aaron is quick to snap back.

Emilio laughs. "Keeping secrets, Henderson? Then again, that is your M.O., isn't it?"

"Fuck off. I'm not dealing with your shit." Aaron storms past him, making a beeline for the door before he catches himself and turns back to me. "Come on, Allie." I step forward to follow, but a hand on my elbow stops me.

"Not happening. You wanna storm out that's on you. But she's not going anywhere with you like this."

Before I can argue—because, yeah, Aaron is angry but it's not like he'd hurt me—he's cursing out a, "Whatever." And leaving me behind.

Un-freaking-believable. I consider chasing after him. He's my ride after all, but a firm shake of Roman's head has me deciding against it. Was it too much to ask to have a normal day for once? No mean girls or asshole fathers or stupid boys to ruin it?

My stomach rumbles again. "Come on, vanilla." Roman steers me toward a nearby booth. "Let's feed you. I'll take you home after."

TWENTY

Roman

A flare of something eerily close to jealousy burns hot in my chest at the thought of Allie on a date with Aaron *fucking* Henderson. No. Scratch that. I'm not jealous. I'm pissed. Who the hell does Henderson think he is?

I told him to stay away from her. Emilio made it public knowledge that she belonged to the Devils. He saw us together at Shadle Creek. He *knows* she's mine. And he's still sniffing around.

It's like the guy has a death wish. After what happened that summer before junior year—when the asshole nearly got all four of us killed—you better believe I'm not taking his shit anymore. I can't believe I was ever friends with that asshole.

I pull Allie closer to me, conscious of my mounting anger. My arm wraps around her narrow waist as I lead her to our usual spot. Lust stirs and my dick twitches as I take in her slim legs and narrow waist, breathe in the strawberry scent of her shampoo. She isn't wearing a lick of makeup, exposing a faint sprinkling of freckles on the top of her nose. God, she's so fucking beautiful.

And she was here with him. The get-up she's in is all for *him*.

I grind my teeth together as we take our seats. Heather returns, takes our drink orders, and slaps a few menus down on the tabletop before retreating to the counter. She isn't trying to flirt with Dom anymore and that's fine by me. Every chick in this place is team Henderson. His aunt owns the place, so I'm not surprised.

For a while there we stopped coming around, but the Sun Valley Diner has the best burgers, and after sweating my ass off on the field, I decided I'd earned a little reward. It's a good thing we came into enemy territory, too, or who knows what Aaron would have tried to pull with Allie. I don't trust the fucker. He might seem squeaky clean now, but I'm not buying it. He's just good at hiding his demons.

She's quiet as the guys jump right into talking about the upcoming game. It's the biggest one of the season and we're all hyped for it. The Saints are the only school with a shot of ruining our record. So far we're undefeated, and once we beat them, it'll be smooth sailing all the way to state. Scouts will also be there, and while we all have a scholarship lined up, it's never a bad idea to have a back-up.

My parents are even showing up for the game, which was one hell of a surprise when my mom told me. Neither of my parents support my decision to go pro. Hell, neither supports my decision to go to college. My pops wants me to go straight into the police academy following graduation. *Not fucking happening.* He might enjoy being a boy in blue, but I have zero plans to follow in his footsteps. Mom does the whole *I just want to see you happy* bit, but really, she wants me to do whatever will make my pops happy to make her own life easier. If she really cared about my happiness, she wouldn't nod and smile and tell me how my father knows best every night at the dinner table. He does not fucking know best. Not where my life is concerned.

They humored me during my freshman and sophomore years. Even came to a few of my games. But when that pending scholarship offer came through end of junior year from Suncrest U and they realized just how serious I am about playing football, everything changed. *Football isn't a career. It's a game. I'm almost eighteen now. I need to be a man. Show some responsibility.* Blah, blah, fucking blah.

Pops is married to his badge. All the man ever does is work. And I get it. It's how he provides for his family. But as the Sun Valley Police Chief, he's got time for little else beyond work. Certainly not time to see his only son play ball. But he's coming to Friday's game—the first one he'll be at all year— and I know once he sees me on the field, sees how good I am, he'll finally drop the subject of me going to the academy. Friday's game is more than just a chance to secure scholarships. It's a chance to prove to my pops that this is what I was born to do.

Allie's quiet as the guys talk until Emilio asks what we've all been secretly wondering. "So, you and Henderson a thing now?"

She stiffens beside me and swings her head toward him, frowning. She better not say what I think she's about to because no, no fucking way is she going to date that douchebag. She's way too good for a tool like him.

I brace myself for the admission, not that it'll matter, because Allie Ramirez is mine. She can like Henderson all she wants, I'll wedge myself right in the middle if I have to.

But instead of confirming their relationship, she says, "We're just friends." I raise a brow and she sighs, shaking her head. "Why is that so hard to believe?"

Our waitress drops off our orders before making a hasty retreat.

Emilio pops a fry into his mouth before saying with a grin, "Because Aaron wants to bone you." He chews, swallows, then eats another. "Can't say I blame him. You're hot as hell, Allie." She blushes. "But I know who you belong to. Henderson does, too, and he's still making his plays." He taps his temple with his index finger. "Not smart on his part but Henderson never was the sharpest crayon in the box."

"I don't belong to anyone."

I snort, leaning back in the booth and spreading my legs to get comfortable. "Yeah, you do." She frowns, looking from Emilio to me. "Time to get with the program, vanilla. Admit you're mine. It's not nice messing with a guy's emotions like that. Letting Henderson believe he has a chance."

"I'm *not*," she snaps.

"Yeah, you are. Admit it."

She scoffs before hissing, "You do not own me. I do not 'belong' to you. I am my own person with my own autonomy."

"Keep telling yourself that, but look where I am and look where you are. This is a thing between us and I for one do not fucking share."

She sets her jaw, turning away from me. Gripping her chin, I force her to meet my gaze, fully aware of Dominique and Emilio's interested stares. "You. Are. Mine. Got it?"

She jerks away. If it weren't for the fact that she's trapped beside me in the booth, I'm sure she'd have already stormed off. "Screw you."

"Already have. And I'm happy to make a repeat go at it, too."

She makes a sound of disgust in the back of her throat, but it's all for show.

"Don't pretend you're anything but flattered. You don't want Henderson. You don't want anyone else. Just admit it already. You want me. I want you. Stop being a child and we can all move on."

Swallowing hard, she swings her glare back to me. Her eyes narrow and her expression is considering before she bites out, "Fine."

Woah. "Fine?"

A shrug. "Yeah, fine. I want you. You're hot and the first time around the sex was good." Her nose crinkles. "Not so much the second time but we all have our off days."

"Burn." Dominique gives a rare chuckle.

"Right to the *cojones*," Emilio adds.

"That wasn't very nice," I bite out.

"Neither is being left without an orgasm. And just so you know, I'm all about second chances in life, but don't expect a third." Her smile is slow as it morphs into a warning. There's that fire I knew was buried inside her.

A slow grin stretches across my face. "Alright. I'll try and remember that."

"Be sure that you do."

I demolish my food. Coach has us running two-a-day practices to prepare for the game and within minutes Dom, Emilio, and I have all cleared our plates, but I notice Allie has barely touched hers. Maybe half a chicken strip and a few fries. She catches me staring and looks away.

"I thought you were hungry?"

She shrugs. "Yeah. It's not really sitting right with me."

I haven't known Allie long but she looks thinner than she did when she first arrived at Sun Valley High, but I brush it off. If the food isn't settling with her then it isn't settling. I'm not her mom. She can take care of herself.

"So, Allie, you coming to watch us play this weekend?"

She perks up in her seat and when Heather returns to clear our plates, Allie passes her unfinished food to her with little concern. I frown but don't comment. The girl needs to eat, but maybe she'll grab a bite when she gets home?

"I wasn't really planning on it..." she begins.

"You have to come. If you're one of us then you gotta represent. No excuses. Game's Friday night at seven. Plan on being there."

She worries her bottom lips then freezes when my thumb pulls down on her abused lip, my eyes meeting hers. "Come to the game."

"Is that an order?" she quips.

I run my tongue along my teeth. "If it is?"

She shrugs, tearing her napkin into small little squares. "I might have other plans."

I growl and pull her against me. I don't know why it's suddenly important that she be there but it is. "You don't have any other plans. You're coming to the game. End of discussion." She doesn't say anything else, but I catch the small smile playing on her lips and triumph floods through me. She'll be at the game.

TWENTY-ONE

Allie

I slip into English class with seconds to spare when an unfamiliar face pauses beside my desk. "Um... you're Alejandra, right?" a girl asks.

"Allie," I correct her while nodding and she slides into the seat beside me.

"I'm Kasey."

I frown. Why is she talking to me? "Uh, okay."

The bell rings and the last of the students claim their seats, but there's no sign of Mrs. Beck anywhere, and as soon as the rest of the class realizes she's MIA, they all begin talking, visiting their friends' desks, and tossing crumpled paper balls around in a game of catch.

My gaze wanders over the heads in the room and I meet Roman's stare. I swear it burns right through me. Heat flashes through my chest with each passing second and my heart rate picks up before Kasey draws my attention back with a small wave of her hand. "So, yeah. Hi."

I raise both brows. "Hi."

"I know we haven't talked before. I kept meaning to introduce myself but you seemed a little standoffish and"—her eyes dart around the classroom—"well, anyway. I was just wondering if you had a thing for Aaron Henderson?"

I scowl at her. Was she for real right now? "Why? Do *you* have a thing for Aaron Henderson?" I don't need to turn to know that Roman's stare is still boring into me but I decide to ignore it, giving Kasey my full attention.

She chokes on a laugh, her blond curls bouncing around her heart-shaped face as she claps her hand over her mouth. "What? No! He's my brother."

"Your brother?"

She laughs. "Yeah, sorry. I probably should have led with that. I kind of assumed you knew."

I'm shaking my head. "No. I didn't. He never mentioned he had a little sister."

She sighs. "Yeah, we're not very close. Four years between us and all. But he's a good big brother. Maybe a little absent but what can I expect? You know?" No. I didn't know. I didn't have any brothers or sisters.

"So that makes you a..."

"Freshman. Yep."

I raise a brow. "And you're in this class because...?"

"Oh. I have a non-schedule first period. I usually hang out in the library since I ride to school with Aaron but Mrs. Beck asked me to T.A. for her today so here I am."

Oh. Okay.

"Anyway, so...umm... do you?"

I tilt my head to the side before her earlier question comes back to me. "Oh. No." I shake my head. "We're just friends."

Her smile drops and she purses her lips together. "Oh."

Why does she care?

I reach out and touch her forearm offering what I hope is a reassuring gesture. "It's not like that with us. On either side. You don't need to worry about me stringing him along or anything. He knows I'm only looking for friendship."

She nods but doesn't look wholly convinced. "Is it because of..." She flicks her gaze toward Roman just as the classroom door opens and I'm saved from having to answer.

"Good morning, class. Sorry for the delay. Please open your books to..."

Class goes by as usual. Kasey helps Mrs. Beck pass out this week's assignment. A ten-page persuasive essay on a controversial current event. Should be easy enough. And then, before I know it, the bell rings, signaling the end of the period and everyone rushes from their seats to head to the door.

I take my time shoving my books in my bag when a familiar sense of awareness has goosebumps breaking out along my skin. I look up and spy Roman waiting for me near the door with a devilish smirk on his face as he looks me over from head to toe with open want.

When I get close to him he takes my hand and drags me out the door before shoving me into the first empty classroom we come across.

"Hey! What—"

His lips land on mine and a small whimper escapes me. One hand settles on my hip, the other coming up beneath my hair, dragging me closer. I tense, but when he groans against my lips I melt into him. The bell rings but neither of us come up for air.

"What are you doing to me?" I arch against him as his lips trail down my neck, teeth nipping at my collarbone.

"Whatever I want." His fingertips slide inside my jeans and he pulls back to meet my gaze. His tongue peeks out to lick his lips, as his fingers get dangerously close to my needy center.

"Roman." My eyes dart up to look at him through my lashes. And then he's there. Right there. His fingers dip inside me before making a hasty retreat as he swirls my clit with my own juices.

"Just making up for before." There's a wicked smile to his voice.

I cling to him, the muscles in his biceps flexing as he works me over with skilled fingers. "We're supposed to be in class," I rasp.

"Are you asking me to stop?"

I moan and my body tightens, chasing away my release. God, no. I don't want him to stop. But when I don't respond, he must take my silence as agreement and withdraws his hand from my jeans. A strangled sound of protest leaves my lips and he chuckles before kissing me into silence as his hands work quickly to unbutton my pants and shove them down over my thighs, leaving me exposed.

My head falls back against the classroom wall and when he shoves two fingers deep inside me, curling them to find just the right spot, I shudder in his grip. He kisses my jaw before trailing his lips down my neck, his free hand coming up to play with my breasts. He pushes down the stretchy material of my top, giving him better access to pinch my right nipple.

I gasp, my knees going weak.

He circles my clit, his movements quickening. I cry out when out of nowhere, my release slams into me. He covers my mouth with his hand, muffling my cries as his fingers milk every last drop of my orgasm from me.

"I need to fuck you," he says, pulling me forward and bending me over the nearest desk, my bare ass in the air and on full display. I shiver, a whimper leaving me as I hear the telltale sound of his belt being unbuckled. His jeans sliding over his hips.

"Condom?" I rasp and he curses behind me.

"I'll pull out."

I'm about to object but then he presses against me and I arch back to meet him as he slides his dick inside my pussy in a single fluid thrust.

We groan in unison as he flexes his hips, holding me in place. "God you feel incredible," he says. His hands tighten on my hips with bruising force as he pulls back and then thrusts inside me once again. "So fucking wet."

I'm panting, barely able to catch my breath as he pounds into me. Each thrust harder than the one before until the desk is sliding beneath me with the force of his movements, screeching across the floor. I cling to the edge and he grinds his hips against my ass.

I cry out his name, losing myself to the feel of him inside of me, completely forgetting that we're at school and that anyone can walk in on us. His hips slam frantically into me and I know he's chasing his own release when suddenly he jerks back and then his hot cum is coating my ass, dripping down over the backs of my thighs.

He slides his dick over the trail of cum he coated me in before smacking me lightly on the rear. I groan and peer over my shoulder. Roman's smirk greets me as he considers my still bare ass. "You should probably clean that up," he suggests. I narrow my eyes as he laughs. "I might be persuaded into helping you out under a few conditions." He tucks himself back into his jeans before folding his arms over his chest, leaving the top button unbuttoned, but saying nothing.

"Do you ever want to do this again?" I ask.

He grins. "Every day of the week."

"Then get me something to wipe your cum off my ass or I won't let you near me with so much as a ten-foot pole."

"You say that now, but—"

Voices can be heard in the hallway. *Crap.* Everyone is supposed to be in class. "Now, Roman."

Thankfully, he does as I ask and finds a roll of paper towels in a closet and helps to clean me up before tossing them in the trash. I shimmy back into my jeans and am adjusting my top just as the door bursts open and Silvia Parish's startled brown eyes meet my own.

She takes in the scene, her eyes narrowing on our rumpled clothes and my unruly hair. When Roman steps closer to me, they narrow farther and I can't help the grin that spreads across my face.

"Did you need something?" he asks, not a care in the world that she knows exactly what we were just doing. "You're interrupting."

"We all heard you fucking in Calc," she sneers at me. "You sound like a dying rhino."

Feeling extra bold with Roman beside me, I roll my eyes and flip her off. I don't have time for her mean girl antics today. "Whatever." Not my strongest comeback, but it's better than wilting under her glare.

She whirls and leaves as quickly as she came. Roman leans down, smacking my ass and giving me a meaningful look. "If that's what a dying rhino sounds like, I better be hearing it again. *Soon.*"

I shiver in response to the blatant desire in his gaze before Roman walks out of the room. I decide to stop by the bathroom and just skip Calc entirely. A look at one of the clocks in the hallways shows me that there's only ten minutes left until the bell rings for lunch, so I decide to loiter for a bit and save myself some embarrassment.

I wash my hands and splash water on my face before running my fingers through my hair in an effort to smooth it out. The door opens behind me and I don't pay it any attention until a body slams me forward and my stomach collides with the porcelain sink. I stumble and am shoved harshly to the ground. My hair covers my face as a foot slams into my chest. *Shit. Ow.* I suck in a pain-filled gasp and another kick comes at me from behind, slamming into my back with the force of a sledgehammer.

I curse and roll, narrowly avoiding the third kick when a fist slams into my cheek. My head snaps back and my vision blurs. Someone grips my hair, jerking my face up as my eyes meet Silvia's.

"Bitch." I spit blood in her face and she reels back. Then I kick out, connecting with her shin and she stumbles back into her two asshole friends who decided to join her. I scramble to my feet and rush out the bathroom door just as the bell rings and the hallway crowds with people.

I suck in a breath and clench my hands into tight fists to keep them from shaking.

Careful to keep my head down, I lose myself in the sea of bodies, hugging my ribs as I fight through a wave of pain. *Fuck.* I think I'm going to vomit. I stumble toward a classroom door and lunge for the first receptacle I see to throw up my breakfast in.

Acid burns my throat and tears fill the corners of my eyes making it hard to see. The next thing I know, a boy crouches beside me, a comforting hand smoothing down my back, but I flinch at the contact. "What the hell, Allie? Are you okay?" Aaron says.

I hold a hand out to keep him at bay as I dry heave over the trashcan, my stomach intent on puking some more, despite it now being empty.

When the heaving stops, I sink to the floor still clutching my aching stomach and lean my head back against the wall. Aaron crouches down in front of me. His eyes are wide and filled with worry.

The door opens and Dominique steps inside, his eyes immediately zeroing in on me. "What's going on here?" His nostrils flare and he rushes toward me. "What the fuck did you do?" He turns a hot glare toward Aaron who stands and takes several steps away.

"I didn't do anything. She stumbled in here and I followed her to see if she needed help."

He reaches for me, but I shake my head and slowly come to my feet. I use the counter as support to steady myself as my head spins and everything blurs for a few seconds. Nausea rolls through me again.

The door opens again and Emilio steps inside. "Yo, Dom. What's taking you so—fuck!"

I lift my head and take in his wide-eyed stare. "Someone better start talking before Roman gets here." The door opens again and Roman walks in. Emilio whistles. "Too late."

Roman spots me and his eyes flare. "What the fuck happened to you?"

"Nothing." I shrug, but the movement causes me to wince.

"Nothing?" Roman stalks closer, his hand reaching out, tilting my jaw toward the light. His thumb grazes my lip and I hiss. He releases me. "This doesn't look like nothing."

The other three boys crowd me until Dominique shoves Aaron back. He curses but stays put as all three Devils level me with varying shades of anger. "Spill, Alejandra," Emilio says, and woah, we must be serious because Emilio never uses my name. It's always Allie or vanilla.

I swallow and look down at my sneakers. "It's nothing. I was walking out of the bathroom as someone else was walking in. The door slammed into my face." Three sets of disapproving eyes meet my gaze.

"You're lying," Dominique says. And yeah, maybe I am. But I don't need any of them making things worse by creating a scene. Silvia is the petty mean girl type and she's mad she isn't getting her way. I can handle her. I wasn't expecting an attack like this but looking back, after the hallway incident, I should have seen it coming. I won't make that mistake again.

I shake my head at Dom's accusation but then stop when the room spins. "No, I'm not. You guys are making a big deal out of nothing. I got smacked in the face with a door and I'm on my period. Can we drop it now?"

"That the story you're sticking with?" Roman asks, unconvinced.

"Yep."

He glares. "For the record, you're not on your fucking period and I don't like liars."

I shrug. "Whatever. Look, I just had the pleasure of throwing up my breakfast and would love to wash my mouth out. Can we move this show along?" I shove past them and head for the door, grateful when no one rushes to immediately follow.

TWENTY-TWO

Roman

"She was jumped," Emilio says as soon as Allie leaves the room.

A snort from behind has all three of our heads turning. Aaron shakes his head, his jaw clenched and his hands fisted at his sides. "Yeah, she was. Wonder who's fucking fault that is?"

"What the hell is that supposed to mean?" I advance on him, but he doesn't cower, which only serves to piss me the fuck off.

"You know exactly what I mean, Roman. Or did you forget we used to be friends? I know how that head of yours works. You don't think I know you wanted her targeted when she first showed up here? That you didn't plant your little seeds in the school to make her life difficult?" He briefly looks up to the ceiling and laughs, but the sound is harsh and mocking. "Every fucking girl in this school is going to go after her now. And you"—he digs his finger into my chest—"you're the one who put the target on her back." He shakes his head. "I might have my demons, but at least I'm not a selfish prick like you." He storms out of the classroom, leaving me reeling with his last statement.

"Fuck," I yell as soon as Aaron is gone from the room.

Two sets of grim stares meet my own. "We didn't really consider how chicks would respond when you claimed her," Dominique tries to reassure me, but we all know what Aaron said is true. I did this. Me. No one else. I knew what would happen and I did it anyway. I might not have known the girls would stoop to jumping her, but I should have suspected this after what went down with her and Silvia before. Stupid. I am so fucking stupid.

"I need to fix this." Neither one disputes my statement. The question now is, how?

Emilio rubs the back of his neck. "I didn't make things better when I told the school to ice out Silvia. This could be retaliation for that. She can't do anything to us, but..."

I shake my head. "I appreciate what you're doing, but, no. This is on me." I fucked up and I'll own it. "Besides, we don't even know if Silvia was involved. We need more information."

Emilio snorts. "One of us is going to need to be with her at all times," Emilio says.

"How the fuck are we supposed to manage that?" I ask, anger burning a hole in my gut. She was hurt. Someone put their fucking hands on my girl and hurt her.

"Yeah. It doesn't look like Allie will be forthcoming with that," Dom remarks.

"We start by finding her and then make sure whoever did this doesn't decide to have another go at it," Emilio says and I nod.

I don't give a shit if Allie wants to sweep this mess under the rug. I want to know who did this and I'm going to make *damn sure* it doesn't happen again. Everyone at this school needs to know they can't hurt my girl and get away with it.

We head out to find Allie but she's elusive. She isn't in the lunchroom and she's not in her next class either. After searching for twenty minutes straight, I find out from the front office that she signed herself out for the day. I release a harsh sigh of relief. At least with her home, I don't have to worry about someone else coming after her.

I fill the guys in when we meet up later after school and we come up with a plan to shadow her during the next school day. I've got her covered before school and during first. I'll walk her to second and Dom will follow her after second to third. Emilio's next to her fourth period class so he'll have eyes on her until she makes it to class and then I'll catch her as soon as she's done for the day.

We shouldn't have to worry about anything happening to her during classes. No one is *that* stupid. And fourth period she's got Welding with Aaron. I don't like the idea of relying on that fucker, but whatever his motives, he seems to care for her, and thankfully there aren't any catty bitches in that class for her to have to deal with.

It's a solid plan and I should be cool with it, but I can't get the idea of her abused body out of my head. Every time I close my eyes I see her face. The bruises. The split lip. It's like a dagger to the stomach, and thinking of what she must have felt makes the blade twist inside me.

Practice that afternoon is grueling. I push all my anger and frustration into completing each pass and running hard until my heart feels like it's going to burst out of my chest, but it doesn't matter. I'm responsible for a pass-interception that I should have completed and then I fumble a fucking catch. Coach is screaming at me to get my head out of my ass and I'm trying but, *fuck*. I'm so out of it.

"We cannot afford for you to play like this come Friday," Coach shouts.

I grit my teeth to keep from lashing out. I know he's right but—*Fuck*. I tear my helmet from my head and throw it on the field.

"Roman!" Coach shouts, but I ignore him, stalking to the locker room to strip out of my gear and shower before the rest of the team finishes.

"Valdez, get your ass back on the field," he tries again.

Dominique heads toward Coach to smooth over my little outburst, but I don't stick around long enough to see if it works.

I need to see Allie, and recognizing that makes me feel all sorts of ways that I don't want to think about. It's three days till the big game. I should be focused on plays. Football is all that matters.

I know she's home. I know she's safe. I need to let this insatiable need to see her go but, dammit, I fucking can't. I'll be useless on the field until I know without a shadow of a doubt that she's okay.

Forty minutes later I'm pulling up to her house—if you can even call it that. I used my dad's Sun Valley residents service app that he doesn't know I have installed on my phone to look up Gerald Ulrich's address. Having a father who's the chief of police comes with a few perks, but what I pull up to is not a home. It's a fucking mansion.

The place has got to be five thousand square feet or more. It's got twin pillars flanking the front door and massive floor-to-ceiling windows on all sides of the house. The lawn is perfectly kept and rose bushes ring the grass. This place rivals even Dominique's, and that's saying something, because that fucker has more money than any person can spend in a lifetime.

For a minute I idle in front of the place, staring at the front door as though I can *will* her to step out of it. I press down the gas, letting the roar of the engine fill the street, and a flutter of movement at one of the second-story windows pulls my gaze.

Allie peaks through pale pink curtains and I wave, still willing her to come outside. The curtains close and I wait. She knows I'm here. She'll come.

A few short minutes later she's closing the front door behind her. Wearing white jeans and an oversized hoodie, she stops beside my car and frowns. "What are you doing here?" She tucks her hair behind her ear, exposing the purple bruise on her lower jaw.

But all I see is red.

"Get in."

She shakes her head. "What do you want, Roman? Shouldn't you be at practice or something?"

I try and tamp down my irritation at her refusal. "Nah. Ended thirty minutes ago. Come on." She's still not moving. "Get in the car, Alejandra." Something about saying her full name gets a reaction out of her, and with a muttered curse, she's opening the passenger side door and sliding inside. "Put on your seatbelt."

She does.

Thank fuck for small favors.

We ride in silence for the first ten minutes before I take her to a different side of town where the houses are smaller, some with bars on their windows and heavy iron screen doors covering their wooden counterparts.

"Where are we going?" she finally asks just as I pull onto a familiar street.

"My place." I'm not entirely sure why I'm taking her home with me. We come from two different worlds. But I want her beside me. I need to know that she's okay.

I pull into the driveway of a three-bedroom, ranch-style home and put the car in park. "Come on."

Allie gets out hesitantly, checking her surroundings with an inquisitive stare. "This is where you live?"

I nod, searching for any sort of reaction that my life isn't good enough, but I see none from her. I release a breath. There's no judgment in her gaze as she takes in the stucco exterior of my home or the fact that the garage door is wide fucking open and my garage looks like a second living room packed full of mismatched sofas with a pool table in the middle.

A car door slams one house over and a voice shouts, "Yo, what's for dinner?" as Emilio jogs toward us.

"What's—"

"We're neighbors," I tell her as he nears.

"Please tell me your mom's going to feed me. Coach is killing me with these two-a-days and I need some fucking calories in me before my stomach decides to eat itself."

"Come on, *cabrón*. Let's see what she's got."

Allie follows behind but I don't miss the curiosity on her face as I lead her through the garage and straight into the kitchen. As soon as we're inside, we're enveloped in the heady smell of my mother's cooking.

"*Mamá,*" I shout into the house, knowing she can't be far. I check the stove, lifting the lid off a large stockpot, finding fresh warm tamales steaming inside.

"Hijo, no toques," *Don't touch that,* she admonishes just as she turns a corner. I'm about to ask her what's wrong, because my mom only ever makes tamales for two occasions. A holiday like Thanksgiving or Christmas, or because my pops is upset about something—usually where I'm concerned—and she's trying to smooth things over the only way she knows how. With food. But before I can ask, she spots Allie and her eyes widen in surprise.

"You brought home a girl?" Her accent is thick but her English is clear as she takes Allie in from head to toe and a wide smile spreads across her face. Fuck. I don't think I thought this all the way through.

"Mija, let me see you." My mother pulls Allie toward her, not bothering to introduce herself or offer any sort of hello before spinning her around and taking her in.

Allie accepts this like it's completely normal, a hesitant smile on her face as she circles back around to face my mother. My mom is a small woman, a few inches shy of five feet making Allie, who's tiny compared to me, look tall for once.

"You're beautiful," my mother tells her, leaning in to give Allie a kiss on the cheek.

Allie returns the gesture. "Thank you. I'm Alejandra." Her voice is small but her smile is genuine.

"And how long have you been dating my son?" she asks, and I groan while Emilio chuckles.

"*Mamá!*"

"What? A mother should know these things."

I shake my head. "No, she shouldn't. Don't scare away the first girl I've introduced you to."

"Sorry, Mrs. Valdez, Allie here is mine." Emilio tosses his arm around Allie's shoulders.

My mother's frown is immediate, forcing me to bite off a laugh. "Tell him you won't feed him unless he gives her back."

Her eyes, lined with age, spark with mischief and she smiles.

Emilio groans. "Not cool, bro. Not. Cool."

I tug Allie from his arms. She comes willingly and I tuck her beside me, leading her to the table. I'm just as hungry as Emilio. He wasn't kidding when he said our two-a-day practices have been killer.

When Allie's back is to my mother, my mom's concerned eyes meet mine and she makes a small gesture, brushing her thumb under her own jaw. I tilt my head, letting her know with that small gesture that I know why the bruise is there and that she has nothing to worry about.

She trusts me, so with a satisfied nod, Mom returns to the stove, dishing up three plates of food while we take our seats. Within a few short minutes, rice, beans, and tamales are in front of me and I don't hesitate to dive in. Emilio eats like he's been starved, which earns him a beaming smile and a second helping. Mom won't eat until Pops comes home from work, so after making sure we're all settled, she retreats to her room.

I wish I knew what was up, but our family is private and she would be embarrassed if I brought up family matters in front of guests, so I'll wait to talk to her when Allie's gone.

The first few minutes we focus on our food. Allie's bites are small, her chewing almost methodical as if she's savoring the flavors. I've noticed she doesn't eat a lot at school but she's eating now, so it doesn't look like there's reason to be concerned.

"You're such a lucky asshole," Emilio says, now on his third tamale and I smirk.

"Consider yourself lucky I put up with you or you'd miss out on all of this."

Allie laughs. "It is really good."

"Better than my albóndigas?" I ask and she blushes.

"I don't know. That's a hard one. I'm not sure I could choose."

"Roman's ma's tamales. Hands down. She only makes them like twice a year. I would kill for these."

I ignore him, leaning toward Allie and capturing her lips with my own in a quick kiss. When I pull back her eyes are wide and uncertain as her fingers come up to touch her mouth.

"What was that for?"

I shrug. "Because I wanted to."

Emilio, having missed the exchange, talks on about how amazing my mom's food is and how I'm a greedy bastard who doesn't share often enough. Some of it is a joke but there's a thread of painful honesty there too. Emilio's mom bailed when he was seven, leaving behind her husband and four children. He has two older brothers and a little sister. And let's just say his dad isn't the domestic type.

But Emilio's always been welcome here and my mom loves feeding the fucker. As we eat, Allie relaxes, her smiles coming more easily as Emilio and I bitch and moan about practices. Every now and then she sends me questioning looks. I know she's waiting for me to ask her what happened back at school, but I want her comfortable first. I'm also waiting for Dominique to show up. I have a feeling I'm going to need all the help I can get to pry the names I need from Allie's mouth.

When we finish eating I draw Allie back outside to the garage and pull her down beside me as Emilio takes a seat on the opposite couch, his expression now serious. The sun is setting and a cool breeze floats through the open space.

My knee bounces and I'm itching for a smoke but refrain from pulling one out. I haven't taken a hit since Shadle Creek weekend and it's better not to blow my little streak.

As soon as Dom's black Escalade pulls into the driveway, Emilio shifts over to make room for him. Dom steps out in black slacks and a black button-up shirt with the sleeves rolled up. He heads toward us and Emilio whistles at him.

Dom doesn't react aside from flipping him off. Seeing Dom dressed up isn't all that unusual. His family is the sort to dress for dinner and use fine china, so I appreciate that he came here straight afterward and didn't take the unnecessary time to change.

He sits back on the sofa and gives me a look that says, *now what?*

Allie catches it and turns to look at me. "What's going on?" Her tone is wary.

I run my fingers through my hair and sigh. "We need to know who jumped you today."

She starts to stand but I pull her back down beside me. "No more running. Someone hurt you and we want to know who."

"Why do you care?" she hisses.

Is she kidding me right now? "I care because you're my—"

"I'm not *your* anything."

Clenching my jaw, I cup her face and force her to meet my gaze. "We've gone over this. You're mine. My girl. Got it?" She swallows hard but doesn't respond. "Anyone who fucks with you is asking to be fucked with by me."

"Us," Dom corrects and she whips her head around toward him.

"Why?"

I open my mouth to speak but she cuts me off. "And yeah, I get it. You're a possessive asshole. I'm yours until you decide I'm not. I know. But we've gone over this, too"—she indicates the space between us, a small frown on her face— "and we both agreed this is for fun. We're passing the time. You don't need to go all alpha protector on me. I can take care of myself."

Silence.

No one says a thing as I glare into her dark brown eyes, pretending it doesn't bother me one bit to hear her say that whatever we have between us doesn't fucking matter. Like she said, we're just passing the time. I'm not catching feelings for some girl I barely know and clearly she's not catching any for me. Good.

I release my grip on her jaw before I add to her bruises and give an exaggerated eye roll. "Stop reading into this, vanilla. If I can't protect what's mine then how can I expect anyone to take me seriously. I have a reputation to uphold."

Emilio opens his mouth to say something but I send him a murderous look, shutting him up.

Allie's brows furrow as she considers my words with a sigh. "I can handle this on my own."

"Right. Because you've done such a great job already."

"Will you just drop it?"

All three of us shake our heads.

"We're going to find out one way or another. Why are you so adamant to face this alone?" Dominique presses.

"Because I can. It's mean-girl shit. You're blowing it out of proportion. Just because three girls decided—"

"Three?" Emilio questions and Allie's eyes widen, realizing her mistake. "Names, Alejandra?" he presses.

"I don't even know all their names," she mutters, folding her arms over her chest like a petulant child not getting her way.

"Maybe not, but you know at least one, am I right?"

She glares at me and I smirk.

"Maybe."

I turn to Emilio and Dom. "Can you guys give us a minute?" They nod and head back inside. Once they're gone I turn Allie toward me, pulling her close until her chest is pressed against my side. I rub my thumb over her jawline before dragging it against her bottom lip. "Who did this?"

Her eyes plead with me to drop it, so I go for a different tactic and crash my lips against hers. She immediately kisses me back as I tug her onto my lap, her legs now straddling my waist. She rocks against me and I'm instantly hard inside my jeans. I devour her mouth, drinking down her soft moans. When I finally break the kiss, I rest my forehead against hers, our chests heaving, her small hands clinging to the fabric of my shirt. "Who?" I try again, capturing her mouth once more and then pulling away. "Tell me, Allie."

She groans, chasing after my lips but I deny her, instead trailing kisses up the column of her neck. "Allie?" I scrape my teeth against her skin and she shivers in my arms. "Come on, baby. One name. Tell me who did this and I'll help you forget all about it."

"Silvia," she says.

I smile triumphantly before gripping her ass. I stand, wrapping her legs around my waist as I head over to the door, slapping a hand down on the garage door opener to give us some small measure of privacy. Dom and Emilio will know what we're doing once they hear the sound of the door closing and they'll make sure we're not interrupted.

TWENTY-THREE

Allie

H e's getting under my skin. It's been a few days since the bathroom incident and one of the Devils is always at my side. I know they're doing it to protect me, but it's getting annoying. I can't even go to the bathroom without having one of them try and tag along. The first time I went to go pee I had to forcefully shove Emilio out of the bathroom and that was only after he'd stormed in and kicked everyone else out making sure it was clear.

It's a good thing I wasn't worried about my reputation here at this school before, because a guy forcefully clearing a bathroom usually only ever meant one thing.

Even Aaron has been extra attentive and sticks around until he spots one of the Devils, and then it's like a handoff. I don't know if they somehow hashed out my babysitting details or if this is some unspoken guy thing, but I'm ready for it to be over. The one positive in all this is that I've somehow managed to make a female friend. Roman likes me sticking around at their practices until he can take me home himself and since it's not like I have anything better to do, I agreed.

Somehow, Kasey Henderson wound up keeping me company the first day and we sort of just hit it off. I've managed to convince her to stick around two other times and realized it's nice having a girlfriend. It makes me miss Adriana even more, but that's not a friendship with any chance of recovery.

The big game is today and it's all the guys are talking about. "You're still coming to support, right?" Emilio asks, tossing a french fry at me.

I nod and take my seat beside Roman at the lunch table. He pulls me close and I lean my head on his shoulder, feeling more tired than usual. I poke at my food, not making any real effort to eat before pushing my tray toward Dominique who's already finished his. "Here, you need fuel for the big game."

He grins and picks up my burger, eating the whole thing in four bites. I don't bother hiding my laugh. Dom is practically a garbage disposal when it comes to food. They all are.

I know I should probably try and eat some of my lunch but the very idea of it makes bile rise in my throat. I've lost more weight and my clothes are starting to hang loose on my body. Between the lack of appetite and the running I've taken up, I'm getting leaner. I still have curves but I've lost some of the softness around my stomach and thighs, not that I'm complaining.

"Why aren't you eating?" Roman asks, surprising me.

Saving me from having to respond, Kasey picks that moment to plop down beside me, setting her tray down on the table with a loud smack. "Urgh, can you believe her," she practically snarls.

I lift my head, giving her a questioning look.

She rolls her eyes. "Sarah. She's all over Aaron and it's disgusting. I can't stand her."

I look across the cafeteria and spot Sarah standing behind Aaron who's sitting at a table. Her arms are wrapped around his neck, her breasts pressed against his back. "I take it you're not her biggest fan?"

Her lip curls in disgust. "Definitely not. She's a bitch and she's only all over Aaron because she thinks it'll make him jealous." She points a finger toward Emilio before shoving a fry in her mouth, still glaring in her brother's direction.

"Me?" Emilio's balks, eyes wide and a horrified expression on his face. "I don't want none of that."

I lift my water bottle to take a sip just as Kasey snorts. "You slept with her last weekend. She's my neighbor. I totally saw your walk of shame the next morning." I choke on the water and Roman slaps my back a few times before the coughing subsides.

"You slept with that piranha?" I ask.

Emilio glares at Kasey, stabbing a finger at her in return. "Not cool, baby Henderson."

"Gross. Don't call me that."

"Hold on. You slept with Sarah Draven?" I ask again.

Emilio sighs and Roman fights a grin. "What baby Henderson left out is, there was a party. I was drunk. That basket of crazy over there took advantage of me."

I snort. "*Riiiight.*"

"Hey, at least I learn from my mistakes. You're still sleeping with this asshole."

Roman shoots him a glare and Kasey snickers. I give Roman a quick kiss on the cheek and his glower instantly softens. "I happen to like this asshole," I tell him and everyone else at the table makes gagging sounds.

I roll my eyes and steal a fry off Kasey's tray only to throw it at Emilio who somehow manages to catch it in his mouth.

"So, the game...?" Emilio says, trying to shift the focus off himself. "Who are you going with, because you can't show up alone."

I roll my eyes but notice Roman scowling. I guess he hadn't considered that. "I'll be fine. Nothing has happened since the whole bathroom incident and nothing is going to happen. You three went all psycho on Silvia and she's been avoiding me ever since." Every head turns to look where she's currently seated, alone and in a far corner picking at her lunch with a look of complete misery on her face.

All three give me smug smiles. As soon as Roman learned Silvia was behind the attack he went all caveman and pulled in every guy on the football team to make sure that her status as an outcast stuck. She's a social pariah now. I almost feel bad. Her own friends have abandoned her and the school pretends she doesn't exist. People will walk into her without batting an eyelash. I noticed in second period even our teacher ignores her. I have no idea how the Devils managed that but they did.

"No way." Roman shakes his head. "You can't show up alone. All three of us will be on the field. We won't be able to protect you."

"I don't need protection—"

"I can go with you," Kasey says. All eyes swing toward her.

"Are you sure?" I ask. "You hate football." I know because she's whined on at least four separate occasions about how boring it is and how stupid it is that the school treats the players like gods. Kasey isn't fond of athletes in general, which has made her little addition to our group pretty interesting, to say the least.

"Yeah, I'm sure. I like hanging out with you. Besides"—the corner of her mouth lifts into a smirk as she turns her attention toward Dominique—"then I can watch him throw an interception and give him shit for it."

Dom glowers and our entire table erupts into a fit of laughter.

"Not fucking likely," he deadpans.

I don't know what's going on with those two. Likely nothing because Dom will be eighteen in a few short months and Kasey's only a freshman, but she seems intent on getting under his skin any chance she gets, despite the fact that he usually ignores her.

The bell rings signaling the end of lunch and we make our way out of the cafeteria. Roman stops me just outside my third-period class and plants a lingering kiss on my lips that leaves me breathless.

"Don't be late tonight," he tells me, nipping my lower lip.

"Are you suddenly worried I won't show up?" I ask, fingering my bracelet.

He smirks. "Nah, I know you'll be there, but it never hurts to have some reassurances."

I tug my bracelet off and take his hand in mine, trying it around his wrist. "Consider yourself reassured. This is important to me. You can give it back to me after the game."

He kisses me deep and slow, leaving me breathless before walking backward toward his own class. "Later, baby."

TWENTY-FOUR

Roman

F riday night came too fucking fast. I'm sitting in the locker room and can barely hear what coach is saying as he gives his little pep talk before we rush out onto the field. I tighten my laces, my gaze meeting Dom's. We nod, both ready to lay it all out on the field. Tonight's a big night. If we win, it'll be smooth sailing from here on out. Coach drones on and on about how proud he is of each of us. How we've played an incredible season. And then he yells at us not to fuck it up.

Emilio elbows me in the ribs, a grin on his face as he sucks on a *palerindas*—a tamarind-flavored sucker—his game day ritual. Personally, I can't stand the things, but Emilio's an addict and always has a few in his bag.

I bounce my leg, waiting for coach to hurry up so we can get out on the field. Tonight the Devils play the Saints and I'm determined put those fuckers through hell.

The stadium lights light up the field and hundreds of people in the bleachers as I jog beside my team. I scan the crowd, not seeing Allie yet, but I know she'll be here. Seats are packed, everyone on the home side decked out in red and black with devil horns on their heads.

I make sure Allie's bracelet is tucked beneath my glove before following the other guys to the center of the field. Dom is our captain and quarterback and all eyes are on him as we huddle up and run through the details of our first play.

I'm hyped as fuck and bouncing on the balls of my feet, ready to leave the Saint's defense in a cloud of dust. One last scan of the bleachers shows that Allie still isn't here, but I shake off the irritation as soon as I spot my pops in the stands. I puff out my chest and when Dom calls the play and snaps back, I'm off. I sprint wide to the left, before spinning to catch the ball I know is aimed right for me. My hands connect with the laces and I clutch the damn thing like my life depends on it before taking off straight for the goal posts.

I'm tackled twenty yards from the end zone but I'm still grinning because we picked up way more ground on the first play than we should have. Looks like the Saints are going to have an off day.

It's the end of the second quarter and we're ahead by seven. The stadium is packed, making it harder to find my girl, but as I take my seat on the bench, Dominique points out Henderson's little sister. "Baby Henderson's here. That means Allie is, too."

I nod, scanning the surrounding crowd for her dark brown hair. The spot beside Kasey is vacant. Maybe Allie went to the restroom? The idea alone is enough to have me clenching my hands into tight fists. "Yeah, but do you see her?"

He looks and shakes his head. "No."

"Me, either. Which means she's off somewhere at this packed fucking game alone right now."

"Maybe she just went to grab a soda?"

"I don't care if she needed to take a shit. She knows the deal. She's not supposed to go anywhere at this school alone."

He nods, a scowl on his face letting me know he doesn't like this any more than I do, but there isn't anything either of us can do about it from the field. Coach calls us back to the locker room for our half-time pep talk and I have no choice but to follow the rest of the guys.

When we return for the beginning of the third, the seat beside Kasey is still fucking empty. Worry worms through me, followed quickly by anger when I catch my pops getting up from the stands, his phone to his ear because of course he can't leave work at the office.

I'm tracking his movements as he leaves through the gate entrance and miss Dom's words as he calls out the play before the snap. Fuck. I take off, hoping I'm heading in the right direction. When Dom throws, I realize I'm way the fuck off and have to kick it into gear to reach his intended mark. My fingers glance across the ball but I fumble the catch. Thankfully, one of my teammates is close by to recover it. I kick at the field, unearthing a chunk of grass as I curse and head back to the start-up line.

The rest of the game goes similarly, but I'm not the only one affected now. It's like everything went to shit the second half. Dom throws an interception and we miss two field goals that we should have had in the bag. Emilio lets two running backs slip past him, allowing the Saints to score. We're still in the lead but we're down to the wire and if we don't score, there's a good chance the Saints will on their next play and we'll lose. There isn't enough time on the clock. I have to score.

I know the play. I've done this maneuver a million times before, so I focus on my breathing, narrowing my field of vision as I zero in on where I need to be and how to get there as quickly as possible. My pops never returned after stepping out and I still haven't caught sight of my girl. Focusing all of my anger and frustration into our last play I sprint up the field, adrenaline rushing through my veins. My hands find the ball and then I'm running up the field, racing along the boundary line.

Two players are hot on my heels and I have no one from my own team anywhere close to help. One of the assholes—number eleven—is gaining on me, but with the ball tucked under my right arm I shove out with my left, shoving him away and then TOUCHDOWN!

My team rushes me. Helmets knock into mine and fists

knock me in the shoulder. There's less than two minutes on the clock and the other team has no time-outs left. I cheer with my team. We won. We'll run out the clock, but my job here is done.

I'm riding a high and smiling like an idiot until I look back up at the stands.

Kasey's nowhere to be found now, and neither is Allie.

My smile tightens. And I turn back to the guys, accepting their good-natured high-fives and shouts of congratulations, all the while thinking in my head, *where the fuck is she?*

TWENTY-FIVE

Allie

I'm running late getting to the game. Kasey was going to meet me at my place and we'd drive over together but something came up with her aunt, so she sent a text letting me know she'd have to meet me at the school.

I call an Uber and get the oldest grandma in the history of Uber drivers who happens to drive five miles an hour below the speed limit the entire way, but I get there just as the first quarter ends and make my way over to the bleachers where Kasey said she'd be.

"Hey. Sorry I'm late." I claim the empty seat beside her.

"Damn, Allie. Looking good," she says, taking in my painted stomach. I blush. It hadn't been planned, but I knew that some of the girls painted their boyfriend's or favorite player's number on their midriff, so I painted Roman's—a number four—and a small red devil on my abdomen.

"Thanks. Think he'll like it?"

Her brows wiggle. "I think he'll *love* it." She smirks, then winks. "Also, don't hate me, but I might have to leave early."

Oh. I look around, instantly realizing I don't have anyone else to hang out with here if she leaves, but I promised the guys I'd be here so I can't very well bail.

"My aunt is running short-staffed at the diner," she tells me. "I don't usually work there but she's in a bind. That's why I was late. I filled in after school for one of the girls who was a no-show. I can stay for most of the game, but I'll need to leave before the end of the fourth so I can get there before the football crowd shows up."

"Oh. That's totally fine." It's great, actually. I won't be alone the whole game. Just for part of the fourth. No big deal.

I look out on the field and instantly find Roman—number four. My heart quickens and I watch him run up the field, scoring for the Sun Valley Devils. The entire stadium cheers, including me. I jump up and down like a moron screaming his name in the hopes he'll see me.

"Oh, and here. I brought us these to make the game more interesting." Kasey opens her purse to show me the stash of mini booze bottles tucked away inside.

"You snuck alcohol into a school game?"

She grins. "How else was I supposed to get through this game?" Pulling two out, she hands one to me. A mini

Malibu rum. I roll my eyes but accept it. "To Dominique throwing an interception."

"I can't toast to that."

She shrugs. "I can. You can toast to Roman scoring the winning touchdown."

I laugh but concede. "Okay. I'll toast to that." Cracking the cap, I take a drink, downing half of the rum in one swallow before tucking the bottle into my pocket. "That's kind of awful," I tell her.

"I know, but it was all I could find on short notice. Aaron keeps a stash of these in the bottom drawer of his dresser."

My phone buzzes in my pocket. I look down and recognize Julio's number flashing across the screen and smile.

"Hello?"

"Hey—" His words are hard to hear through the thundering noise of the crowd.

"Give me a second to get somewhere quiet," I shout into the phone. "I'll be back. I need to take this," I tell Kasey. She waves me off, her attention focused on her own phone as her fingers fly over the keyboard. Standing, I make my way through the stands, slipping through the bleachers and heading for the parking lot gate.

The half-time show is starting up and everyone is on their feet dancing to whatever song the cheer squad has going on.

"Excuse me. Sorry." I brush past a group of parents and finally make it outside the gate. It's still loud out here but the noise level is no longer deafening.

"Sorry about that. How are you?" I ask as I stride further across the darkened lot toward the corner of the school. The lights barely illuminate the space but it's still hard to hear Julio over the crowd so I resign myself to a phone call in the dark.

"I'm good. Now, tell me about this guy you mentioned you're seeing."

I laugh, hearing the protective tone in his voice. "Chill with the big brother vibes. Nothing serious is going on."

He snorts. "Allie, you don't date. Ryker was the exception and we saw how that went."

I groan. "Please don't remind me." If I could forget ever being with Ryker, that'd be the day.

"I'm serious, though. Is he good to you?"

A smile spreads over my face as I think about Roman. He's still an asshole to everyone else in this school but in the small pockets of time we happen to get alone, he's different. Still cocky and possessive but also kind, thoughtful, and surprisingly funny. Just thinking about this past week we've had together is enough to make butterflies dance in my stomach.

"Yeah, Julio. He is. I don't know what it is about him but..." I trail off and narrow my eyes in the dark as I spot two men ten yards away from me. They're not doing anything, just standing there watching me, but still ... goosebumps spread across my skin.

"You still there?" Julio asks.

"Ye...Yeah. I'm here. Sorry, umm, what was I saying?" I turn away from the men and head back across the parking lot, finally realizing I'd pulled myself away from the safety of the crowd. Everything looks different now. Darker, more sinister. My heart races in my chest and I can barely make out Julio's words as panic bubbles inside me.

I scan the lot and see Silvia across the parking lot, but there's no way I'm going to her for safety. I'm not that stupid. I don't see anyone else close by, though. I chance a look behind my shoulder and just as I turn, my phone is snatched from my fingertips. The call is ended and my phone is tossed carelessly to the ground. "Hey!"

The man who took it grabs me by the throat and slams me against the brick wall of the school. My head slams against the hard surface and my vision blurs, a strangled cry pouring from my lips.

"This her?" Another voice asks.

A grunt. "Yeah. It's her."

The man holding my throat whirls me around, one arm bands beneath my chest, pinning my arms to my sides while the other one grips my throat. He shoves me forward. "Come on, we'll take her over here."

I try to scream but all I can muster is a wheezing sound. I spot Silvia across the lot again. Her face is trained away from me and I'm silently begging her to look my way. To see what's happening right now. But she never turns, her gaze caught on something or someone else.

I try to cry out again, shouting her name but nothing comes out. My head is pounding and I squirm against his hold but he has me in a vice-like grip. My vision clears and I can see that he's leading me further from the parking lot into a more remote area where the lights don't reach. My stomach drops.

I fight harder, kicking out with my legs, and when that doesn't work I drop my weight, but he still doesn't release me.

"Girl's got some fight in her," the second man says. I twist to see him but all I can make out is a dark shadow.

The man holding me grunts and his grip on my throat tightens to the point that I know it'll leave a bruise. Spots form in my field of vision and I claw at his fingers, desperate for air. "Just means this'll be more fun." His hot breath heats the side of my neck and I recoil. What does he mean, more fun? What are they planning to do to me?

Tears track down my cheeks, but I'm not resigned to my fate. Not yet. I try kicking again and this time I manage to hit his knee.

The man holding me curses and the hand around my throat loosens enough that I can finally suck in a deep breath.

I make it count and scream with everything in me. "Help! Somebody help me!"

The fist comes out of nowhere. A crack along my cheek that leaves me reeling.

"Dumb bitch." He releases me and I crash to the ground, my hands meeting cool grass. I choke on a sob and reach up with a shaking hand to cradle my cheek.

The men don't give me any time to recover. I'm shoved face first down in the cool, wet grass, my injured cheek pressed hard against the ground. I cry out again but it's cut off when his hand comes up to cover my mouth. "You're going to be nice and quiet if you want to leave here alive," he spits at me. The threat in his voice settles deep in my bones, freezing me in place.

"Please—"

"That's it. Beg for it."

I try to shake my head but I can't move. His weight has me pinned in place. "Please." I hiccup. "Don't do this."

He releases my throat and leans back. His legs straddle my own and his other hand shoves beneath me to release the button of my jeans. *This can't be happening.* I struggle against his hold, squirming and kicking, but he's just so much bigger than me. My struggles make little difference. Deciding I have no other choice, I scream again. "Help. Som—"

Crack!

He grabs the back of my head and slams my face into the ground. *Hard.* Pain lances through me and sheer terror rips my insides apart.

"I won't tell you again. Shut the fuck up," he growls just before tugging my jeans and underwear down, exposing my bare rear to the cold night air.

Panic tightens my throat, but I manage to say, "Why are you doing this?" in a choked-out sob. My head is throbbing and black is quickly filling my field of vision, but I fight to stay awake and aware. I can't black out. I refuse to pass out and be at their mercy.

The other man is chuckling beside us. "This is a message for dear old dad." Ice freezes in my veins. "We want to make sure he knows that when he fucks with what's ours, we'll fuck with what's his."

What? I struggle to comprehend what he's telling me, but as soon as I feel the other man press himself against my naked rear, my mind blanks.

No. No. No.

One hand pins me down, the other is beside my face as he braces himself against me. I hear the sound of a foil wrapper being torn open followed by more chuckles.

Tears prick the corners of my eyes and I struggle to breathe over the mounting pain in my chest. This isn't happening. *This isn't happening.* I repeat the words over and over again in my head but it doesn't make them true.

A sharp intrusion makes my stomach lurch. I gasp and without realizing what I'm even saying, I beg him to stop. To let me go. I promise him anything and everything I can think of if he will just let me go. He doesn't. Fighting doesn't do anything but make him rougher. He grips me tighter, his hand bruising as he grabs my hips and forces his way inside of me. The other man presses his boot to the side of my face, holding me down.

My breaths are heavy. He moves behind me, grunting like an animal and vomit threatens to rise in my throat.

Everything hurts. My vision continues to swim as I force the bile down. I lock my gaze on his hand and force my mind to think of something, anything else.

The full moon manages to illuminate his tanned skin. The calluses on the side of his thumb. He has short fingernails with a thin line of dirt beneath each of them. I focus on the scars that cover the top of his hand. On the age lines. I force myself to count every hair follicle.

Time passes. I keep counting. I keep tracing the lines on his hand, blocking out the sounds he's making. And then he stops. I sob in relief as his weight leaves me until he says, "Don't fucking move."

I don't. I keep myself planted on the ground, my breathing shallow and my cheek still mashed against the lawn of the school. I need to move. To run and escape but my limbs are locked and frozen in place. I'm drowning in the realization that I was just—

Then the second man steps closer.

No. The word echoes in my mind before a raw animalistic sound pours out of me. He straddles my hips like the man before him did and I'm already shaking my head as another sob lodges itself in my throat, but just as he reaches for me, a voice speaks out in the distance.

A man.

His voice comes closer. I can't tell what he's saying but his words get louder as he nears. "Help," I try to call out, but my words are little more than a whisper. My throat aching and scraped raw from crying.

"Shut up." The man behind me says with a growl. "Do you think he's spotted us?" He directs his questions to the other guy. I shift my head, still unable to see either of their faces. Both men are dark shadows in the night. A heavy presence I'm desperate to escape. I can't go through this again. I don't care if they kill me. I can't—

"*Help!*" This time my words are louder.

The two men curse and the one behind me shoves up from me, using my back to press himself forward. I groan from the weight of him, my spine protesting his movements. "We need to get gone," he says.

"Hey! Stop!" The newcomer shouts and the two men curse. Footsteps pound across the pavement toward me. I can't tell how far away he is but a trickle of hope spills into me. I move to push myself up when one of the men grabs my hair and jerks my head up, my scalp stinging and fresh tears forming in the corners of my eyes.

I cry out.

"Be sure to relay our message. If Ulrich fucks with one of our deals again, we'll be more than happy to make another visit," the man says before dropping me harshly back to the ground.

They run in the opposite direction just as a new man runs up alongside me. "*Dammit.*" He curses and reaches for me but I recoil from his touch. "I'm not going to hurt you. I work for the Sun Valley P.D. Everything is going to be okay." He tears off his jacket and throws it over my exposed skin before flipping open his cell phone. "I need an ambulance at Sun Valley High. Sexual assault. Yes."

I wrap his coat around myself as I struggle to lift my pants back into place. My fingers are numb and my hands shake, making it nearly impossible. When I finally pull them up I gingerly roll to my back. Dark night sky greets me.

I swallow hard and the man comes into my field of vision. His phone is still held up to his ear. He's saying something but I can't hear him. Darkness crowds my vision and this time, I welcome it.

TWENTY-SIX

Allie

Janessa storms into my hospital room with a no-nonsense air to her and for some strange reason, my shoulders relax.

She looks to the nurse who's still completing my admittance paperwork and asks, "Can we have a moment? Alone."

The nurse sends a sympathetic look my way and bobs her head before saying to me, "I'll give you and your mom a few minutes and then I'll come back and we'll get started. Okay, Allie?"

I nod, not bothering to correct her as dread courses through me. She means we'll get started with the rape kit and God, I don't even want to think about everything that involves.

I stare down at my hands, noting the bruises on my knuckles. The bloody tears on my fingernails. I suck in a shuddering breath and start counting each bruise on my hands and arms. One. Two. Three. Four...

When we're alone, Janessa pulls a chair closer to me.

Five. Six...

Taking a seat, she reaches out for my hands but I stiffen and jerk away.

She nods to herself and takes a deep breath. I keep my eyes trained on my hands. I know what she's going to say.

"Your father couldn't—"

"I know," I whisper, not needing her to finish her sentence. Gerald is in an important meeting. He can't get away. I've heard it all before. I shouldn't have expected anything different.

So why is my stomach twisted up in tight ugly knots?

I swipe a tear away from my face.

I'm his kid. You're supposed to care about your kids, right? When your daughter is attacked you're supposed to be there. Mom would have been here. She would have held my hand and smoothed my hair back. She would have told me to cry. That it was going to be okay. And she would have held me.

But none of this is going to be okay. *I* wasn't going to be okay.

Another tear escapes and I furiously swipe that one away, too. Mom isn't here so I can't cry. No one will hold me. No one will promise me that I'll make it through this. I can't break down because no one will be there to help me pick up the pieces.

Janessa releases a breath. It's a resigned sound. "I'm sorry this happened to you, Allie. So terribly sorry."

I sit there. What am I supposed to say to that? Am I supposed to comfort her because she feels bad for me? Am I supposed to say I'm sorry it happened, too? Should I tell her how angry I am with myself for being there in the first place? That I'd known better. That I shouldn't have—

She interrupts my train of thought with a question. "Do you know who did this to you?"

I shake my head as bitter acid coats my tongue. Isn't that the kicker. That bastard did this to me and I don't even know who he is. He didn't know me. We'd never met before but he still did this.

"Did you see his face?"

"No," I choke out with a hard shake of my head. I ignore the spinning sensation that hits me with the movement and bite back the bile in my throat. The nurses think I have a concussion. He gave me a concussion when he slammed my head against the brick wall of the school. And that's the least of it all.

"Do you remember anything that might identify him in a lineup?"

I hang my head again. All I remember is his voice. His words. The feel of his body against mine. The pain of him inside of me. And his hand. I remember his hand. I stared at it while he … no. I don't want to relive it. I don't want to remember.

I shove the memories as far down as they'll go and tuck them away with the emotions I refuse to let free right now.

I shake my head.

"Have they done a rape kit, yet?"

I swallow hard and whisper out another, "No."

She nods to herself. "Do you know if he used a condom?"

My brows pinch together. Why does she want to know that? My mind goes back to that moment. To him pushing me down and ripping my pants off of me. I was turned away from him. He shoved my face down on the ground. Pressed my cheek in the dirt. But I remember the sound of a foil packet. I heard the distinct sound of him tear something open behind me before forcing himself—

My breaths come out as shallow pants and suddenly Janessa is right in my face.

"Allie. Allie." She snaps her fingers in front of me.

I can't breathe. I claw at my own throat, desperate for air.

Janessa grabs the back of my neck and forces my head between my legs.

I cry out at the sudden movement but don't fight her. I can't. I still can't breathe.

"Breathe, honey. Just breathe." Her grip tightens on my neck and inside I'm screaming for her to let go. Not to touch me. But I can't get the words out. Seconds tick by. Then minutes.

When my breathing finally slows down she lets go and steps back.

"It was just a panic attack," she says as I lift my head back up.

My vision blurs for a moment but then she comes back into focus.

"Take another breath."

I do as she tells me and when I no longer feel like my lungs are going to collapse in on me, I mutter out the answer to her last question.

"I... I think he did. I think he used one."

"Good. That's good."

She pulls out her phone and her fingers frantically type across her keyboard before she puts it back in her purse.

Then she leans down and lifts a small bag from the ground that I hadn't noticed when she first walked in. "Here. I brought you some clothes. Let's get you dressed and I'll take you home."

I nod, accepting the bag but then I stop. "What about the...?" I make a small wave with my hands unable to say the words aloud. Tears prick the corners of my eyes again as

I brace myself for what I know will be another form of violation and shame blooms in my chest.

I can't do it. I just can't.

They're going to look at me and touch me. I've seen the movies. There will be pictures. Doctors will see me without my clothes. I'll be exposed. I can't I just. I can't.

Janessa takes a step closer and saves me from my panic. "We don't need to worry about that today."

I give her a tear-filled, half-hearted smile. "We don't?"

She shakes her head. "No, sweetheart. We don't."

Relief sweeps through me before reality sets in. "But...if we don't, how will they find him? How will..." I trail off. Because they have to find him, right? He can't get away with this. He'll do it again. What if he finds me again? He said he would come back if...

She places a tentative hand on my arm and I stiffen and jerk away from her.

There's an apology in her gaze as she asks, "Allie, were you drinking this evening?"

I swallow past the lump in my throat and answer honestly with a nod. "But I wasn't drunk. I didn't even have one whole drink." I remember that Kasey snuck mini liquor bottles into the game. She'd given me one. I only took a sip. Drank maybe half of it before I got the call from Julio. "I—"

"I know, honey. I know. But you *were* drinking and you're a minor. You don't know who did this and since you think he used a condom, there won't be any semen to use to find him, if he is even in the system."

I stare at her. Stunned. Is she... no. *No.*

"You're a young girl. You're beautiful and smart and you have your whole life ahead of you. But this, this could ruin you. This could ruin your father."

My father. That's what this was really about.

"If Ulrich interferes in our deals again, I'll be happy to make another visit..."

Cold dread consumes me. He's going to stay out there. He's going to get away with this. Because of Gerald. Because of my dad.

No. No. *No.* That's not right. He'll find me. If Gerald messes up again. I don't even know what he did. Why the man came after me. But I do know deep down in the marrow of my bones that he'll do it again and I have no way of knowing. No way of protecting myself because I don't even know what he looks like.

I shake my head. No. *No!* I can't breathe.

Janessa cups my cheeks as tears fall freely down my face now. "Allie. If we do a rape kit this goes on record. There's no taking it back. You'll be questioned. You'll be blamed. It's not right. This wasn't your fault. None of it was your fault. You need to believe that." Her eyes glass over and I want to shove away from her because how dare she look at me like that. I was the one raped. I was the one who had something taken away from them. Me. Not her. She has no right to act like this hurts her. It only hurts me.

"I know you're dealing with a lot. I know this is a lot to take in, but I need you to see how this looks on paper. You were drinking while underage. You were dressed provocatively." I think back to what I'd been wearing. The ripped jeans and crop top hadn't seemed provocative at the time. It was our big rival game. Everyone dressed up. My stomach had been painted with a red devil and a number 4. It was Roman's number. So many other students had done something similar. But ... was she right? It was a lot of skin, wasn't it? My entire midriff had been showing.

Oh God.

"Honey, even if they find this guy, if they press charges, his lawyer is going to drag you through the mud. They'll tarnish your name. Your reputation. And this trauma will consume your life for six months or more. You'll have to tell a courtroom full of people what happened. Every single detail over and over. The defending attorney will twist your words and turn the blame on you. They'll make you relive what happened in the hopes that you slip up. That you make a mistake in your story."

She thumbs my tears away and I bite back a scream as I digest her words because she's right. I know she's right. But it feels wrong. He shouldn't be free. He shouldn't get away with this.

"They won't find enough evidence to find who did this. If he didn't use a condom, if they had his...his fluids, it still might not be enough evidence to convict. I don't want that for you."

I shudder and turn away from her. I choke back my sobs and straighten my spine, letting everything she says sink in and settle deep in my bones. *Come on, Allie. Be strong. Don't fold now. You've been through too much. You cannot fold now.*

"He did this because of my dad," I tell her, because I have to tell someone. Her eyes widen in shock but I don't give her a chance to respond. "When he..." I pause before forcing the word out. "After he *raped* me, he told me why. He said Dad fucked up some deal of his." Another deep shudder as I repeat the message he gave me. She gasps in response.

Then I push the next words out of my mouth uncaring of how broken and bitter I sound. I'm allowed to feel bitter.

"But you're still right. It doesn't matter because he was smart and I didn't see him. I was raped because of my own father—because of my father's *business*—and it doesn't even matter."

Silence.

I reach for the bag again and move toward the attached bathroom to get dressed. When I brush past her I barely make out her words but they're there, hanging in the air between us. "I'm so sorry, Allie."

Yeah. I was too. But sorry wasn't going to change a damn thing.

I catch my reflection in the mirror before jerking away as I strip down, trying to bottle up all my emotions. The urge to shower is strong. I want any traces of him scrubbed off my skin. When I first got here the nurse told me I had to wait. How important it was that I not shower or even wash my hands until they have a chance to gather their *evidence*. But that doesn't matter anymore. I turn on the sink, waiting until steam rises from the faucet. I pump a large amount of hand soap into my hands and begin washing. I get lost in the motions, making sure I scrub my hands up to my forearms until my skin is coated in a white foaming lather. The water is scalding when I shove my hands beneath it but I don't care. I force myself to rinse the soap off leaving my hands and forearms beneath the spray until they're pink and angry. I've endured worse.

If I could shower in the sink I would but that will have to wait until I get to Gerald's.

When I come back into the room, Janessa and one of the nurses are facing off against one another. They turn to me and I stop.

"Allie. I was trying to explain to your—" the nurse begins.

"She is a minor and the decision has been made. We're leaving."

I bow my head. I don't have it in me to argue with anyone. Let them figure it out.

I slip my feet into my shoes and hear the distinct buzz of a cell phone as Janessa uses her *take no prisoners* tone with the nurse.

I don't bother listening to their conversation. I know how this will go and I'm already resigned to my fate.

I locate my phone on the bedside table, grateful it was recovered at the scene, and unlocked the screen.

Four missed messages.

> **Roman: Where are you? What the hell, Allie?**

> **Roman: You said you'd be here.**

> **Roman: After everything that's happened will you at least let me know if you're okay?**

> **Roman: Tracked down Kasey. She said you bailed for some phone call. Where are you?**

I glance at the time. It's just after ten. The game would have ended almost an hour ago. He would have come out of the locker rooms, expecting to find me waiting for him, but I wasn't there. How long had he waited for me?

My fingers shake over the keyboard. What do I say? I can't tell him where I am. What happened. I can't tell anyone. But I don't want to lie to him, either.

Another text flashes across my screen.

> **Emilio: Way to fucking support our boy.**

Then another

> **Roman: You know what, whatever. You do you.**

A fresh wave of tears cascades down my cheeks. I can't stop them. I swipe them away but they just keep coming.

Janessa calls my name and I turn to her, shoving my phone into the pocket of the pants she brought for me, then I follow her to the door. On my way out, the nurse hands me a small pill and a glass of water. I don't ask what it's for. I know.

I place the pill in my mouth and take a drink, swallowing it down before handing the cup back to the nurse who nods like I've done something good, but she's still not happy.

Janessa watches the exchange with a tight-lipped frown but she doesn't say anything.

A pair of police officers and a man that must be their boss meet us halfway down the hallway. I don't recognize the officers but the man with them, he's the one who found me.

I remember that. He's wearing a uniform like the others. It's similar to the boys in blue but there are more pins on it. More stars on the shoulders. He has an air of authority the other two don't have.

I want to thank him. He helped me. But I can't make the words form. All I can do is stare at his hands. They're rough and tan and—

I take several steps back.

Janessa turns her head to look at me but all I can see are his hands.

They're not the same, Allie. They're not the same.

I know that. My mind knows that. But my heart is racing out of my chest because they're not the same but they're similar and I can't stop looking at them. He takes a step in my direction and my muscles lock up.

My head snaps back to look him in the face and he freezes.

"Miss?" His hands are lifted as if in surrender and I can see the worry in his gaze. He takes another careful step closer and my chest heaves. He's approaching me like I'm some rabid animal. I need ... I need ...

Janessa takes two steps to her left and suddenly she's blocking him from my view. She says something but I don't hear it. I can't hear anything over the roaring in my ears.

His hands aren't the same. I tell myself again and again like a mantra that will somehow make this all better. I try to think of something else. Anything else. But then my mind latches onto Roman and how mad he must be with me right now. How disappointed all of them are. I promised I'd be there. They'd wanted me to be there. And then I wasn't.

Janessa tugs on my sleeve and I glance up, she guides me around the officers and I don't miss their pity as she ushers me outside the hospital doors. I don't want their pity.

When we're outside I slowly start locking myself down. I will my mind to go numb. To block out everything I'm feeling. To forget everything that happened. I just want to forget it all.

TWENTY-SEVEN

Allie

I wake with a start. My chest heaves and my eyes pop open. Daylight filters in through my bedroom curtains, letting me know it's morning. Or maybe afternoon. It doesn't matter.

I stare up at the ceiling, willing myself to go back to sleep. I don't want to be awake. It hurts too much.

There's a knock at my door.

I ignore it.

Another knock.

I roll to my side just as the door opens. "Allie," Janessa calls.

I squeeze my eyes shut hoping she'll think I'm asleep and leave me alone.

She doesn't.

I hear her steps fall across the carpet as she comes closer. My bed dips under her weight as she sits on the corner. I stiffen when she reaches out and touches my leg. "Allie, you need to eat something. Why don't you come downstairs? Your father ordered breakfast. It'll be good for you to get out of bed."

I say nothing.

She tries another tactic. "Some friends of yours from school have stopped by."

They have? A part of me wants to know who. Wants to know if it was Roman. If he's still angry with me? He hasn't messaged me since that night and I miss him but ... every time a man has come close to me I've panicked. Gerald tried speaking to me once. I freaked out. I curled into a ball like a child and sobbed. I still don't know why. It just happened and I couldn't stop it.

He hired a doctor to come look at me. That didn't go well either. For the past three days the only person that I've allowed in my room has been Janessa. I don't like it when she's close, and I really don't like it when she touches me, but at least her presence doesn't send me into a mindless panic. It's enough.

So, while I might want to see Roman, I don't want him to see me like this. I don't want to risk losing myself again. With him. But curiosity burns through me so I open my eyes and ask, "Who?"

She shifts her weight. "A few boys. Two Latinos and a black guy. They said they were your friends?"

I nod.

"What did you tell them?"

"That you weren't seeing visitors right now."

I swallow. "Anything else?"

She's quiet for a moment and I hold my breath. "I didn't tell them what happened but ... one of the boys got angry when I refused to let him in. He started shouting. I might have yelled at him. Told him you didn't want to see anyone. Even him." She grips my leg in apology. "He didn't seem happy. I'm sorry, sweetheart. I just didn't know how else to make him leave."

I blink back the moisture in my eyes. "It's okay."

She sighs and stands to leave. "Will you at least think about coming down to eat?"

I nod, knowing I won't. I haven't left my bed since that night to do anything more than use the bathroom or shower. Something I've been doing at least three times a day. Sometimes more. I can't seem to get the feel of his hands off of me. The smell of his skin.

Janessa starts to say something else but I can't listen to her anymore. I'm losing myself to my memories. I want her to go away. I need to go back to sleep. It's the only place I feel safe anymore. Childishly I cover my ears. "Please," I whisper. "Go away."

Time passes from one day to the next, even when it feels impossible. Even when it seems like I'm losing myself with each passing hour. Each passing minute. I don't understand how the sun manages to rise each day when I can barely open my eyes to greet it.

I lose count of how many days go by.

Some days Janessa comes to try and get me to come downstairs. Some days she doesn't. I manage to drink the bottled water she brings me. On occasion the tea. But I rarely touch the food. The few times I've tried have resulted in me bent over my toilet heaving whatever I consumed right back out. My body doesn't feel like it's mine anymore. I know this isn't normal. I know I need help. But I can't find the energy or want to ask for it. I'm numb and I'm afraid to be anything else but numb.

Roman doesn't message me. Neither does Emilio. Dominique reached out once asking me if something happened. If I was okay. But I didn't respond. What could I say?

I wake to the sound of heated voices in the hallway outside my bedroom door. Rubbing the sleep from my eyes I try and muster interest in what they're saying. I stare at the closed door, pulling my covers tighter around myself as if that's enough to keep me warm. But it's not. All I feel is a bone-aching chill. It never leaves.

"She needs more time."

"She doesn't need time. There's nothing wrong with her and she's done nothing but sleep. It's been nearly a week—"

"What else would you have her do? The girl is traumatized."

"She needs to get over it."

I don't hear what they say next. I look at the clock on my bedside table. It's just after seven in the morning.

I take a deep breath.

I'm okay.

I will get through this.

You're strong, Allie. You're strong like Mom.

I take another deep, shuddering breath and force back a fresh wave of tears. *Why am I crying?*

"You're strong like Mom," I whisper to myself. I wipe my tears away and make myself get out of bed. I'm numb. I can be numb and move. I can be numb and do things. Go places. Right? Maybe.

Mom died. My boyfriend cheated. My boyfriend dumped me. My best girlfriend turned her back on me. I lost my home. I had to go to a new school in a new town. My dad never has time for me. I was ra...

I force myself to finish the thought.

I was *raped*.

I'd been through so much in such a short amount of time. But it was done. Over. Finished. All of it had already happened. I'd push forward. *One day at a time, Allie. You can do this.*

Numb. So fucking numb.

Janessa's voice rises again. There's mention of a therapist.

I don't know what Gerald says in response but I can tell by Janessa's tone that she doesn't agree.

That's okay.

I'm okay.

Or at least, I will be. Time heals all wounds, right? That's what all the inspirational quotes and memes on social media say.

The day I arrived in Sun Valley I told myself all I needed to do was survive this year, graduate, and then I could go home.

That is still the plan. I can go home. Things will be better once I'm back in Richland. There won't be a school full of people who hate me. There won't be bad men lurking around corners, hurting me to get to my dad. I will be safe. I just have to survive here a little bit longer.

Letting that resolve settle inside of me, I shower. The hot water scalds my skin, but it's still not enough to warm the bone-deep chill. I scrub at my arms and legs, wishing I could clean myself, but I've already learned it doesn't matter how many times I wash my body, I still feel dirty. I can't get the smell or feel of him off me.

I spend thirty minutes in the shower before giving up and drying off. I put on a pair of jeans and a long-sleeved purple top, careful to cover every inch of skin I can reasonably manage and add a silk scarf to cover the bruising on my neck for good measure.

Leaving my hair down, I blow it dry and add a heavy layer of concealer along my jaw, my right cheek, and beneath my bottom lip. It's not enough, so I add a layer of foundation on top and then another layer of concealer on top of that. It covers the bruises but I can't do much to conceal the swelling. With some lip liner and gloss, it should be less noticeable. I hope.

Even with a full face of makeup, my skin is still a little discolored but if I keep my head down like I usually do I should be fine. No one will give me a second glance.

There's a knock on my door and before I can answer, it swings open.

Janessa walks in to find me sitting on the floor in front of the full-length mirror in my room.

"You're ready?" she asks, sounding surprised.

"Yeah." I stand and reach for my backpack. My eyes lock on my hands and I freeze, staring at them as though for the first time. My knuckles are bruised. My nail beds torn and cracked with dried blood.

Makeup can't cover that. I frown. I'll have to keep my hands in my pockets if I want to avoid any questions. Dread wells up inside of me. I can't handle any questions.

I grab a zip-up hoodie from my closet. One of the pieces I picked up with Aaron during our Target run.

Janessa frowns when she sees the black garment and then steps over to my closet. She flicks through the clothes hanging there and pulls out a soft white sweater with pale pink sleeves.

Turning, she hands it to me, gently taking the hoodie and placing it back inside my closet. "This goes with what you're wearing," she tells me.

I want to scream.

But I don't.

Screaming doesn't do anything. It doesn't help. I know that, so I nod and slip my arms into the sweater, feeling another piece of myself die inside. Why does the sweater matter so much?

When we step outside to head to school, an unfamiliar car sits in the driveway.

Dominique stands there, leaning against the hood of his black Escalade, arms folded over his chest.

I freeze.

"Allie," he calls out and tilts his head back to his car. "I'm giving you a lift. Come on."

My heart rate picks up and my eyes turn to Janessa, pleading with her to say something. Anything.

I can't go with him. My breathing becomes erratic. *I can't.*

Understanding washes over her face. She gives me a barely perceptible nod and turns to him. "I'm sorry, young man, but you need to leave."

Dom smirks. "I'll get right on that. As soon as Allie gets in the car." He flashes her a dazzling smile. "I'm a friend from school. I've given her rides before. She's plenty safe with me, ma'am."

Janessa flicks a look to me as if to ask, *what now?*

But how the heck should I know. I have no idea what to do in this situation. I wasn't prepared to face him. I had an entire pep talk ready to give myself on the drive to school today. Before I saw him. Before I saw anyone. My hands are clammy and a cold sweat drips down my spine.

My heart hammers in my chest. Faster. Harder. My breaths quicken and I know a panic attack lingers right there on the edge. I can't let him see me like this. My temples pound, a headache now coming on strong, beating inside me like a battering ram.

"Allie?" she whispers.

I can't. I can't.

I know Dom is safe. He's my friend. He's safe. I know that. But the idea of being in a car with him right now is sending my mind into a spiral. I can't.

I turn and rush back inside the house, ignoring both of them as they call out for me.

I can't.

I'm not ready.

I just can't.

TWENTY-EIGHT

Allie

More time passes. I don't know what I was thinking trying to go to school. I was an idiot.

It's been three days since. Maybe four. I don't know for certain and I try not to care. There's a knock at the door and I sigh, but when I roll over to tell Janessa to go away, my breath freezes in my lungs.

Julio steps inside, Janessa right behind him. "Allie," she hedges.

I swallow hard and push up into a sitting position, clutching my blankets tight to my chest. "What are you doing here?" I whisper, my eyes zeroed in on Julio as he stands just inside my room.

His dark brown eyes soften and he takes a step toward me. I lock up with that one small movement. He stops and turns to Janessa, a question in his gaze.

"She has a hard time with men right now."

He nods. Taking a step back, he leans against the wall before sliding down to the floor and folding his hands in his lap. "Hey," he tries again.

I shift in my bed, putting a few more inches between us. "Hi."

Janessa hovers in the doorway. "Do you want me to stay?" she asks.

I take a deep breath. Exhale. Then take another one and shake my head. "I... no. I'm okay."

She nods but doesn't look convinced.

"I'll stay right here for however long she needs," he tells her. "I won't push."

"I'll be right downstairs if you need me," she tells me and then pulls the door shut behind her.

Julio and I stare at one another for several seconds before he finally breaks the silence. "Are you okay?"

That one question has my eyes brimming with tears. I look away and swipe at my cheeks.

"Fuck, Allie." Julio hangs his head, his chest rising and falling with heavy breaths. "I..." He looks at me, his eyes stark and raw with pain. "I don't know what to say. How to fix this."

I choke on a laugh. "She told you?"

He nods. "I tried calling you a few times but your phone kept going to voicemail. Then this chick calls me out of nowhere asking if I'd be willing to come here for a few days. See if I can help." He shrugs. "Allie, when she told me what happened to you. What you went through..."

My eyes sting and shame blossoms in my chest. Pressing my lips into a tight line I look down at the covers clenched between my fingertips. He must think I'm so weak. So dirty.

"Hey."

I don't look up.

"Hey!"

I shake my head. I don't want to see the pity or disgust I know must be in his gaze. If Julio looks at me differently... I can't handle this anymore.

"Allie. Babe. I love you. You are my best friend. Let me be here for you."

A tear slips down my cheek and I furiously swipe it away. "You shouldn't be here," I tell him.

"Alejandra. Por favor. Déjame ayudarte." *Please. Let me help you.*

I want help. I do. But—

"How?" I choke on the word. "How can you help me? Julio, I feel like I'm dying inside and I wish I was dying on the outside, too. I don't want to be here. I don't want to feel this. Anything. *I can't.* I can't do this anymore. I just—"

He pushes from the ground, but stays by the door. A sob mixed with a whimper passes through my lips. He freezes. Hands clenched into fists at his sides, his eyes plead with me but I don't know what he wants.

A tick forms along his jaw and he scrubs a hand over his face leaving behind a weary expression. "I want to hold you. Can we... do you think we can try?"

I have no freaking idea. Closing my eyes, I slow my breathing while my mind races, rationalizing his request. The only person who's touched me is Janessa. But Julio is my friend. I trust him. I know him. I ...

"Can I see your hands," I ask.

He frowns, confused but raises them palms out to face me. I shake my head. "Turn them around."

He does without question. I take in the backs of his hands already knowing what I'll find. Both hands are inked, one sporting a large skull with red roses on either side. The other is tattooed with a strand of rosary beads and a cross resting between his thumb and index finger.

I focus on the ink, tracing the lines of the designs with my gaze. I force myself to recognize the differences between his hands and those of my attacker. Beyond the ink I take in the gold band he wears on his right middle finger. His clean, short nail beds.

My breathing slows and my shoulders relax. Julio is patient with me, letting my eyes drink their fill. Several minutes pass before I feel confident enough to let him step closer.

With exaggerated slowness, he walks to the edge of my bed. When he reaches it, he inclines his head, asking if it's okay to sit. I nod.

Beside me now, we both wait. When I don't have a panic attack, he shifts closer, leaning beside me against the headboard.

I swipe at my eyes and hold myself perfectly still as he slowly and carefully places one arm around my shoulders. Neither of us moves. My deep, deliberate breaths are loud in the quiet room, but he doesn't seem to mind. We sit there and as the minutes pass, I slowly shift until I'm turned toward him, my ear pressed against his chest over the sound of his beating heart. His grip around me tightens and I manage to breathe through it.

One hand comes up to mindlessly stroke my hair. "I'm so fucking sorry, Allie," he says.

I nod against his chest. "Me, too," I whisper, almost afraid to break the silence in the room. "But I'm really happy you're here."

"And I'm not going anywhere. I'll stay as long as you need me."

I spend the morning with Julio and for the first time since the attack, I feel like I can breathe again. He tells me he's staying all week. Longer, if I need it. He already got it cleared with his parents and teachers and he's staying in the guest room in the pool house. There are plenty of empty rooms in the main house for him to stay in, but he seems content to stay in the pool house, so I don't question it. It's probably Gerald being Gerald. I'm surprised he allowed Julio to visit in the first place, so I'm not about to say anything that might jeopardize that.

I'm happy Julio's here. I missed him. I hadn't realized how much until he arrived.

Julio fills me in on the particulars of his stay. He'll be going to school with me. I don't know how but Janessa got him cleared as a visiting student. I guess the plan is for him to attend all my classes with me for the first week so I won't have to face it alone.

I still don't know if going back to school is a good idea. But when I broached the subject of getting my GED, Janessa shot it down and said it wasn't even worth trying to bring up to my father. Anything less than a diploma meant I couldn't get accepted into an Ivy League school—not that I'd personally applied to any—but Janessa seems to be under the impression that I'll be attending one. The idea of college right now seems so out there that it's not worth thinking about. I'd always planned on doing two years of community college first. It's all I can reasonably afford but I don't tell her that. Right now, I just want to focus on today. Maybe tomorrow. Anything past that is too much.

The following morning when my alarm goes off, I force myself to get out of bed. The heaviness in my chest I've had since the attack is lighter. It's still there, but today, it feels bearable.

I've had enough time to wallow in my own misery. More time than I ever gave myself after Mom died. It'll have to be enough. I need to graduate. Missing so much school is going to make that hard enough as it is, and I refuse to let the men who did this to me take anything else.

After spending all day yesterday with Julio, I've convinced myself I'll be okay.

We didn't talk about the assault. He knows what happened and I don't have any desire to relive the memories just so he can hear the story from my own mouth. Thankfully, he never pushes me. Not that I expected him too. Julio is the strong silent type. He's the mountain that refuses to move no matter how hard the wind blows. Growing up, he was my rock. The big brother I never had. He gets me. He gets what I need.

And being held, knowing that I was safe in his arms, that the world couldn't hurt me as long as he was there, gave me the reprieve I needed to pull myself together.

We spent most of the day watching Netflix and eating junk food. Well, he did at least.

I still haven't been eating, but I did pick at some of the popcorn for his benefit.

I know Julio noticed. But he didn't say anything and I'm grateful for it. My ribs stand out in sharp relief beneath my chest. I can count each one while in the shower. It's not healthy but I don't know how to make myself want to eat.

Sometimes even the scent of food gets to me and sends me running for the bathroom.

When I go downstairs in the morning, I expect to find Janessa waiting to take us to school, but instead, she hands me a set of keys and gives me a small smile.

"Your father pulled this from the garage for you at my suggestion." She tilts her head to the set of keys. "This way, if you need to leave, to get away, you can."

I stare at the keys in my hand. Tears form in the corners of my eyes and I swipe them away. I keep crying. I'm always crying. I hate it, but I never thought I'd be so relieved to have access to a car. Before all of this, I would have refused it. I didn't want Gerald's money. I didn't need it and I like earning my own way in life. It's why I'd been applying for jobs in the first place. But I couldn't afford a car on my own right now. Not even a beater. And this, this would give me an escape.

"Thank you."

Her smile widens just a bit. "If you ever want to talk..."

Julio comes in the back door. "Hey." He lifts a hand in greeting and walks toward me.

My stomach tightens as he approaches but I do what I did yesterday every time my body reacted to his proximity. I look at his hands and the anxiety subsides. Then to Janessa I say, "Thanks. But I'm good."

She nods. Hands me a to-go cup of coffee and Julio and I both head outside.

I find a silver Audi RS 5 in the driveway. I push a button on the key fob, somewhat surprised when the Audi chirps back. He's letting me drive an RS? Why can't he be like normal dads and just get me a Jetta? Preferably a used one.

"Damn," Julio draws out. "This is sick."

I roll my eyes. "Yeah, yeah. You can drool over the interior. Come on or we're going to be late."

TWENTY-NINE

Roman

_____

E milio sidles up beside me. "She's back," he mutters under his breath. My jaw tightens and all our heads turn to see her step out of a silver car a few rows down from us.

"Is that a..." Emilio starts.

"Brand new Audi RS 5? Yeah. It is," Dom answers and a quick look his way shows he's not all that happy to see her, either.

Guess she's still living the good life or maybe now she's just happier to embrace it. She's dressed in that rich preppy shit she wore the first week of school.

I guess we're back to that again, too.

I shrug my shoulders and catch Emilio and Dom's gazes. "Doesn't matter what she's driving. She's here. I want some fucking answers." That chick that works for her dad blew us off when we showed up, but I'm not buying the whole

Allie-doesn't-want-to-see-me crap. Something else has to be going on. I tried waiting around for Allie to leave the house, hoping to catch her and corner her into talking to me, but she never fucking left her house. Not once. Not that I ever saw, at least. And I was there, every fucking day for eight days straight. I went full-fledge stalker and don't even care.

I push off from the hood of my ride, intent on speaking with her, but then I catch sight of a guy getting out of the passenger seat of the same vehicle.

"What the fuck?" Emilio says beside me. He scratches the back of his head. "This is new."

"Yeah," I bite out. "It is."

I watch as he moves around the car until he's right beside her. He reaches a hand out to her. It's tentative, like he's unsure if she'll accept his touch and for a second my heart races in my chest. She's going to brush him off. I know she is. If this were a thing, if he was competition, he wouldn't look so hesitant to touch her. I grin. The fucker has no idea what he's trying to get in between.

Allie's mine. She has a lot to answer for and I'm pissed as hell with her, but she's still mine.

I take another step toward them and my boys follow suit. But then she smiles up at the guy and accepts his hand. She threads her fingers with his and the two of them turn their backs on us and head to the school's front entrance.

I stop in my tracks, my eyes glued to their hands. Their fucking entwined fingers like this is middle school or some shit.

What. The. Fuck.

Dominique puts a hand on my shoulder and squeezes. "You alright, bro?"

"I'm fine."

Emilio swears beside me. "Who the fuck is that dude?"

I grind my teeth.

"We still need answers," Dom says beside me. "You guys didn't see her last week. Something happened."

"I don't fucking care. Ice her out." Anger bubbles up inside me. "I don't have time for petty bitches and their games. That's not how we roll." Both of them nod their agreement, but Emilio looks hesitant.

"There's gotta be an explanation," he hedges. I glare at him and he puts his arms up, palms out in surrender. "Whatever you say, man. We'll ice her out."

I nod. She ghosted us. Ghosted me. And for what? This guy? I don't know him. Don't even recognize his face. Not once have I ever seen him near her before. But she blew me off for *that* guy. She made me look like a fool. And now, hand in hand, she's making sure the entire school knows she's dropped me.

She didn't even have the decency to call. My pops showed up to the game. He never comes to my games. He never has the time. But he came to our rival game against the Saints and I had it all planned out. He was going to meet my girl. I told my fucking parents about her. My mom knew Allie was supposed to be there and she no-showed. Fucking no-showed. No call. No text. Nothing.

A tick forms in my jaw and I glare at her retreating form. As if she can sense my attention her head swivels to look over her shoulder and her eyes lock on mine. Pools of chocolate brown meet my stare head-on and she flinches.

I hope she sees just how pissed off I am. How done I am with her.

The guy beside her slows his steps. I watch as she untangles her hand from his and he frowns at her. She says something to him. She's shaking her head and glancing over at me again. He says something back and they argue for a moment before a decision is made.

She turns around and heads in my direction—the new guy hot on her heels. She chews on her bottom lip, worry lines deepening with every step she takes. Good. She should be worried. If she's expecting a warm welcome, she won't find it.

The guy has a blank expression. I can't get a read on him but he stays close to Allie. Almost like he wants to protect her. His hands are tatted and he has two diamond studs in his ears. He's dressed in dark denim jeans and a black hoodie with the words Richland printed on the back. Then it clicks. This dude is from her hometown. Is he the ex? The ex that doesn't look like he's an ex anymore?

They're almost to us when Dom asks, "What's the plan?"

I shake my head. I don't know. She's coming over to us but she's with him. They clearly have some sort of relationship with each other and I have no fucking clue what's going on. Was I some side piece of hers? She said in the beginning, she didn't want anything serious. We didn't use labels. I never called her my girlfriend, but fuck, she was my girl. She'd been *my girl.*

None of it matters now. "Stick to the plan. Ice her out. I'm done."

They nod and we each grab our bags, heading straight toward them. Allie's steps falter and her skin pales, highlighting the sharp angles of her cheekbones. Has she lost more weight?

When we're right in front of them she says, "Ro?" My name on her lips is whisper-soft and it does something to me, twisting my insides around, but I don't respond. I don't react. Instead, I push right between her and her new guy and head straight to the doors. My steps never slow.

She gasps before saying a little bit louder, "Roman?"

I keep going. Then the asshole with her calls out, "Bro, what's your problem?"

I whirl on him. Dropping my backpack on the pavement, I close the distance between us and get right in his face. He holds his ground and fury flashes in his eyes.

Allie sucks in a breath and takes several steps back. She's as white as a sheet but I can't find it in me to fucking care.

"I don't know who the fuck you think you are, but this is my school. My town. Don't talk to me again. Ever. We clear."

He doesn't answer, meanwhile Allie's all but hyperventilating beside us as she watches the exchange.

Slowly, so fucking slow, I turn my head to glare at her. "The same goes for you. Don't speak to me. We're not friends. We're not anything. I don't fraternize with whores." She jerks back as if I've slapped her and the next thing I know a fist smashes into my face and I stumble back a few steps. Dom and Emilio rush up beside me and I shake my head, blinking hard to clear my vision as it meets the angry glare of the guy she came with.

His nostrils flare and his hands clench into tight fists at his sides as though he's barely keeping himself from hitting me again.

I spit and my blood smacks the pavement. "You're gonna regret that."

"Don't call her that again. Are we clear?" His tone is hard, his eyes murderous.

I can't help it. I laugh. "Whatever you say, *cabrón*. Just know she was underneath me two weeks ago. Who knows how many guys she's had since?"

"You worthless *sonovabitch*. Do you have any idea what she's—"

"Julio, don't!" she cries out and we both turn to see her tear-filled gaze. "Please. Don't."

Guilt tears into me at the sight of those tears before I push it away. No way am I going to feel sorry for her. She's got *Julio* now. That's this fucker's name. So not the ex.

His eyes soften as they drink her in and he moves toward her. He cups the back of her neck and draws her face toward his chest. She goes willingly, wrapping her arms round his waist and fuck, it's like a punch to the gut. Seeing that, seeing her in his arms hurts more than that fucker's punch to my face ever could.

I don't say anything. I have no fucking words. I turn around and head back to the entrance, refusing to look back.

"Watch your back," Dom warns him before moving in step beside me.

"What the hell was that?" Emilio mutters when we're out of hearing distance from the happy couple.

I don't answer him.

When Silvia Parish walks past me, rather than ignoring her like I usually would, I call her over. Her eyes are hesitant, but they brighten when I give her a smile. She slows her steps, waiting for me.

"Hey, Ro," she purrs.

I see the confusion in my boys' gazes but I ignore them. "Ready to be out of the dog house?" I ask her.

She pouts. "That was really mean of you."

"Yeah. Well, maybe later I'll make it up to you. What do you say?"

Lust darkens her eyes and she nods her head in agreement. "Mmmmm. I'd love to." She settles in beside me. "Are you and the little do-gooder over?"

I shake my head, then look down at her and give her a devilish grin. "Nothing to be over," I tell her. "Shit never even started."

THIRTY

Allie

_____

If Julio wasn't with me, I wouldn't have survived today. He follows me to all my classes. A few girls give him interested looks but he ignores them, his full attention on me.

Roman is a no-show first period. A part of me wonders if he's off screwing Silvia in the locker rooms or something. I know he's mad but he didn't need to say what he did.

I want to talk to him, to explain why I didn't call or text. I know if he knew my reasons, if he knew everything that happened, he'd understand. At least, I hope he would. But I can't convince myself to expose myself like that to him. His words cut deep. He wanted to hurt me and he did. What if he doesn't understand? What if telling him what happened only confirms what I am in his eyes? A whore.

Julio tries to comfort me throughout the day. Every time I catch sight of Roman, Dominique, or Emilio, he distracts me with a question or a dumb joke. Sometimes it works. But most of the time, it doesn't.

"Hey," he tilts my chin up, forcing me to meet his gaze. "You don't need them. Seven more months and you're coming home with me."

I nod. I'll be eighteen in four months. Graduate in seven. It feels like forever and a day away but in reality, it's not that far. Falling out like this with the Devils hurts, but maybe it was for the best.

We eat lunch in the library without incident. Well, Julio does at least. I manage two bites of pizza before throwing my tray away, unable to stomach the food any better than I have been at Gerald's.

Spanish goes by without a hitch. When I get to Welding, Julio draws a little more attention than he had in my previous classes, but this time, since it's a class full of guys, Julio doesn't ignore them.

"This the new beau?" Aaron asks, a smile on his face. It's a forced smile but it's a smile nonetheless. I stiffen as he nears but Julio positions himself between us, easing some of the tension before he answers Aaron for me.

"Nah, man. Allie's like my little sister. I'm a friend from back home." He reaches out a hand and Aaron shakes it. His smile morphs to one that's more genuine as he gives Julio a once-over.

"Sister, huh? You two could have fooled me. All the hand holding, the looks..." He trails off and I know there's a question in there, but he doesn't come out and ask it.

Julio and I have been affectionate since he arrived. I'm not entirely sure why. Back home, we never really held hands, but we've cuddled watching movies together and neither of us have ever shied away from physical contact. But it's always been platonic. Saying I'm like a sister is one hundred percent accurate. I don't have any biological siblings but if I did, I imagine my relationship with them would be like what I have with Julio. Easy. Comfortable. And with zero romantic feelings for the other person.

"I've known J since grade school." I shrug. "I don't think either of us realized how people might take things."

Julio snorts beside me. "We also don't care."

Aaron seems to mull that over. "So... how's Roman handling this? I saw him earlier with—" He cuts himself off and looks away. Rubbing his hand over the back of his neck he offers me an apologetic look. "Sorry. I know it's none of my business but I think you deserve to know." He pauses. "Roman was all over Silvia Parish at lunch today."

A rock falls to the pit of my stomach. "It didn't take him long to move on."

Aaron's face twists into a grimace. "Did something happen? All the Devils have been acting weird. I know you and he were—"

"No. Nothing happened. Things ran their course. That's all."

Julio's vibrating with anger beside me. I know he wants to say something. He's made it clear what he thinks about Roman, but thankfully he keeps quiet about it all.

"Well, for what it's worth, I hope you're doing okay. Roman is an asshole. You deserve better."

Julio whistles and the teacher's head jerks in our direction with a glare. In a quieter tone he says, "You can say that again. That guy is a grade-A asshole."

Aaron high fives him and I stifle a groan as the two dive into a heated conversation about just how much of a dick Roman is. *Great.*

Just as class ends Aaron's phone chimes with a message. He pulls out his cell and scowls. "Shit."

"Something wrong?" I ask.

He ruffles his sandy blond hair before shoving his phone in his back pocket and grabbing his skateboard. "One of our dishwashers at the diner just bailed. No notice either. Tonight is going to suck."

"You work at a diner?" Julio asks.

He nods. "Yeah. My aunt owns it—the Sun Valley Station. Best burgers in town. I work there after school sometimes to help her out." He shrugs. "I don't really need the money but it gets me out of the house."

An idea forms and before I can talk myself out of it I say, "I can help. I mean, if you think she'd want to fill the position. I'm looking for a job."

His brows furrow. "You are?"

I bob my head enthusiastically.

"Allie, you sure this is a good idea?" Julio whispers beside me. I give him an affirming nod. This is a great idea. Exactly what I need.

"Yeah. I've put in a few applications around town, but I haven't gotten any callbacks."

"I've seen your place and your new ride. You're not hurting for cash. Why would you want to scrub dishes at a diner?"

"Because I don't want to have to rely on my bio-dad for everything. I barely know the guy. You know what he's like. Would you want anything from him?"

He shakes his head with a grimace, probably remembering Gerald's words when he'd last been over.

"If you helped me get this job you'd be doing me a huge favor."

His lips twist as he considers it. "You'd be able to work tonight?"

I nod.

"Alright. I'll talk to her. I can't make any promises but plan on working the closing shift. It's four to eleven."

"Thank you. You have no idea how much I appreciate it."
The bell rings signaling the end of class and we all get up,
gathering our things.

Aaron smiles and steps forward. His arms open as if to hug
me and instantly I stiffen. Julio intercepts the touch,
reaching out to shake Aaron's hand while pulling him into a
bro hug. Aaron's eyes widen in confusion over Julio's
shoulder.

"Thanks for helping my girl out, man. I'm glad she'll have a
friend around after I head back home."

"Uh, yeah. Of course."

Julio steps away and then tugs me toward the door.

"See you tonight," I tell him, rushing to leave.

THIRTY-ONE

Roman

I sit on the hood of my El Camino, my legs wide and Silvia standing between them. Her manicured hands rest on the top of my pants and she's leaning into me, trying hard to be seductive.

I ignore her. She thinks I'm lingering because I want to be in her fucking presence when in reality, that is the last thing I want. Keeping her close today is already biting me in the ass. She's a stage-five clinger with a serious complex but Allie's Audi is four cars down and I want her to see Silvia between my thighs.

I want her to see just how over her I am, so I wait.

"Yo. We going to practice?" Emilio asks, tossing his bag into my backseat. Dom's already in the locker room. He's our QB and he can't afford to show up late. Coach would rip him a new one.

"Yeah, we're going."

He gives me a sideways glance until he spots Allie and the new fucker walking beside her. Realization dawns on Emilio's face and he does me a solid. Walking toward the gym doors he shouts, "Come on, fucker. You can bone Silvia later."

Allie's head jerks toward his voice. Then she follows his gaze and sees what I wanted her to see. Hurt flashes in her eyes. What the hell does she have to be hurt about? I might not admit it to anyone else, but she's the one who dropped me. She showed up with some random, held his fucking hand, and now wants to act like this is all on me.

Not happening.

I grip Silvia's hips and draw her closer. Nuzzling her neck, I keep my eyes locked on Allie's as I let my other hand wander until I'm grasping Silvia's tight ass.

She moans in my embrace and presses herself closer to me. "Roman, you feel so good."

I bite back my scathing response, hating the feel of her body pressed against mine when it should be Allie instead.

I scrape my teeth along the column of her neck. She visibly shudders. So fucking dramatic but it works to my benefit.

Allie stands there, ten feet away from her car, watching us. It's like she's frozen in place and I take full fucking advantage. When Silvia's hand dips down to stroke my dick over my jeans, I shift, making sure Allie has a nice view.

Her cheeks heat, a pretty pink blush staining her cheeks but whether in anger or embarrassment I have no fucking clue.

Julio calls her name. When she doesn't respond, he tugs on her hand and draws her to her car. Her eyes stay locked with mine the entire way until she finally steps inside and the tinted windows block her from my view.

As soon as her car leaves the lot, I push Silvia away and head toward the gym.

"Hey—" she squeaks.

"I got practice." I'm already halfway across the parking lot.

"Oh. Okay. Call me later!"

I throw a wave over my shoulder. I won't call her, and yet she'll still be waiting for me tomorrow when I get to school. So damn predictable.

THIRTY-TWO

Allie

I got the job.

Just as Julio and I are walking in the door, I get a text from Aaron.

> **Aaron: My aunt said you can work tonight as a trial run. If it works out, the job is yours. Closing shift 3x a week.**

> **Me: THANK YOU SOOOOOO MUCH!**

"You look happy," Julio says as we drop our bags beside the kitchen island. I grab two glasses from the cupboard and fill both with water before handing one to him. "Thanks."

"I am happy. Aaron said I got the job. Finally, something good. Ya know?"

He nods but his brows are pinched together as he looks down at his glass. "I don't want to rain on your parade, but are you sure this is a good idea?"

I stiffen. "Why wouldn't it be?"

He runs a hand through his dark brown hair and lifts his gaze. "Allie, you've been through a lot."

"I know that," I snap, not liking the direction this conversation is going. Not two minutes ago I was elated. Now, he's popping my balloon and for no reason.

"How are you going to handle being around everyone? The customers? The other staff? What if Aaron goes to give you a friendly goodbye hug again?"

I chew on my fingernail. "I'll figure it out," I tell him, determined to make this work. "I'm fine. I didn't have any major breakdowns at school today. This will be good for me."

He doesn't look convinced, but he lets the subject drop. I check the time and notice I have forty minutes to get ready and be at the diner. "I need to get ready. Do you want to drop me off and you can keep the car in case you want to do anything?"

He shakes his head. "No. I have some independent study homework I need to catch up on. You okay to drive yourself?"

I nod. "I'll be fine."

He still doesn't look convinced, but says nothing as I jog upstairs to change.

The Sun Valley Station is packed for a weeknight. Nearly every booth is filled and only two barstools remain empty at the front counter. I recognize a few students from school but, thankfully, I don't spot the Devils. I don't think I could deal with seeing Roman right now.

Aaron waves me over as soon as I walk in the door. "Hey, follow me." He catches the attention of one of the servers and calls out an, "I'll be right back."

She nods and Aaron leads me through a set of swinging doors and down a private hallway to an office. He knocks twice on the door before opening it.

"Aunt Emma, this is Allie." A middle-aged woman with ash-blond hair looks up from her desk. Her features are severe. Sharp nose, high cheekbones, and thin lips. A pair of reading glasses sit perched atop her head.

"You go to school with my nephew?" She leans back in her seat, setting aside the papers she'd been looking at to give me her full attention.

"Yes, ma'am."

"Ah, manners on this one," she says to Aaron before turning back to me. "Do you have any work history?"

"I was a barista back in my hometown for a summer." It's not much but it's something and it did teach me to work at a fast pace.

"Did Aaron fill you in on the particulars? This is a dishwashing job. It's not glamorous. You won't be waitressing and you won't be earning tips. From time to time you might buss tables if the girls up front need the help but for the most part, you'll be in the back. You good with that?" She gives me a scrutinizing once-over.

I hadn't known what to wear so I put on a pair of black skinny jeans and a long-sleeved black t-shirt and paired it with white sneakers. I assumed black would be safest.

"Sounds good," I tell her.

"Okay, then. Aaron will get you an apron and show you to the back. If you keep up today, the job is yours. It's minimum wage but you'll get a dollar raise once you last six months. Schedule changes each week but you'll be guaranteed three shifts."

I nod. "Thank you."

Aaron leads the way back through the hallway and into the kitchens. I'm greeted by two cooks, but both are elbow deep in work so they only offer me a wave and a smile. I stiffen when I realize it'll be just the three of us back here, but my shoulders relax when Aaron leads me further into where the washing station is.

It sits away from the cooks in a small corner. "Servers and busboys will stack dishes here." He points to a low counter already piled high with dirty plates and glasses. "And then when you're done with them, you put them here. Silverware and glasses all get put inside the automatic runner so they're sanitized but you'll wash plates and bowls by hand."

"Sounds easy enough." I give him a smile. "I think I got it."

"Okay, and if you get stuck or need help, I'll be up front." He places a hand on my shoulder and I instantly lock up. Panic rushes into me and Aaron doesn't miss my reaction. His hand immediately lifts and he takes two steps back.

"What just happened?"

I open my mouth to answer but nothing comes out.

"Allie, you're really pale."

I wrap my arms around myself and look away. Julio was right. This was a horrible idea. What had I been thinking?

I worry my lower lip struggling to give Aaron an explanation for my behavior when he says, "Something happened to you while you were gone?"

I meet his concerned gaze knowing my own is glassy-eyed with unshed tears and nod.

"Fuck." He rubs the back of his neck. "That's why your friend stepped in when I went to hug you today?"

Another nod.

"Okay. Okay." He paces in front of me as he takes this all in and I brace myself for whatever he has to say next. "I don't need to know what happened. It's none of my business. If you decide you want to tell me at some point, you can, okay? I'm here, for whatever you need." My heart melts at his confession. I knew Aaron was a good guy. "But..." A shake of his head as he expels a harsh breath. "You don't want to be touched. Is that it?"

I nod. "Yeah. Pretty much."

"Is that why your friend is here in town? To help you out with whatever you're dealing with?"

"Yeah."

"I'll help, too. Whatever you need. I know he can't be with you twenty-four seven. When you're here, I've got your back. Okay?"

A tear slips down my cheek and I swipe it away. "You're a really great guy, Aaron. Thank you."

THIRTY-THREE

Roman

She's not eating. I don't know why I care but the girl never eats. Not at school anyway. Her cheekbones are sharper. Her clothes fit looser. Something is up and I have no fucking clue what.

I know my boys notice. They give her the same concerned glances I do when they think I'm not looking.

The urge to force her to tell me what's wrong is strong, but she's still with that fucker, Julio. And worse, she's hanging out more with Henderson. One of them is always with her. She's never alone. Not in her classes. Not at lunch. Hell, even when I spot her going to take a piss, one of these assholes is always right outside the door.

I'm tempted to find a way to distract them so I can pull her away but I talk myself out of it. I shouldn't care that she's losing weight. What difference is it to me? She wasn't eating a ton before. This is just more of the same. Maybe she's still upset over her mom. That's probably all it is. I can't say I blame her, but it is not my problem. Not anymore.

Just then, Silvia struts toward me. I groan. The girl is clingy as shit. "Yo, Rome," Emilio calls. "The wife is coming."

I flip him off and ignore the annoyance Silvia's presence brings. Sarah is right beside her, making stupid eyes at Emilio. He tilts his chin at her in greeting and the girl swoons. Pathetic.

Kasey Henderson walks by just then and sneers with a dramatic eye roll. "Getting desperate, boys," she calls out before heading to the table Allie's sitting at. I ignore her comment and throw my arm over Silvia's shoulder and as expected, she presses herself into me, her breasts and the inch-thick padding in her bra mashing up against my chest.

"Are we going to get to spend some time together this weekend, Ro?" she asks, fluttering her lashes in what I'm sure she thinks is a seductive manner, but really she ends up looking like she's got something stuck in her eyes.

I shrug my shoulders. "Dunno. I got plans with the boys. We'll see."

Her bottom lip juts out and I know she's not happy. Chick's been trying to screw me all week. I've kissed her but that is as far as things have gone and only ever in public. If I'm going to lower my standards to a girl like her, there's gotta be a reason for it, and ensuring it gets back to Allie is reason number one. Silvia wants more. She wants to fuck. But the idea of screwing her makes my dick limper than a soft noodle.

I can barely manage to shove my tongue down her throat as it is.

A few weeks ago, I'd have fucked her in a heartbeat. Silvia's got a tight ass, curves, and a decent rack. Her teeth are straight, and she's got long, sleek hair I'd normally enjoy wrapping around my fist. But now, all I see when I look at her is a pathetic girl who can't seem to understand just how uninterested I am in her.

She's a means to an end. A way to pass the time. The season's over and I don't have football practice anymore to use as a distraction, so instead I try and come up with creative ways to screw over the girl who decided to stomp on my fucking heart.

When Allie's gaze turns my way, I lean into Silvia's touch and capture her lips with mine. She moans dramatically into the kiss and I force myself to close my eyes, pretending it's Allie I'm kissing. Allie whose mouth I'm tasting.

Silvia moans again, not bothered in the least that we're in a crowded cafeteria and she sounds like a porn star. I wish she would shut the hell up. When she moans for the third time I pull away. Her pupils are dilated and her smile wide as she struggles to catch her breath. I flick my gaze back to Allie's table but it's empty now. She's gone.

THIRTY-FOUR

Allie

The week passes and before I know it, it's Saturday night. I work the closing shift again at Sun Valley Station, only this time, Aaron has the night off so he can go watch the girls' basketball game. The season just started and Kasey plays on the JV team, though not by choice. She hates sports but I guess her parents are forcing her into some extracurriculars. Aaron's going so he can make fun of his sister later.

I was originally given the night off too, and Aaron invited me to come, but I couldn't stomach the idea of attending another school event.

The diner is slow the first few hours I'm here, but I know once the game is over that'll change. Everyone will either go out and party or come here for food since other restaurants in the area will be closed, so I take advantage of the reprieve and make sure all the dishes are clean and stacked so that when the rush hits, I'm ready.

Julio had to head back home this morning. I was bummed to see him go but he can only take so much time off from school. He offered to stay longer but I didn't want to take advantage of him. I appreciate the week he gave me, though. I've only had one panic attack since Monday and true to his word, when Julio wasn't around, Aaron did his best to step in and help make me comfortable.

The volume in the front of the diner increases and I chance a look at the clock, noting that it's just after nine. Less than two hours until closing and we're just now getting busy.

I keep myself occupied, scrubbing dishes down while I listen to some older *My Chemical Romance* songs. I'm bouncing to *Black Parade* a little over an hour later when Emma pops her head in the back and says, "I have to leave early and handle some stuff. Julie will be the one closing up with you tonight."

I nod. Julie's one of the waitresses who works here full-time. She's in college and from what I've gathered, also a family friend so she's trusted with a key and closing out the register.

Tonight's cooks, Rodrick and Ben, let me know they're heading out when they fulfill the last order of the night and I wave goodbye to them. They've mostly kept to themselves since I started working here and a part of me wonders if Aaron said anything to them about me. I wash the last of the dishes just as the double doors swing open and Julie bounces into the room.

"Are you almost done?" she asks.

I nod. "Yeah, just a few more."

She eyes my stack of dishes with a frown. It's not that big and should take ten minutes tops to get through. "I'm supposed to meet some friends at a party and I'm already running late. Are you okay if I head out? The doors are already locked and the till is zeroed out. All you have to do is make sure the door is closed all the way when you leave."

"Yeah. That's fine."

She squeals. "Thank you so much. You're a doll. I'll see you next week."

And then she's gone.

I finish up the dishes, no longer in a hurry, and then collect my bag and hoodie. I shut off the lights and I'm just about to open the door when I spot a man standing across the street. All the lights are out inside the diner so I'm confident he can't see me, but it's like he's staring right at me anyway, even though I can't make out his eyes.

Goosebumps break out all over my skin.

The streetlight casts him in shadow, hiding his face but illuminating enough of his body that I can make out his dark washed jeans and flannel shirt. He's big. Built like a man and not one of the boys I go to school with.

Fear freezes me before I stumble back a few steps away from the door. The man never moves. I glance toward the parking lot, spotting my Audi right where I left it. In the furthest spot on the lot because I hadn't wanted to be parked close to anyone.

The ten yards or so between it and me feels like a mile.

Can I make it to my car before him? If I run I probably can. Maybe. What reason does he have for standing out there, lurking?

"Come on, Allie. Pull yourself together," I mutter to myself. Just because I was attacked once before doesn't mean it will happen again. But my attacker's words echo in my mind as if he's standing over me again. *"I'd be happy to make another visit,"* he'd said. What if this is him, or his friend? What if Gerald messed up again?

Gerald and I never talked about what caused the attack in the first place. He just said he'd take care of it and then he never brought it up again. I should have brought it up again. I should have made sure something like that could never happen to me another time.

Oh God. I'd been so stupid.

I slump into one of the booths toward the back, away from the windows, and pull my phone out with shaking fingers. I dial Julio's number before I realize he can't help me and hang up. Okay. Plan B. I'll try Aaron.

I call him and wait. The line rings once, twice, six times.

Voicemail.

Dang it.

I try again.

Voicemail again.

I wipe my clammy hands on my knees and stare at the screen of my phone. I don't know who else to call. Feeling desperate I try Janessa. She doesn't pick up. Against my better judgment, I try Gerald next.

"You've reached the voicemail box of..."

I hang up.

My heart skips a beat. The man is still out there. What is he waiting for? A knot of dread expands in my chest. It crawls through me and my entire body begins to shake. I squeeze my eyes shut. I need to get it together. I can't think if I panic.

My breaths are ragged as if I've just run a marathon. My chest heaves up and down. I press my forehead down on the cool surface of the table and force myself to slow down my breathing. I can't have a panic attack. Not here. Not now.

Think, Allie. Just think.

The idea to call Roman leaves me as quickly as it came. I swallow hard and chew on my bottom lip until I'm certain I've bitten through the tender flesh and the tang of copper fills my mouth.

I try Dominique.

He answers on the second ring. "Allie?"

"Oh, thank God." I choke out the words on a sob.

"What's going on?"

His voice is hard, and a sense of urgency has me rushing to say, "I just got off work and there's a man outside. I think he's waiting for me. I let Julie leave early and I'm alone and my car is far away and—"

"Breathe, Allie. Take a breath. Slow down."

I try to do as he instructs but I can't seem to slow down.

"Where are you at?"

"The Sun Valley Station."

"Okay. I'm on my way. I'll give you a lift. We can get your car tomorrow morning."

I nod even though he can't see me. "Thank you."

"Just hang tight. Go in the back. I'll be there in ten."

THIRTY-FIVE

Allie

I'm huddled on the floor in the kitchen hiding behind one of the cook stations. My knees are pressed to my chest and I have my arms wrapped around them as though through sheer will, holding myself tight will keep me from falling apart.

My phone chimes and I lift it to glance at the illuminated screen.

> **Dom: I'm here.**

"Thank God."

I squeeze my eyes shut once before forcing them open. Dominique is here. I'm safe. He's a big strong football player and whoever the man is outside won't want to mess with him. He's probably gone by now anyway. I'm okay. Everything is okay.

Me: Be right out.

I push myself up from the ground, my legs still shaking as I shove my phone in my back pocket and try and catch my bearings.

I take several deep breaths and press my hand over my chest. My heart is racing but there isn't anything I can do about it. I force myself to move toward the front of the diner. My steps are slow and I keep checking my surroundings to make sure I'm still alone. I know the man couldn't have gotten inside. The doors are all locked. But I still feel the urge to double and triple check.

I spot Dominique's Escalade parked right out front and a small sigh of relief escapes me. I'm almost to the door when a police cruiser pulls up behind it. I stop. Did he call the cops? I look around and don't spot the man outside any longer. Inwardly, I groan. I'm going to have to explain the false alarm to an officer. He's going to think I'm an idiot for getting all worked up over nothing.

Dominique is sitting in the front seat of his car seemingly not paying attention. His eyes are on his phone, the screen casting light on his face in the darkened vehicle.

I watch as the officer gets out of his car. He draws his gun from his holder and moves around the vehicle until he's facing Dom's driver-side window.

What the—

The officer starts shouting. Dominique raises his hand in the air and then steps out of his car. I move to the corner of the diner to get a better look and notice another police cruiser pull up. This one follows suit and two men exit that car, both with weapons drawn.

Dominique is shaking his head vigorously, hands still lifted in the air.

He turns around to face me and I see stark fear in his eyes. *No. No. No.*

I pull my phone out of my back pocket and rush outside just as Dom lowers himself to his knees, his hands coming to rest behind his head. I look up and down the street but aside from Dominique and the police, the street is empty.

"Ma'am, I need you to step back inside the restaurant."

What? No. I shake my head. "What's going on, officer?" I ask, my feet rooted in place.

Dom is on his knees, but the police have three guns drawn and trained on my friend. My phone is still clutched in my hand so as discreetly as possible I dial Roman's number. His dad is the chief of police. I remember him telling me that. Instinctively, I know I have to call him. I know he can help.

I don't bother waiting to see if he answers, I put the phone on speaker and turn all my attention to the officer closest to Dominique.

"Ma'am. Get back inside the diner." His voice is hard, his eyes narrowed as he looks me over.

"I...I can't. It's locked now. Why are you pointing your gun at him? He didn't do anything wrong." As I'm talking I hear the call connect and Roman swears on the other line quietly enough that only I can hear him.

"This man is suspected of auto theft." The officer tells me. "We got a tip and he fits the description."

I frown at that. No way would Dom steal a car. His family is loaded. He has no reason to.

"Officer, I know him. Dominique Price is not a thief. He's here to give me a ride home. I called him at the end of my shift here at the Sun Valley Station." I say all of this, hoping Roman will hear and call his dad. Maybe he can show up and help defuse the situation, or make a call so these guys back off.

Dominique isn't saying anything but his normally dark complexion has taken on an ashen quality. His eyes are wide and he's not looking at me. I'm not even sure he's aware of what's going on anymore.

I take a step toward Dom when another officer shouts, "Ma'am we need you to stay away from the suspect."

Suspect? Dom isn't a suspect. He's a kid. He's seventeen. He's just a kid like me.

"But I ... I know him." My voice wobbles. "Why are your guns drawn? He's not dangerous. He's not..."

"Ma'am. Please step back. It's for your own safety."

"Put your guns away and I will. He isn't doing anything to justify this type of force."

At my words, Dominique flinches and all three officers start shouting.

"Get back."

"Get on the ground."

"Keep your hands in the air."

They're not talking to me. They're shouting at Dominique, but he barely moved.

Dom's eyes flick to mine.

"I'm not leaving you," I mouth.

His lower lip trembles. My eyes prick with tears. Dom, strong, quiet Dom is on the verge of tears. This cannot be happening.

Then one of the officers gets angry when Dominique doesn't move to comply but he's already on his knees. What more do they want? "Get on the ground. Get on the fucking ground," he shouts, stepping forward. "I said, get on the fucking ground." His hands shake and I can see hatred burning in his gaze.

No. *No!*

I drop my phone, purse, and sweater so there's no way any of them can think I'm hiding anything. Then I move closer.

"Ma'am!"

"Miss!"

I keep my arms raised as I walk toward Dominique, my steps measured. I don't look at the officers. I don't look at the guns. I keep my gaze locked on Dom and watch as he tracks my movements with his eyes but he doesn't move. He's still as a statue.

When I'm right beside him I finally look up and meet the gaze of the closest officer. Then I step in front of Dom, protecting him with my body.

My voice shakes as I say, "His name is Dominique Price. He's seventeen years old. He goes to Sun Valley High." My heart is pounding in my chest. I can barely hear myself, but I push more words past my lips, determined to make them understand. "He's here to pick me up from work. He was giving me a ride."

The officer closest to me, an older white man with dark brown hair shot through with streaks of silver, eyes me warily.

"He's driving a brand-new Escalade. We have reason to believe the vehicle is stolen."

"It's not!" I shout the words. I don't know why I'm not scared anymore. But I'm not, all I'm feeling is anger. Cold and visceral. They have no right to do this. To make Dom feel a certain way when he didn't do anything wrong.

"Miss. I understand you know this man but—"

"He's a *kid*. A seventeen-year-old kid. The car is his. His family has money. Why are you doing this?" I can hear the hysteria in my voice but can do nothing to quash it.

"We have reason to believe—"

"How? Why? Because he's black?"

His eyes narrow. "This has nothing to do with race. We received a call—"

I cut him off. "Do you know the chief of police?" I ask him. "Do any of you know Police Chief Valdez?" I shout.

One of the men nods so I push on. "His son, Roman, goes to Sun Valley High. He's best friends with Dominique Price. This is Dominique Price. Chief Valdez has known Dominique forever. Please, just put the guns down and call the chief. He'll clear this up. He'll tell you—"

Another cruiser pulls in. Two more officers exit and add two more guns raised in our direction.

I can't catch my breath. Panic rises in my gut.

My voice is frantic now. "Call the chief. I'm not letting you shoot my friend. This is not happening." The last part I say to myself.

It takes every shred of courage in me to turn my back on them but I do. I turn around and the crouch down behind Dominique. I take in his broad back and raised hands. I look at his hands. Always hands. *This is Dom.* I tell myself. *He's my friend. I can do this. I have to do this.* Wrapping my arms around his waist I use my body as a human shield.

Panic floods through me at the contact but I close my eyes and shove it away. It's just Dominique. Dominique is safe. He would never hurt me. I'm touching him. He's not touching me. I'm okay. I'm okay. I'm okay.

To him I say, "Don't move. I've got you. I won't let them shoot you for being black. I've got you."

He trembles beneath me. Seconds stretch into minutes, but I don't move. Neither of us do. I can hear the officers in the background arguing amongst themselves, but I block out their voices.

My legs begin to shake but I hold on tighter, refusing to move away and abandon my friend. Then a familiar voice calls out from the crowd. "Allie?"

I turn my head but still don't release Dom.

"Roman?" My word is a whisper and I feel Dominique's shoulders slump in relief.

Roman shoves through the cluster of officers, a severe-looking older man right behind him. A man I recognize. *Oh shit!* The man who found me that night. That's Roman's father? I can see the resemblance now.

"Drop your weapons and stand down. Now," he orders the men.

A breath whooshes out of me as one by one the officers holster their weapons.

"Everyone but the first officer on the scene, get the hell out of here. Beat it."

No one argues, and once I can see that they're clearing out and there aren't any more guns trained our way, I loosen my hold on Dominique and stand. My heart pounds in my chest now for an entirely different reason.

Police Chief Valdez meets my gaze. There's concern there but it's fleeting. Then he turns and starts in on the officer forced to stay behind.

Roman is there, yanking me into his arms. "What the hell were you thinking? Fuck. Were you trying to give me a heart attack? Seeing you like that just shaved ten years off my life."

I freeze in his arms and close my eyes. Silent tears track down my face. I... I can't... I can't breathe.

He releases me and turns toward Dom, completely unaware of the meltdown taking place inside of me.

"What the hell happened?" Roman asks.

No answer. I swallow several times trying to force the lump in my throat down.

"Dom?"

He's not getting up. Roman sends me a worried look and I force my feet to move. I step around him until I'm standing in front of him and I bend down to catch his gaze. "Dom?"

His jaw is locked. His eyes glassy and far away. I send a worried gaze toward Roman but he shrugs, unsure of what to do. I bite my bottom lip. Words aren't getting through to him.

I take a deep shuddering breath and swipe the tears from my face with the backs of my hands before turning my attention to his. They're still held above his head.

I shove past my fear and with shaking fingers, reach out and cup Dom's cheeks in my palms. "Dominique?" His gaze flickers to mine. "It's okay. You're okay. They're gone. It's okay."

His hands slowly lower but his arms are trembling. He sucks in a shuddering breath. "I need..."

I know and I force myself to give it to him. I wrap my arms around his neck and hug him close. His strong arms wrap around me in an almost painful embrace. I bear it and when my limbs lock up and my breath becomes erratic, I just squeeze him tighter.

"It's okay. I've got you."

THIRTY-SIX

Roman

Allie took off ten minutes ago. I tried to convince her to let me give her a ride but as soon as Dom released her, she took off straight for her Audi with barely a backward glance.

I was tempted to go after her. I don't know what the hell came over me but seeing her like that, in the line of fire, I've never been so fucking scared in my life. My girl was in danger. *My girl.*

Fuck all the bullshit with her and Julio. Fuck the fact that she ghosted me. She's mine. She ran off tonight but as soon as I get Dom settled, she and I are going to have words.

It's just the three of us now. Dom, me, and my pops. We're sitting in Dominique's Escalade but I'm in the driver's seat. No way am I letting him drive himself home tonight. Dom gave my dad a recount of what happened, and one thing for sure is heads are going to roll Monday morning when my dad gets to his office. He assures Dominique that all of the officers will face consequences. I'm almost positive the first asshole on scene will lose his badge. You can't be a racist prick on my dad's force. He has zero tolerance for that shit.

"You boys going to be alright tonight?" my dad asks.

"Yeah. I'll drive Dom home and crash at his place. What were you doing here, anyway?" I ask him.

Color is coming back to his face. He seems a little more like himself. "Allie called me. She was freaked out. I guess there was some dude outside and she didn't feel comfortable leaving the diner by herself."

A stab of pain hits me in the gut when I realize she was afraid and she called him. Not me. But before I say anything, my pops curses.

I flick my gaze toward him, and he asks, "Are you two close with her?"

We both shake our heads. "Used to be. We don't talk anymore," I tell him.

He frowns but I have no idea why. What does he care whether or not I talk to Allie?

"What's that mean exactly?" he asks.

I shrug, not wanting to get into it with him. Allie and I were on the outs but after tonight, I plan to rectify that. "Nothing. It's whatever."

His frown deepens and his eyes flicker with disappointment. "That girl's been through hell," he says.

Anger rises up inside me. "How would you know?"

He scrubs a hand over his face, and I know he's going to give me some non-answer. Hell, no. Not this time. If he knows something about my girl, I should know it, too. "Pops, how do you know Allie?"

His mouth tightens. He's quiet for a minute so I press again. "If something's going on, I should know. You have to tell me."

"The night of your game. The one your mother and I came to watch you play in..." he hesitates.

"Yeah? What about it?" I remember that he'd stepped out to make a phone call and then left shortly after. Mom said a case came up or some shit.

"She was assaulted in the parking lot."

Wait. What?

My chest seizes and my mouth drops open. "What do you mean, assaulted?" Was that why she wasn't at my game? She'd been hurt? *Fuck.* She'd been hurt and I'd been a complete asshole. No wonder she didn't message me back.

His face hardens. "I don't want you spreading rumors about this girl, feel me?"

Dread settles deep in my stomach. "What kind of assault are we talking about here?" There's only one that would warrant his tone, and I need him to confirm it.

"We believe she was raped."

I suck in a breath. And then I fucking explode. "What? Are you fucking kidding me right now?" I jump out of the driver's seat and start pacing in front of the car, unable to remain still.

My dad and Dom both get out after me.

"Fuck." Then his words settle over me and I whirl on him. "What do you mean you think?" Either someone is raped or they aren't. There isn't really a gray area here.

"She wouldn't consent to the rape kit. She told the nurses she was raped upon arrival and it was clear she'd been when I found her. She was—" He shakes his head. "It doesn't matter. But she told the nurses about the assault when we got there. I rode in the ambulance with her. She had all the signs of a rape victim. Torn clothes. Bruises. All of it. But before the nurses could start the kit, some woman in a suit stormed in and tore out of there with her like she was on a mission. When me and another officer tried to confront her, she shut us down. The girl's a minor. We couldn't question her without parental consent and they weren't giving it."

I pull at my hair and resume my pacing. "And she was okay with that?" Goddammit. This is so much worse than I thought. Raped? Fuck. I iced her out and she'd been raped.

She'd been in trouble today and she'd called Dom. Not me. I fucked up. She's been hurt and I royally fucked up.

My dad lifts his shoulders and releases a weary exhale. "I don't know. She was in shock. She shut down. I can't say I blame her." He shakes his head. "Whoever hurt her made sure to leave their mark. I can't fault her for calling you when she saw a man outside." He directs that statement to Dom, and I notice his eyes are no longer distant. Instead, they're alight with remembered fury.

"The guy who hurt her?"

Pops shakes his head. "Still out there."

Fuck.

THIRTY-SEVEN

Allie

It's Saturday morning. Against my initial hesitations, I decide to go on a run to clear my head. I couldn't sleep last night. I kept replaying what happened at the diner again and again, visualizing all the ways that things could have gone. It was bad enough, what happened. But it could have been a thousand times worse. Deep down, I know that, and it's left me shaken.

I can only imagine how Dominique must feel. Speaking of... I spot a familiar black Escalade as I round the corner of my street, my sneakered feet smacking against the pavement.

I wipe the sweat from my forehead, but I don't slow down. Not until the car gets close enough for me to spot Dominique through the windshield. I let out a small breath of relief. I was pretty sure it was him, but it helps having the confirmation.

The Escalade pulls up beside me and slows, keeping pace with my jog as one of the windows rolls down and Roman hangs an arm out of the passenger side window. My heart stutters in my chest, despite everything that's happened. I spot Emilio in the backseat. Looks like the gang is all here.

"Allie," Roman calls my name. His voice is hard and I instantly bristle at his tone. "Get in the car."

"Pass," I tell him, picking up my pace. I swallow hard, forcing myself not to focus on the sound of his voice. Longing sweeps through me, but I push it aside and keep my eyes trained ahead of me.

"Allie." There's a warning in his voice. He's angry. Does he blame me for what happened last night? *Probably*.

"Go away, Roman."

The Escalade jerks to a stop and Roman jumps from the car. I squeal when he rushes me and between one second and the next, he has me hoisted over his shoulder and unceremoniously throws me into the backseat beside Emilio before slamming the door and getting back in the front seat.

"Bro, what the fuck?" Emilio snaps. "What happened to playing this cool?"

"Buckle up." Roman barks, ignoring him.

I rush to right myself and then press against the door as far away from Emilio as I can get as Dom pulls the car back onto the road. My breaths are loud and heavy in the quiet space and I can feel all their eyes on me.

"Let me out." Adrenaline floods through me and I close my eyes. *It's just the guys.* I'm fine. They're not going to hurt me. Even if Roman is angry with me, he wouldn't hurt me. Not like that.

It doesn't matter. Telling myself I'm safe doesn't stop the panic coursing through my veins. I'm hyperventilating now.

"Allie, it's okay. We just want to talk." Emilio unbuckles and slides closer to me and I lose it in a haze of blind terror.

"Let me out. Let me out!" I scream and my fingers claw at the door. Finding the handle, I jerk it open. Dominique slams on the brakes just as I throw myself from the car. I slam against the pavement, asphalt scraping against my skin and three sets of doors open and slam shut. Curses fly but I'm already scrambling to my feet, uncaring of the scrapes or bruises I know I have. Blood drips down my forearm and all three guys step toward me.

"Stop! Don't come any closer." I hold a hand out toward them, urging them to stay away. My other hand clutches my head as I struggle to get air into my lungs. My head is pounding, an incessant beat growing louder and louder as each second passes.

"Allie, we won't come any closer. Breathe. We won't hurt you. You know that." Dom's voice cuts through some of my panic. I step back on the pavement until my feet meet grass and then I collapse. Pressing my head between my knees I rock back and forth, sucking in air.

"I'm okay. I'm okay. I'm okay." If I say it enough, it'll be true.

"What do you need?" Dominique again.

I shake my head.

"Allie?" Emilio's voice is higher than usual. I look up and all three are standing maybe fifteen feet away with a mix of worried and confused expressions.

I swallow hard. "Hands." My voice shakes. "I need to see your hands."

Three scowls greet me but without hesitation, Dominique holds his hands out and takes two steps forward. "Okay. Here are my hands."

I take in his darker skin. The contrasting pink of his palms. I force myself to recognize how different his hands are from the men who hurt me. He takes another step. Then another. My breathing slows and I shudder.

Dominique crouches down in front of me, hands still lifted. I reach out and take one of his hands in my own. I turn his palm over. Safe. Dom is safe. Emilio steps closer, his hands lifted as well.

The sun-kissed color of his skin has my chest rising and falling faster and faster. I close my eyes. "I'm sorry. I—" I shake my head. Dom waves him back and without me having to ask, he steps further away from me.

"What is it about hands?" Dominique asks.

I shake my head. I don't want to talk about it. I know I'm freaking out and I know they want answers but I can't—

"We know you were assaulted." His voice is gentle, but his words are like a slap.

What? All the blood drains from my face.

"Baby—"

I jerk my head toward Roman. His voice is filled with pain as his wide, haunted eyes meet mine. His hands are clenched into white-knuckled fists at his sides. He steps closer and I flinch.

Cursing, he rounds to the opposite side of the car. "Dammit."

"You're not helping. Get your shit together," Dominique tells him. He turns back to me. "Can you explain what it is about hands. We just want to help. We didn't know. Not until last night..."

Last night, after Roman's dad showed up. He must have told them. Shame washes over me in cascading waves that leave me drowning in self-loathing and disgust. They know. All three of them know. Tears fill my field of vision and I press the heels of my palms against my eyes, fighting to keep them from falling.

"Allie—"

"Your hands are different," I choke out. I gasp for breath and force more words past my lips. "The man who hurt me... I only saw his hands. I... Your hands are different. I know you won't hurt me. I'm not saying Roman would. I know it doesn't make sense but...." I give him a pleading look, begging with him to understand.

Dom's eyes tighten and he runs a hand over his tightly braided hair. "Your mind gets it but your body doesn't." He shakes his head. "It's okay. I get it."

My shoulders slump in relief. "Your hands are different. He wasn't black. It's easy for me to convince myself you're safe."

He nods. "And with Roman and Emilio?"

I shrug. "I think he was maybe Latino, too. I don't know, but his hands, they were tan. Darker than mine. Like..."

"Like theirs."

I nod, unable to look at either of them. God, what they must be thinking right now.

"The guy who's been with you all week—?" Dominique doesn't finish but I know what he's asking.

"Like a brother. I've known him since grade school. And he has tattoos." I trace the back of my hand. "They cover the tops of his hands. A skull and roses... rosary beads..." I say all of this hoping he understands. I know I'm not making complete sense but I don't have another way to put into words why hands matter.

He nods again. "Okay. Okay. Let me think." He stands and goes back toward his car. He says something to Roman and Emilio and Roman explodes, throwing his hands up in the air and cursing. He pulls at his hair, but when he looks at me, all of his anger evaporates. In its place is stark need and devastation.

My chest tightens. He's not hiding any of his emotions from me. Not this time. He lets me see all of it. Every painful piece of what he's feeling. And it leaves me reeling. I don't know how to interpret his anguish. Is he upset because of what happened? Because I'm such a mess?

He doesn't come any closer. Just stares at me with unmasked emotion, and it's suddenly too much. Seeing him hurts too much.

I swallow hard and push back up to my feet. My eyes stray to his clenched fists and I notice that he's still wearing my bracelet. The one I gave him before the game. I try not to read into it but does that mean—

"Allie, baby." His voice is raw. "I never—" His voice cracks and he looks away. "I fucked up. I thought some things and they weren't true and I wasn't there when you needed me." He turns back to me and I can see the despair in his eyes. "I messed up. But I'm here now. I want to be there for you. You have to let me be there."

I shake my head. I can't deal with all of this right now. Wrapping my arms around myself, I take a step away, retreating back the way I'd come. "I... I can't do this. I'm sorry."

"Allie!"

I pause, hating how weak I feel right now. How broken and shattered I am inside.

"I won't hurt you. I would *never* hurt you." He takes a tentative step forward and I jerk away. He stops and offers me a sad smile. "I would never hurt you. You've gotta know that."

"Wouldn't you?" My own voice cracks as the words spill out on their own. I'm not sure if I'm asking or challenging him, but he did hurt me. He's been hurting me.

Roman's face falls. He rubs the back of his neck and averts his gaze. "I'm so fucking sorry. I didn't know. If I'd known I never would have... Allie, I never meant..."

"But you never asked." Tears fall freely down my cheeks. I don't even bother to wipe them away. I want him to see them. I want him to see every ugly broken thing about me and know he had a part in it. I want him to hurt the same way he made me hurt. Because just like Ryker, he left me. Right when I needed him the most. "I tried to talk to you. That first day I came back to school. As soon as I saw you, I walked straight up to you and do you remember what you said? What you called me?"

Anguish fills his gaze, but I can't find it in me to hold back.

"You called me a whore." I shake my head, more silent tears falling down my face, enough so that Roman is a blurry shadow in front of me, his features no longer recognizable. "I can't do this. Just... leave me alone. I think I've been through enough."

I turn and jog home. Thankfully, no one follows.

THIRTY-EIGHT

Roman

S he won't meet my gaze. I try and talk to her at school, but she gives me the cold shoulder, and hell knows I deserve it. I try and catch her eyes in first period but not once does she look my direction. To make matters worse, Silvia is waiting for me outside the class and the look on Allie's face when Silvia makes an attempt to kiss me sends a spear of self-loathing straight to my gut.

I push Silvia away but the damage is already done and before I can call out to her to wait up, Allie is gone, swallowed up by the crowded sea of people in the hallway.

"Silvia," I bite out.

"Yeah, babe?" she purrs, stroking a hand over my chest. I pull her hand away, my lip curling in disgust. "I've had my fill. I'm moving on. I suggest you do, too."

Her eyes widen before narrowing into slits. "Let me guess, you're going back to daddy's little princess?"

I take a menacing step toward her. "Say one more thing about Allie Ramirez and I'll make sure you regret it. You've already had a taste of what it's like to be on my bad side. Want to be there again?"

She swallows hard and shakes her head.

"Good. Now make yourself scarce. I've moved on."

I don't bother waiting for an answer and head out to find Emilio. He's smoother when it comes to girls. Maybe he'll have an idea of how I can get Allie back.

I catch Allie talking to Dominique in the halls as they head to lunch, but as soon as I approach, she takes off and sits at Henderson's table. I try to ignore how gutted I feel at her dismissal, but it's hard. Dom pats me on the shoulder. "She just needs time, man."

I nod, knowing he's right but it doesn't mean I have to like it. I messed up royally when I pushed her away. I won't make that mistake again. Won't give up on her or what we have. I've never felt about a girl the way that I do about Allie. It's why even when I was pissed as hell at her, when I thought she'd moved on with Julio, leaving me in the dust, I still couldn't get her out of my head. She lives there. Takes up space and refuses to move the fuck out.

At lunch, I sit with my face in my hands, going over all the ways I can win her back. When the lunch bell rings, I track her with my gaze, watching like some love-sick puppy as she leaves the cafeteria, Kasey and Henderson close on her heels.

I shove away from the table and storm after them.

"What do you think you're doing?" Dom shouts somewhere behind me.

I shake my head. I have no fucking idea but I have to do something. Allie slips into her third-period class and I walk past it, my eyes trained on Henderson, and just before he reaches the door to his own class, I jerk him back by the fabric of his shirt.

"Hey, man—" Startled green eyes meet my own when he sees who grabbed him. "What the hell, Roman?" He jerks away, adjusting the collar of his shirt.

"You've been hanging out with Allie a lot lately." I meant it as a question, but it comes out as an accusation and Aaron's jaw tightens.

"Why do you care? You've been a complete asshole to her ever since she came back. Do the girl a favor and leave her alone. She's been through enough and she doesn't need your shit."

I slam my fist into the locker beside him. "I didn't know!" A few people in the hall turn to look at us and I snarl at them. "Move the fuck along." Heated faces turn and rush to their classes, effectively clearing the hall of everyone but the two of us. "I didn't know what happened to her. Not until just recently."

"And that's supposed to somehow make this all better? Fuck you, Roman."

"Henderson—" It's a warning.

He shakes his head. "No. You fucked up. I don't know why you're even talking to me. I'm not going to help you fix your mistakes. I don't owe you any—"

"Yeah, you do."

His eyes narrow.

"You owe me and you fucking know it. You want me to stop hating you? You want the Devils to stop hating you for what you put us through the summer before junior year?"

His mouth presses into a sharp line and he gives me a single sharp nod.

"Then help me talk to her. She doesn't feel comfortable with me." He snorts and the urge to punch him in his smug face is strong, but I ignore it. "I care about her. I want to be there for her. Help me talk to her and I'll forget what happened. We'll wipe the slate clean."

He considers this. It's no secret I hate him. I've hated him since junior year. He used to be my friend. We were like brothers. All four of us. But then he had to go and fuck it all up. He'd just gotten his license. He was the only one of us old enough to drive and we were all heading to Shadle Creek to camp for a week over summer.

But the fucker did drugs. None of us knew. He hid his addiction because he knew what we'd say about it, and on the way up to Shadle Creek, high as a fucking kite on coke, he hit a truck head-on. We were in a WRX. His first one, not the one he drives now. The force of the impact sent Emilio shooting out the window and broke Dominique's arm in two places. He had to have surgery to repair the break and spent all summer in a cast. It could have ended his chances of playing football and we all could have died. Emilio surprisingly came out the least scathed. Scrapes and bruises. A concussion, but nothing life threatening. And me, I had the pleasure of a ruptured spleen, and after surgery that shit took four long weeks to recover from.

To make matters worse, as I was freaking the fuck out trying to help Dom out of the car and find Emilio because we had no fucking idea where he'd been thrown, Henderson was ranting about how much trouble he was in. How screwed he was. We all could have died and all he'd cared about was whether or not he'd be going to jail.

He should have. Maybe it would have straightened him out. But for whatever reason, I convinced my pops to go easy on him. There was history there. Years of friendship I couldn't turn my back on, even though not once did he visit Dom or me in the hospital.

He got a slap on the wrist. Community service and his parents had to pay a fine to the city. But after that, I cut ties, and to this day, the asshole still hasn't apologized.

I never thought I'd forgive him, but to get Allie back, I'll do damn near anything.

"You'd do that? Forget what happened?" He swallows, his Adam's apple bobbing. "Forget what I did, and all I have to do is get Allie to talk to you."

I nod.

"I can't make any promises."

"I don't need promises or assurances. I just need a chance. One fucking chance to make this right."

"Okay."

I exhale a breath. "Okay."

THIRTY-NINE

Allie

Roman calls me now. All of the Devils do. Emilio sends me a joke each morning. Or a funny meme he found online. He wants to make me smile. And while I appreciate the gesture, it's a lot to take in. The sudden shift in their behaviors.

One second they hate me. Now it's like they're smothering me in distant affection.

Dominique is the only one I talk to at school. He sometimes walks me to class when Aaron isn't around. He makes sure no one gets too close. I didn't ask him to play guard dog, and when I told him as much, he just gave me this serious stare and carried on like I hadn't said anything. I've learned not to push. If he wants to make himself late to class each day, that's his prerogative.

Roman messages me each morning. A variation of **good morning, beautiful**, and calls me every night. I don't respond to the texts and never answer the calls. He doesn't leave any voicemails which is probably for the best. Hearing his voice at school is bad enough. If he left me messages, I know myself well enough to know I'd replay them again and again, obsessing over the sound of his voice. Trying to peel back any hidden meaning. It's already what I do with his texts. Sometimes he adds an emoji and it's enough to leave me guessing, hoping. For what, I'm not really sure.

But without fail at nine o'clock each evening my phone lights up and his name flashes across the screen. A part of me has come to look forward to that phone call. When eight fifty nears, I start counting down the minutes, hoping he'll call, and that alone scares me. Because sooner or later, he's going to give up. He'll stop calling. He'll stop texting. And he'll move on. I want him to move on.

I can't afford to need anyone else in my life. I've lost too much, and I don't think my heart can take any more. It doesn't matter that I miss him or that his presence sets my heart racing.

What happens when he's no longer there?

I'm already dreading when the calls stop.

It's been a week since he found out what happened to me. A week of pretending I don't want him. Of trying to convince myself that I'm better off without him. But I'm slipping.

I catch myself staring at him when he's not looking. And I hang onto every word Dom says whenever he mentions

Roman. How he's doing. Where he's at. What they're eating for lunch. It's borderline obsessive and I know it, but I'm desperate to know every little detail.

Aaron has mentioned him a few times, too, which was surprising at first. He's always made it clear how he feels about Roman. I know they have history, and while I'm curious, I also know it's none of my business. But even he's tried to convince me to talk to Roman. To at least hear him out. He thinks it'd be cathartic for me. And maybe it would be. But....

"Hey, Allie?" A hesitant voice calls out and I turn away from my locker to find Emilio standing a few feet away. He mashes his lips together, his eyes on the ground near my feet. "You doing okay?"

"Hey. Umm, yeah. How are you?" I glance around the hallway, class will be starting soon.

He shrugs and looks up, giving me a small smile. "I'm good. I, uh..." he trails off and looks away. "I wanted to try something. If you're okay with it?"

I nod and brace myself.

"I know you said hands were a thing for you. So, I, ah..." He raises his hands so the tops of them face me. He's painted his nails an inky black and has a gold band on his left thumb and another on his right-hand middle finger. "I was hoping this might make a difference for you." He shrugs again with an almost sheepish expression on his face, and I can't help but smile as I take in what he's done, focusing on his nail beds and the jewelry. I take a tentative step forward. When my heartbeat stays steady, I take another. Emotions clog my throat and I take another step.

Emilio bites his upper lip, his eyes anxious as he waits for me to close the last bit of distance between us. When I do, I reach out and take one of his hands in mine, turning it over to trace the lines of his palms. I give him a tentative smile. "You going to wear nail polish all the time now? It might mess with your player status both on and off the field."

He smirks. "I think the black makes me look cool. I'm going for that whole emo-rocker look with some Latino flare."

"Ah, is that where the gold comes in?"

He smiles and hesitantly reaches for my elbow tugging me close. When I don't object, his arms wrap around me and I breathe in the smell of him. Spice and mint. His embrace tightens for a split second and I stiffen but he's quick to release me, taking a single step back. "I missed you, vanilla."

"I missed you, too."

He winks. "So, uh, you maybe wanna—" His eyes flick to someone over my shoulder, and I turn to find Roman standing just outside the door leading to our first-period class.

"He misses you, too," Emilio says behind me.

I shake my head. "I can't fix that E. Rome and I," I brush my hair out of my face and give him a tight-lipped smile.

"We were just each other's way to pass some time. We both said as much from the beginning. A happy ever after was never in the cards. It's time to move on."

"Do you really believe that?" he asks.

I shrug. "Yes. I don't know. Maybe. It doesn't matter now."

He shakes his head. "I've known Roman almost my entire life. I'm closer with him than I am my own brothers. He's not the best at showing how he feels, but he cares about you, Allie. A lot. I don't want to push you. You've been through enough but just ... don't write him off yet, okay?"

I bit my bottom lip and look away. "I don't think I can afford to care about him any more than I already do. It hurts—"

"I know, sweetheart. I know. But I think Rome can make you happy. You deserve to be happy."

FORTY

Roman

I watch Allie with Emilio and jealousy hits me like an oncoming train.

She takes his hands and rather than retreating, she steps closer to him. Reaches out and touches him.

Dominique slaps a hand on my shoulder and my gaze jerks toward him. "You need to fix this."

"I'm trying."

"Try harder."

I tug away from him. "She's letting everyone else in *but* me." Even I hear the bitterness in my voice. The second I see Emilio pull her into a hug, I see red. I want to punch the fucker in the face, to hell if he's one of my best friends.

"I know this hurts, man—"

"Hurts?!" I turn to him, eyes wide, and a sneer on my lips. "You think this hurts? Fuck you. I wish all it did was hurt.

This shit right here"—I wave in their direction—" it fucking guts me. My girl won't talk to me. Won't look at me. She was fucking r—"

Dominique grabs me and shoves me inside an empty classroom. "Keep your goddamn voice down," he whisper-shouts.

I'm shaking my head, hands already forming fists. I need to hit something. Or someone. I need to funnel all of whatever it is that I'm feeling into *something* or I'm going to lose my goddamn mind.

Dom gets in my face and it takes everything in me not to draw back and hit my best friend.

"This sucks. You're pissed off because you know you fucked up. You had a good thing going and she got hurt." I open my mouth but he cuts me off. "But you're still not getting it Rome. *She* got hurt. Her. Not you. You don't get to be pissed off at her or anyone else because you're a jealous asshole used to getting his way. She deserves better than that."

"Get off me." I shove him back. He takes a few more steps away, his jaw clenched and his eyes narrowed.

"This isn't about you. Not what you want or what you think you need. If you want to get her back then stop being a selfish prick and realize this is about her. What she wants and what she needs. That's all that should matter right now."

I work my jaw. The asshole is right and I hate it. My eyes fall to the floor and I force myself to take a deep breath before dropping down, my ass hitting the cool linoleum with my back against the wall. My eyes hit his once more. "What do I do?"

He rubs the back of his neck, a weary expression on his face. "I don't know, man."

"She won't talk to me," I say, my words hollow and empty.

Dom sighs. "You're making this about you again. It's not just that she won't talk to you. She can't. You saw what happened before. She freaked out and damn near had a panic attack."

Fuck.

It's the hands thing.

Something clicks. An idea forming in my head and suddenly, I know what I have to do now.

I push to my feet and head for the door.

"Where are you going?"

"Out."

"What do you mean, out? We have class."

I shake my head. "I'm skipping. I have something I need to do. Just—" I pause. "Watch out for my girl."

I head straight to the parking lot, ignoring Mrs. Jennings when she pokes her head out of her classroom and asks me where I'm going. Season's over. She can give me all the detentions she wants.

I spot Henderson in the parking lot getting out of his Subaru WRX and make a split-second decision to call out to him. "Yo, Henderson."

His head jerks toward me and he scowls.

"Come on, we're cutting."

"What?"

I stalk toward his car and open the passenger side door. "Get in the car, Henderson. I need a ride. Let's go."

Surprisingly, he does as I ask. I give him directions to The Missing Piece and have him park in the first available space we can find. There's no hesitation as I walk inside. I don't even need to think about what to get. I already know. He follows behind, uncertainty written across his face.

The woman at the desk takes one look at the two of us and her smile brightens. She's wearing a low-cut tank top in the middle of winter, exposing her arms, both covered in ink. "Do you have time for walk-ins?" I ask, ignoring the flirtatious smile she gives me.

"I'll check for you," she turns to her computer before her gaze returns to mine. "And what about him, sugar? You both here for some work?"

Henderson shakes his head in a definitive no.

"Just me," I tell her.

"Alright then. Henry has some time. What are you after?"

I give her a quick rundown of what I'm looking for.

She purses her lips. "Are you sure you want that on your hands?"

I nod and she goes and gets this Henry guy who comes to the front, and I explain again to him what I want. He looks at me the way some tattoo artists do when they think you're making a mistake, but he's not going to say anything because he's happy to take my money.

We sit down together and he works on the sketch for both pieces. Laying the stencil on my hands we go over placement and then we're set. He doesn't bother asking me for ID. I've learned that once you have some ink, no one really cares much about adding more.

"Last chance, man. You sure?"

I nod. I explained to Henry what the tattoos meant, it's not every day a guy walks in asking for what I'm after, and the explanation only cements his belief that this is stupid. But that's okay. This girl is it for me. She's not just my beginning, she's my end. I've been fucking around and going through the girls in this town one right after the other until she showed up. That had worked for me these last few years. I never wanted more than one night with any of them. But with Allie, I don't want just one night. I need more. I need her every day. For all of the days that are to come.

She's the first person I think about when I wake up and the last one on my mind when I go to sleep. She's not just some random. She never was. She's the real deal. I know we're young. I know we said we were having fun. I shouldn't be worried about my tomorrow or my forever, but that's what I want with her.

She needs to know she's it for me. I'll make the sacrifices. I'll step up and put in the work. Because she fucking deserves it. I just hope this shows her exactly what she means to me because if this doesn't do that, I have no fucking idea what else I can do to win her back.

It takes four hours for Henry to finish. When he does, he walks me through the usual list of how to care for the ink. What lotions to use. And gives me the reminder that hand tats are notorious for fading faster than anywhere else on the body. I pay him and give him my thanks after he covers the tops of both my hands in a thin bandage.

There's still around an hour left of school and another twenty minutes or so after that until she gets home. I need to talk to her where she'll feel safe. I don't want to do it at the school. We don't need the audience and I know the parking lot holds bad memories for her, so I decide to head to her place. I don't want to spring this on her or make her uncomfortable, but I don't see an alternative.

"I can't believe you just did that," Henderson says.

I shrug like it's no big deal because it isn't. I'd do a hell of a lot more for that girl than just get a little ink.

He gives me a sideways look as I tell him to head toward Allie's place. "You really care about her?" he asks, sounding surprised.

I grunt because I don't have to justify my feelings for her to him.

He parks across the street from the mansion where she lives, and I recline my seat and settle in to wait. A glance at the clock shows me we have some time before she gets home. Henderson turns off the car and the silence between us stretches, becoming awkward.

"We ever gonna talk about—'

I cut him off. "No. There's nothing to talk about."

He sighs. "I fucked up."

"That's the understatement of the century."

He turns toward me in his seat, nostrils flaring. "You've fucked up too, Rome. Don't pretend like you're some saint."

"Never said I was," I tell him. "But I'm learning from my mistakes. Trying to fix them. Can you say the same?"

His face tightens and he looks away, staring out the windshield. "I was in a bad place back then."

I nod. I'm aware. I might not have been at the time. He was good at covering his tracks, keeping his nose clean, but I found out later what he'd been going through. "We made a deal," I remind him. "You help me, we wipe the slate clean. But, Henderson." I wait until he meets my gaze again, wanting him to see just how serious I am. "I won't make this deal again. Whatever shit you still need to clean up, be sure that you do."

He nods, not denying that he's still in some shit he shouldn't be.

Knowing I shouldn't I ask, "You still doing?"

He shakes his head.

"Dealing?"

A pause and then a single sharp nod.

"Keep that shit away from her. Got it? She likes you. She doesn't have many people here and she's been through too much. Don't let whatever you're into rub off on her life."

"I won't. I would never—"

I snort. "Because it didn't fuck up our lives either, right?" That quiets him and he exhales a harsh breath.

"I'm getting my shit in order. I just ... need time."

"It's been a year and a half."

"I know." His jaw tightens. "But I have my reasons, and I'm working on it."

I nod, letting the subject drop. We wait in silence for a few more minutes before Allie's Audi comes into view.

"So, what's your plan here?"

I turn to him and shrug. "I don't have a plan. I'm winging it. If she's okay to talk to me, make yourself scarce. I'll find a ride back later. If she struggles, stick around and try not to listen as I pour my heart out on the fucking pavement."

He frowns, rubbing the back of his neck. "Uh, okay. I guess I can go with that."

FORTY-ONE

Allie

I've been thinking about what Emilio said all day. I want to believe him. Believe that Roman misses me. It's just so hard to do that when it was so easy for him to push me away.

I pull into my driveway and get out, my mind distracted, when I hear a voice behind me say, "Allie?"

I squeal, whirling to see who's behind me and find Roman and Aaron standing a few yards away.

I press my hand to my chest, willing my racing heart to slow. "Don't scare me like that!"

Roman lifts both hands, "I didn't mean to scare you. I just want to talk."

I frown and flick a glance toward Aaron who's standing a few steps behind Roman. He gives me a sheepish look and shrugs. "I'm just here for moral support."

My scowl deepens. "For me or for him?" I thought they hated each other.

Roman answers. "He's here for you. We're patching up some of our shit. Henderson can be an okay dude when he wants to be. But I asked him to come with me because I wanted him to be here for you."

He did? "Why?"

Roman takes a tentative step forward. "Because I want to talk and I know you trust him. That you're comfortable with him around."

"I'm fine with Dominique too, and he's your friend. Why not ask him?"

He shakes his head. "Because I didn't want to gang up on you. Dominique's my friend. He's yours too, but I didn't want you to think he'd be on my side over yours or that you wouldn't have anyone in your corner. Henderson and I have our history, but when it comes to you and me, he's always going to pick you first. He's in your corner. He's your friend. I want you to feel safe talking to me."

Oh. That's ... thoughtful of him.

He runs his hands over his face and I catch sight of the twin bandages over the top of both his hands.

"What happened to your hands?" I ask, worry clenching my stomach. Is he hurt? Did something happen?

Roman lifts his gaze, his dark brown eyes meeting mine. "That's actually what I came here to show you."

Aaron looks nervous behind him, shifting from one foot to the other.

"Ummm...okay." I wait for him to elaborate but he doesn't. His lips are pressed into a tight line, his eyes downcast. He peels back the bandages and underneath I see that he's sporting new ink. I gasp. "You tattooed your hands?"

He nods but doesn't say anything as he removes the second bandage, shoving both in his back pocket. I swallow hard as I take in the new pieces he's added, fighting the urge to get a closer look. They're beautiful. On his left, he has an anchor surrounded in a sea of crashing waves that covers the entire top of his hand. The detail looks amazing and before I can talk myself out of it, I step toward him, curious about the design.

"Do you want to see them?" he asks, holding perfectly still, almost like he's afraid to breathe. I realize how close I've gotten to him and my own heart races, but I fight through the wave of apprehension and nod.

He holds his hand out and with shaking fingers I trace the design on his left hand before jerking away and putting a foot of distance between us. Hurt flashes in his eyes before he masks it.

I inhale a lungful of air. *It's just Roman.* I remind myself. I force my gaze back to his hands, allowing myself time to take in the dark ink and see the stark differences between his hands and those of my attacker. Seconds pass and when my heart settles I move closer to him once again.

"Why an anchor?" I'm whispering and have no idea why.

"Because when you're adrift, when you can't find your way to shore, I want to be the one who steadies you."

My heart seizes in my chest. "You got this for me?" I ask, dumbfounded.

His smile is hopeful.

"I don't understand," I say. "This is permanent, Roman. You didn't have—"

He cuts me off. "I did, Allie. I need you to see how important you are to me. How much you matter and how incredibly sorry I am. I just... I want a second chance. To do everything the right way. To treat you like you deserve to be treated."

A tear rolls down my cheek and I hastily wipe it away. Forcing down the sudden knot in my throat I ask, "And what is this one? Is it an orchid... or maybe a daffodil?" I examine his right hand. This one is smaller though still covers most of his hand.

Roman shakes his head. "No. Not an orchid or a daffodil."

"What is it then?"

"It's a vanilla planifolia." At my confused expression he adds, "Mexican vanilla."

I gasp, dropping his hands. I look away as emotion threatens to bubble up out of me. It's as if he's shoved his hand in my chest and squeezed my heart until it beats only for him. The walls I've built to protect myself begin to crumble.

I catch sight of Aaron. He's retreated toward his car and is sitting on the hood, giving us some semblance of privacy. His eyes meet mine and he gives me a barely perceptible nod as if to say, *yeah, that just happened.* I turn back to meet Roman's raw gaze.

"Why?" I force myself to ask. None of this makes sense. "Why are you trying so hard to fix something that never really started?"

"Because you're worth it. You're worth all of it. All the fighting, the pain, the feelings. You make me fucking *feel*, Allie." He slaps a hand on his chest right over his heart. "Right here. You made my ice-cold heart beat, and it only wants to beat for one person. You. Only you. I don't just want you. I fucking *need* you." He steps forward and presses his forehead against mine, cupping my face in his strong inked hands and I close my eyes, breathing him in. Fighting through the fear of being close to a boy I'm not sure I can trust. "Alejandra Ramirez, I need you in my life."

Instinctively, I know Roman would never hurt me. Not physically. But the fear of giving this boy my heart has the air in my lungs freezing.

"Roman, I can't lose a—"

"You won't," he says with conviction. "You fucking won't. I can promise you that. I don't know how to do this whole relationship thing. I'm learning as I go here. But I won't ever turn my back on you like that again. Never, Allie. Just give me this chance. One more chance. I won't mess it up."

"I'm broken," I tell him because it's true. I'm broken, my pieces jagged and sharp. I don't know if I'm even capable or even willing to be intimate with him after everything I've been through, and he doesn't need that. He doesn't need my baggage. For what, a few months of bliss? We're graduating in a few short months. And then what?

"Let me pick up all your broken pieces and put you back together. Let me be your anchor when you're lost and the world keeps spinning around you."

I pull back, and my heart aches seeing the sheer vulnerability on his face. His hands fall from my cheeks to wrap around me and I'm almost surprised when I don't stiffen. "And when we graduate?"

He presses his face into my hair. "We figure it out. I'm not letting you go, vanilla. I need you too much."

My heart does a free-fall and I pray that this time, he doesn't let it splatter on the ground near his feet. My trust is a bruised and battered thing. But I think I love the boy standing in front of me. And I think he loves me, too. Neither one of us knows how to say it. Words don't feel like they'll ever be enough.

But Roman said he needs me, so I take a leap of faith and let my truth pass over my lips, whisper soft. "Maybe we need each other."

FORTY-TWO

Allie: Four months later

"Happy birthday to you. Happy birthday to you. Happy birthday to Allie. Happy birthday to you."

My smile is beaming as I lean forward and blow out the candles on the cake Mrs. Valdez made for me. It's my eighteenth birthday, and while I don't feel any different than I did yesterday, I know that after today, everything is going to change.

It's been four months since Roman and I decided to give a real relationship between us a try. We've had our ups and downs, and I'm still learning to cope with some of the traumas I've experienced, but I've made a lot of progress.

I don't freak out anymore when he comes up behind me and wraps his arms around my waist like he's doing now, leaning in to kiss my neck. "Did you make a wish?" he asks, his breath is hot against my skin, his voice pitched low and seductive.

A slow smile spreads over my face and I shake my head, turning to look at him. "Nope."

His brows furrow in confusion, and I bite my lower lip to keep from laughing. "I already have everything I could ask for." And it's the truth. All my friends are here. I have the most amazing boyfriend who consistently puts me and my needs first. And I've gotten the help I should have when I was first assaulted. Roman's mom—Maria—made sure of that.

I'm happy and I'm healing. I couldn't ask for anything more.

His face cracks into a wide grin as he turns me to face him, then dips down and presses his lips against mine in a tender kiss. His kisses always start this way. Hesitant and soft. But one nip of his bottom lip has him deepening the kiss and I gasp, opening my mouth to drink him in, silently asking for more.

Voices groan behind us before wandering off.

"Get a room," Emilio calls out and I pull away, fighting hard not to blush.

"Fuck off," Roman says, though there's no heat in his voice.

Emilio rolls his eyes then pries me out of Roman's embrace. "You'll have Allie all to yourself soon enough. Today you have to share."

I squeal as he lifts me into the air, throwing me over his shoulder and racing into the backyard with me, Roman hot on our heels. It's strange to think that a few short months ago I was adrift. Lost to my pain and consumed by my grief. I didn't think I'd find happiness again. Not like this. But I'm not numb anymore. I feel my emotions like a kaleidoscope of sensation and I relish each and every day.

The entire crew moves outside. Roman's parents—Maria and Melchor—Dominique, Aaron, Kasey. Even Julio, Gabe, and Felix made the drive up from Richland to celebrate with me.

Emilio sets me on my feet before gripping my hand and dragging me to the center of the yard. Music is playing on the outdoor speaker system and he draws me into dancing with him as Rombai's *Me Voy* plays. Kasey joins us before long and the three of us sing off key. Despite most of Kasey's words being made up and not actual lyrics, we laugh, dancing without a care in the world because that's how I've chosen to move on.

So much happened that I didn't have control over, and the threat of what tomorrow brings is always there. But my therapist reminds me during our weekly sessions that I need to focus on today and live my life without fear. I've lost so much. More than most people in my short eighteen years. But I don't want to live a life full of fear and what ifs. Which brings us to today. I'm eighteen, and I'm getting the keys to my first apartment this afternoon. Roman is moving in with me, which Maria and Melchor aren't thrilled about since both of us are still in high school, but Maria at least seems to understand.

Living with Gerald isn't an option for me if I want to

escape my past. He's a toxic piece of my life with an ever-present threat hanging over my head that we still need to deal with, and to move forward, I need to separate my life from his.

Janessa set up a meeting with him just this morning and I explained that I was moving out. I thanked him for taking me in after my mother's death and told him I'd made other arrangements now that I was a legal adult. He didn't look happy about it, but Janessa managed to smooth things over and help with some of the awkwardness.

He's letting me keep the car, a birthday gift of sorts. He also gave me access to a trust fund that I have no intention of using on anything beyond schooling, but I'm glad it's there. It helps with some of the stress that moving out brings.

Roman smiles at me across the lawn, a beer in his hand as he stands with Aaron on his right and Dom on his left. Kasey stands surrounded by my boys from back home, soaking up all their attention and I fight a grin when I see Dominique's murderous glare aimed their way.

Something makes me think there's something going on between the two of them, but neither has mentioned anything and I haven't asked. I'm just happy. Content, for once, and looking forward to what comes next for us.

It only takes a few lingering looks before Roman sets his drink down and joins me on the lawn, his hips swaying in sync with mine as his arms wrap around me. "You're so beautiful," he tells me.

I can't help the smile that blooms over my face. "You're pretty good-looking yourself," I remark, giving him an obvious once-over and letting heat build in my gaze.

His eyes gain a wicked glint. "I'm so fucking lucky." He presses his lips to mine again before whispering against my mouth, "And I love you so fucking much."

God, this boy. "I love you, too," I say, flinging my arms around his neck and hugging him tight. No matter what our future holds, I know he'll be by my side, and I can't wait for what our next chapter might bring.

If you want more from the Devils head to

https://hi.switchy.io/SavageUS to grab your copy of

Savage Devil, book 2 in the Devils of Sun Valley High series.

And if you're curious about Allie's friends from Richland, be sure to check out The Savage, Book 1 in the Boys of Richland series. https://amzn.to/3AV8ijI

Turn the page to start Savage Devil ...

Savage Devil

One night.
No names.
No numbers.
That is the deal we make.
After tonight, I'll never see him again, and I want to leave
town with zero regrets.

But, a year and a half later, I'm back with a secret I'm
terrified to tell.

Turns out the guy from that one reckless night is football
royalty. One of Sun Valley's infamous Devils.

I didn't tell him I was moving that night.
And, he isn't someone who handles rejection well.

Something I realize when I bump into him at my new
school. Sun Valley High. Home of the Devils.

And he decides to give me a lesson in why you never cross a Devil.

Head to https://hi.switchy.io/SavageUS
to grab your copy of ***Savage Devil***

"Come on, Bibi!" Monique whines before adding a coat of clear gloss over her full lips. "We're going to be late for the party. The one you insisted we go to tonight," she reminds me now as she toys with her hair. The dark brown box braids hang just past her shoulders. She glowers at me through the reflection in the mirror.

"I have nothing to wear!" Yes, now I'm whining, but sifting through my closet for something sexy—or, at the very least, something that doesn't scream "I go to a stuck-up private school"—is next to impossible. And being a Suncrest Saint —even if past tense—isn't something you advertise when mingling with the Sun Valley Devils. With any luck, we won't run into any of the true Devils tonight. That would cause all sorts of problems, especially since Monique's brother happens to be one of them.

He was in a car accident last week and is home recovering, so we should be in the clear. At least, I hope.

"Obviously." Monique reaches into her overnight bag. "That's why I brought you this." She pulls out a sleek, black, bodycon dress and tosses it my way.

I catch it and hold up the barely there dress, an immediate scowl on my face. "No way. I can't wear that," I tell her with a firm shake of my head.

Hand on her hip, she turns to me. "And why the hell not?"

"Because half the dress is missing, that's why," I hiss, careful to keep my voice down as I give the dress another once-over. Mom and her boyfriend—Miguel—are already in bed, and I don't want to wake either of them. Going out tonight isn't exactly approved. But you know the saying, "better to ask forgiveness than permission." Better yet, if Mom doesn't find out, then there's nothing to forgive in the first place.

In my hands, the dress looks no bigger than a t-shirt. A child-sized t-shirt. Yeah, no way am I wearing this.

Monique huffs out a breath. "At least try it on. What happened to you wanting to step out of your comfort zone today, huh? Weren't you the one who said you wanted to do something daring? Live on the edge?" Her brows lift in an expectant expression. "It's your last night in Sun Valley, Bibi."

Urgh, please don't remind me. "That doesn't mean I want to go out looking like a dime-store hooker," I tell her with a huff as a wave of sorrow crashes into me. Tonight is my last night in Sun Valley. Tomorrow, I'm moving. New town. New school. New life. In Richland, of all places. It sucks.

She rolls her eyes before turning away to finish her makeup in the full-length mirror that hangs from the back of my bedroom door. "Do I look like a dime-store hooker to you?" she asks over her shoulder.

"Obviously not," I snort. Monique is a goddess. Five-foot-eleven with rich brown skin, chestnut-colored eyes, and long braids pulled back into a half pony. She looks like Brandy Norwood from her Moesha days and I would kill to look half as good as she does. Her skin is flawless, and unlike me, she's managed to acquire curves in all the right places. I, on the other hand, am reed thin and straight as a bean pole. Mom swears I'll fill out eventually, but I doubt it. Not with my luck. At least I have boobs. Not much, but they're there.

"Glad we both agree. I'm wearing the exact same dress just in green. Try it on. You'll like it."

I roll my eyes but do as she says. It's not like I have a lot of options here. Most of my things are already packed. And even if they weren't, I still probably wouldn't have anything to wear. "Sexy" isn't really in my wardrobe vocabulary.

"Where did you get this from anyway?" I ask. "And how the heck did you manage to hide it from your mom?"

"Online. And I ordered it when she had a stupid floral shipment arrive for one of her charity things. There were so many delivery people in and out that day, she never noticed my lonely little Fashion Nova box."

"Sneaky," I tell her with a wink.

Monique and I have been best friends since middle school, which is how I know her parents would never approve of her wearing a dress like this. It's all about appearances for the Price family. They even took issue with our school-issued uniform skirts and had hers custom ordered three inches longer than standard. Though the hemline isn't the only thing about the dress they'd object to. They'd also balk at her wearing anything that wasn't designer and didn't cost a fortune. Can't wear the same clothes as the common folk.

Slipping the dress over my head, I smooth down the fabric and eye myself in the mirror.

"Damn, girl." Monique whistles. "You look stunning!"

I grimace. "This is...a lot." Though I can't pull my eyes away from my reflection. Monique is seven inches taller than me, so while her dress comes down just far enough to cover her butt, mine falls to mid-thigh. It's strapless and hugs my body like a second skin, giving the illusion of curves I know I don't have. But...wow.

Monique comes up behind me and pulls the clip from the back of my head, making my long, curly black hair fall around my face.

"This is perfect," she tells me. "It's sexy and screams for the love of God, please take my virginity."

I smack her arm but don't bother fighting my laugh. "I'm not trying to announce I want my virginity taken."

She tosses my hair clip on the bed and hands me a tube of bright red lipstick. "Doesn't change the fact that that is exactly what you're after. Come on, Bibi. This was your idea. Let's be rebels for once. We need this. A last hoorah before you abandon me."

I chew my bottom lip but accept the lipstick and move closer to the mirror to put it on. Squaring my shoulders, I remind myself that I'm leaving Sun Valley with zero regrets. I've spent the last sixteen years of my life being the good girl. The girl who never stepped out of line. Never caused a fuss. Never broke the rules.

I need to breathe. Even if it's only for one night.

At first, I was always on my best behavior because Mom was pregnant. She was older, the pregnancy unplanned, and it wasn't without complications. She needed help and support and I wanted to be there for her.

Then it was because my baby brother was sick. My parents had their hands full dealing with Afonso's condition. I didn't need to add to their plate by being reckless, and I didn't want to take attention away from Afonso. He was my baby brother. He was everything.

Then, right before his third birthday, he died. It gutted our family. Mom needed to grieve. No way would she have been able to handle me acting out on top of everything else. So, I continued to be the good girl. The rule follower. I can count on one hand the number of times my parents have ever needed to scold me.

Less than a year after Afonso passed, Dad left.

My family has been hit in the face with life again and again. There is never a good time to...I don't know...be a kid. To make mistakes. To act impulsively. Guilt worms its way through my chest reminding me now still isn't a good time. But then, when will it ever be? I'm sixteen years old. I want to be young and dumb. Not forever, but for a night. Just this one time. I want to make mistakes I can look back on. I want to know that I was wild and free. That I spread my wings and lived.

Afonso's been gone for three years now. Dad's been gone for two. It's been a whirlwind for Mom and I, but things have gotten better. Mom has a boyfriend. He's kinda weird but she smiles a lot more than she has in years, and I think she really loves him. He makes her happy. And I want her to be happy.

She's been through so much.

It's why I'm not complaining about the move. Well, not out loud at least. And why I stuffed back my tears and smiled ear to ear when she told me the good news. She deserves to be happy. I just...I want that for me, too.

"Okay. Let's go before I lose my nerve."

Monique's smile widens. "Eeeeee! This is going to be so much fun!"

I don't know if I share her enthusiasm, but I'm committed to this course nonetheless. For one night, I'm not going to be Bibiana Sousa—the good girl. I'm going to be the rebel. The wild child. A girl that goes with the flow, lets her hair down, and for once in her life, makes some freaking mistakes.

No one bats an eye as Monique and I stroll up to tonight's party house. I have no idea whose it is, but I also don't care. Suncrest Academy kids don't throw ragers like this, and by crashing a Sun Valley High party, we're less likely to run into anyone we know and have word get back to either of our parents.

"Come on, let's grab a drink." Monique hauls me through the front door and leads me in the obvious direction of the kitchen where a keg has been set up. Grabbing a red cup, she hands it to one of the guys manning the keg and he fills it for her, giving her an interested once-over.

"You here with anyone?" he asks, handing her the beer and tilting his head toward me in silent question. I shake my head, and wave off the offered alcohol, grabbing a water bottle from the open coolers instead. I know plenty of students who have zero issue with underage drinking but...I don't know...coming to the party to hook up with a guy seems risqué enough for me for one night. Drinking when I've just barely turned sixteen feels like I would be pushing it.

"Nope. Just my girl," Monique says, giving him a come-hither look as she takes a sip of her beer. The guys at Suncrest Academy don't give Monique a second glance. I'm pretty sure it's because they're intimidated by her. She's tall, a complete beast on the basketball court, and she has a spitfire personality. But it could also be because they're idiots. Actually, if I had to put money on it, it'd be because they're all idiots.

He tugs her close and she squeaks, though secretly I know she's thrilled by the attention. Like me, Monique is kept in a sheltered little box, rarely let out to play. We might say tonight is my night, but it's equally for her. We both need this escape from the constricting lives we lead, and Monique deserves to feel like the goddess she is.

"I'm gonna go mingle," I tell her, giving her the out she needs to have fun and not worry about me. She makes a face, about to argue, and I shake my head. "Have fun. You can't stick by my side all night, anyway. Remember?"

She rolls her eyes but smiles. "Fine. But find me if you need me, okay? And don't go home with anyone."

"Yes, Mom!" I snicker and turn around, following the sound of music coming from the back of the house.

I cut through the kitchen and dining room until I get to a set of double doors that leads to the back patio. A DJ booth has been set up. People are drinking and dancing, having a good time. I crack open my water bottle, taking a sip as I soak in the cool evening air, letting my gaze wander over the crowd. Everyone is clustered in these little groups as though natural cliques have formed and I kinda hate it. It's so high school.

I continue to scan the clusters when a guy on my far right grabs my attention. He's cute. My age with light blond hair and broad shoulders. He's laughing at something his friend says when our gazes connect. He stares for a second before lifting his cup as if to say hello. I smile. He smiles back. And then he goes back to talking. But every few seconds his eyes come back to me.

I linger where I stand for a moment, debating whether or not to head in his direction. It's obvious he's no longer listening to whatever his friends are saying. And he's not being shy about staring either. His perusal of my body lets me know he's interested but—

No.

Come on, Bibi. You can do this.

I take a deep breath. Be a rebel, I tell myself. I'm not going to just stand here like an idiot hoping he'll approach me. I'm going to be bold. I can do this.

I take a step forward when a voice behind me stops me in my tracks. "I wouldn't waste my time on Carson Bailey if I were you."

I whirl around, a scowl on my face as my eyes land on a boy hovering close behind me. "He has a small dick," he says, a savage grin on his face.

"Who said I was interested in his dick?" I ask, quirking a brow. And okay, yeah, maybe I am, but I don't have to admit it to this guy. Whoever the hell he is.

He snorts. "With a body like yours in a dress like that, you're looking for something, and it's not cookies at a bake sale. My money is on dick."

I roll my eyes. Jerk. "Maybe I just wanted to feel pretty."

He licks his lips, his eyes roving over my body in obvious appreciation. "Nah. You already know you're pretty. You want something else." His dark gaze is challenging as he boldly steps forward, our chests almost touching. A wave of heat floods through me at his proximity, and I take a second to drink him in. He's not just cute like the other guy. He's hot. He has dark brown hair and equally dark eyes that lift the smallest amount at the corners. He's Hispanic. Not Mexican, though. His jaw line is sharp. His brows angular. Not Brazilian like me either.

Honduran, maybe Guatemalan if I had to guess. Latin American for sure, there's a little too much indigenous in his features to be Spaniard but I don't bother asking to confirm.

Dressed in low-slung jeans and a form-fitting black shirt, it does nothing to hide his muscular body. He's most likely an athlete. No surprise there. He definitely has the confident swagger of one.

I force my feet to stay rooted as he towers over my tiny frame. He's much taller than me, maybe six feet. I have to tilt my head back to meet his stare, and a part of me itches to reach up on tiptoe and close the distance between our mouths, the blond boy all but forgotten thanks to his arrival.

My chest rises and falls with each of my breaths. My heart suddenly eager to beat out of my chest. I've never reacted to a boy like this. It's...intoxicating.

The corners of his lips quirk as if he knows exactly what I'm thinking and more surprising, he acts, closing the space between our lips, his mouth pressing firmly against mine. I gasp and he takes full advantage, his tongue exploring my mouth as the taste of sweet oranges and chili explodes across my tastebuds. I moan into his mouth, unable to stop my reaction to him. Man, can he kiss.

One of his hands grips my hip, the other tangles in my curly hair as he pulls me closer, our bodies pressed tight against one another and everything else around me disappears.

Hoots and hollers to get a room cut through the fog of desire and I pull back, breaking the kiss. He releases me with obvious reluctance, his hand still firmly on my hip and a stunned expression on his face.

I'm breathing heavy, my heart racing. That was...I don't know what the hell that was, but I've never been kissed like that. Never felt the need to clench my thighs together and curl my toes. Was it the same for him? I swallow hard and chew on my bottom lip. His gaze locks on my mouth and he licks his lips, my eyes tracking the movement. My hand reaches up almost as if it has a mind of its own, and my fingers curl into the fabric of his shirt needing to ground myself.

"You still want pretty boy over there?" he asks, tilting his head toward...what was his name?

I shake my head. Hell, no. I want him. This guy right here. If I'm going to lose my virginity to anyone, it should be him. Someone who makes me feel lightheaded after just one kiss.

"Good."

Without another word he reaches for my hand and tugs on me to follow as he weaves his way through the crowd, heading toward what I think is a pool house. "Where are we going?" I ask, my voice coming out a little breathless, my lips still tingling from our kiss.

"Somewhere quiet," he says over his shoulder and I notice he's clutching his side and there's a stiffness to his gate.

Is he okay?

I'm suddenly nervous. We're going somewhere quiet which is good. Right? It's what I want only I don't even know this guy. Then again, that is kind of the point of tonight. Only... God. Come on, Bibiana. Stop being such a worrier.

Reaching the pool house, he opens the door and we both slip inside. The room is dark, some outside light filtering in through the sheer curtains. He drags me toward a sofa and sits, a soft hiss escaping his lips before he tugs me down beside him.

"Are you alright?"

The room is silent except for our breathing. I sit stiffly beside him, my fingers still laced with his as my eyes adjust to the darkness. His thumb rubs lazy circles across the back of my hand, then he shifts to face me.

"Just a sports injury. No big deal."

I purse my lips. It's summer. Sports have ended for the year. I guess it's possible some practice over the summer months. I think football does maybe, but...

"Hey." He pulls me closer. "Come here."

He tugs me onto his lap, my thighs straddling his waist. His length presses against my core and I'm barely able to restrain myself from grinding against him.

He trails a finger along the side of my face, down my neck and settles it along the hollow of my throat. There's something strangely intimate about the caress. "What's your name?"

I hesitate.

"You holding back on me, mariposa?" I was right. Definitely Hispanic. His smile is both savage and sinful. There's this energy to him that draws me in, but it also terrifies me. This is supposed to be a one-night thing. Good memories and a fun time, but nothing more. No attachments. But there's something about him that tells me he's someone I'd find myself easily attached to. It's a good thing I'm only in Sun Valley for one more night. Wouldn't want to become one of what I'm sure are his many admirers.

"Hardly, just, why not keep this interesting?" I suggest as casually as possible.

He raises a brow, shadows cast across his face from the moonlight filtering through the room. "You don't wanna exchange names?" If anything, his grin widens.

I shake my head.

"What about phone numbers?" he asks, cocking his head to the side.

Another shake.

He chuckles. "Damn, mariposa. And here I thought I was the player."

If he only knew just how inexperienced I was. Stepping into the role I've set out for myself, I rock my hips against him and he hisses, his eyes glazing over with lust. "You're playing a dangerous game, mariposa."

"Why do you keep calling me a moth?" I ask, a breathy quality to my voice.

He leans forward, nipping at the column of my throat. "Not a moth. A butterfly," he murmurs. His hands find my hips and he presses me down against him, his hips thrusting upward to grind against my center. Electricity crackles between us. He tilts my chin, drawing my lips to his and fusing them together. Stars explode behind my closed lids and every rational thought in my mind floats away.

The more he kisses me, the drunker I am on his taste, and the more I want to throw caution to the wind. This feels good. Right. I don't even know him, but somehow, my body does. It craves him, silently begging for me.

His fingers dig into me, his erection hot between my legs. I weave my fingers through the short strands of his hair, pressing my chest against his, but it isn't enough. His kiss is drugging, pulling me deep into an abyss I have zero desire to escape. When his hands slip beneath the hem of my dress, tugging it over my ass and then my head, bearing me to his dark and hungry gaze, I offer no resistance.

His eyes grow hooded as he lasers in on my chest, a hand coming up to thumb over one taught nipple. I shiver and he grins. The satisfied smile of a boy who knows the effect he has on a girl. He leans forward, capturing my breast in his hot mouth, his teeth grazing my nipple as I rock against him. My body aching and desperate for more friction.

Between kisses, I tug off his shirt. Unbutton his jeans. It takes next to no time for the two of us to find ourselves naked, clawing at one another's skin and he wastes zero time in retrieving a condom from his discarded jeans pocket and rolling it on before pulling me down on top of him and lining himself up with my core.

A part of me wonders if I should say something. Let him know I'm a virgin. I've heard the stories. I know there is usually pain the first time. But I can't convince myself to ruin this moment. I want this. Unequivocally and desperately. I want this.

His cock nudges my entrance and I stiffen, bracing myself for what's to come. His hard, thick length pushes inside of me with slow and measured thrusts. I gasp at the sensations as he stretches me to my limits, to the point where pleasure merges with the sharp bite of pain.

"Fuck, you're tight," he hisses between clenched teeth.

My fingers dig into his shoulders as I seat myself on him. And when I feel that edge of resistance, that last layer of innocence I'm determined to stamp out, I don't let myself think about it. I suck in a breath, steel myself, and press my hips down until he's fully inside of me, pushing past the pain and focusing only on the pleasure.

He groans and slams his mouth against my own, consuming my cries and filling me up until I don't know where I end and where he begins. "Your name, mi pequeña mariposa?" he prompts when I pull back to catch my breath. My little butterfly.

I ignore the question, chasing his mouth instead and shifting my weight on his shaft. A breath hisses between his teeth, but he holds me steady. "You're a virgin."

It isn't a question, so I don't bother responding. Instead, I do the only thing I can—no, the only thing I need—and move.

I rise above him until only the tip of his shaft remains inside me before sinking back down with deliberate slowness.

He drops his head back on the sofa, his Adam's apple bobbing in his throat. "Fuck, what are you doing to me?"

His voice is guttural, coated in desire and laced with hunger.

I repeat the movement twice more before he lifts me in his arms, standing to his full height, my legs wrapping around his waist. He walks us to a table, laying me back, our bodies never losing their connection.

"You're playing with fire," he cautions as he pulls out of me before flexing his hips and driving himself back in. Harder. Deeper. I writhe beneath him, uncertain if I'm desperate to get closer or trying to pull away.

My body is burning, my center slick with need as he thrusts into me again and again. Pressure builds inside of me making me needy and desperate for more. For all that he'll give. "Maybe I want to get burned."

He lifts one of my legs, drawing it up and over his shoulder as I hold the other tight, curled over his hip. His cock sinks deeper inside of me as he leans down, his mouth trailing wet kisses across my breasts, up my throat, and to my lips. He hits a deeper angle in this position. Every thrust and every pivot of his hips elicits new sensations.

The pressure inside of me continues to build until I'm spinning, unable to tell up from down. My visions blurs, stars explode behind my eyelids and my body jerks, jolts of pleasure spear through me without warning. He swallows down my cries until they become little more than whimpers and mewls, leaving me breathless and my body boneless.

My chest heaves. My body is slick with sweat and he's still rock-hard inside of me. There's something primal in the way he's looking at me right now. His hungry stare drinking in my sweat-slicked skin and thoroughly fucked gaze.

"You shouldn't have given me your innocence," he says, a fierce glint in his eyes. "I'm going to ruin you for any man who comes after me."

I bite my lower lip. Thank God I'm leaving tomorrow. This boy could easily become an addiction. This moment, these feelings, it's more than I imagined. More than I ever anticipated. And a hell of a lot more than I'm ready for. But to hell with it.

"Do your worst." I tell him.

His eyes flash. "Burn for me, mariposa. Burn."

Bibiana - 18 months later...

I'm anxious. More anxious than I should be. I try on half a dozen shirts, hating all of them before I settle on a basic, long-sleeved, black t-shirt and an oversized hoodie, resigned to the fact that today just isn't my day. None of my clothes look right on a body that doesn't feel like it's mine anymore. It's been nine months. And while I've managed to drop most of the weight, I'm still...different.

My breasts are larger. My hips wider. I'm soft in places that were once firm and I just...I exhale a loud breath. I've changed. And not just on the outside. Clothes can only hide so much. There are times like now when I feel like an imposter trapped inside my own body.

Luis chooses that moment to wake, and I silently curse myself for my little outburst. Rushing over to his crib that's positioned beside my bed, I lean down to pick him up, rocking him in my arms while making soft cooing sounds. A quick glance at the clock shows me I need to leave in fifteen minutes. If I'm late for my first day of school, so be it. Luis is more important, and I cherish these moments when it's only the two of us so much.

He's nine months old now, and my days of nursing my sweet little boy are numbered, especially with going back to school. I planned on getting my GED when we returned to Sun Valley, knowing Suncrest Academy would never take me back, but the public high school decided they'd accept my online alternative school credits. Surprisingly, I'm not as far behind as I thought, so I'll have the pleasure of attending Sun Valley High. *Yay*. Can you sense my sarcasm?

If I survive the last six months of senior year, I get to graduate. Mom thinks it'll be good for me. To find a sense of normalcy and be a teenager again. As if it's that easy. The thought of leaving Luis, even just for classes, is a hard pill to swallow. In such a short amount of time, this little boy has become my entire universe.

I sigh and hug him close as he nurses. These moments are special. I know that. And despite having his face memorized, I still get lost staring into his eyes and have to stifle a smile at how unlike me my own son looks. His eyes are a dark rich brown unlike my cerulean blue. His hair a softer shade of chestnut than my raven black. He even has his father's full lips and straight brows that make him look like he's scowling more often than not.

But he's precious, and he's mine.

A pang of regret hits me in the chest when I think of how he might never know his father, who might never have him to show him how to throw a football or work on a car. I want those things for my son. I want him to grow up with two parents who love him. He deserves the full package. But...I don't know who his father is. Not by name. And a physical description doesn't get you very far.

When I found out I was pregnant, I had no way of finding the boy I gave a piece of myself to. No way of letting him know he was about to become a dad. All I know about him is that he lived in Sun Valley. And when I told Mom as much after those two little pink lines appeared, she decided it was for the best to just forget all about him.

A thrum of nervous energy courses through me at the possibility of seeing him again. Every time I leave the house, I scan the faces of the people around me, hoping for a glimpse of the boy who inadvertently changed my life forever.

He said he'd ruin me for any man who came after him. He wasn't lying. Even after all this time, I still think back to that night. To the way he made me feel. Maybe I've built it up in my mind. I don't know. But what I do know is that he left a mark. I realized that even before I found out I was pregnant.

Luis finishes nursing and I make quick work of burping him and changing his diaper before picking out his outfit for the day—a pair of soft black cotton pants and a red onesie—and head to the kitchen where I know my mother is waiting for me.

She sees me as soon as I step into the room, and her smile brightens when she catches sight of Luis in my arms. "Oh, he's awake." She holds her arms out. "Come to Grandma, a*morzinho*," she coos. My little love. I can't help my smile. She used to call me that when I was a little girl.

Luis pulls away from her at first. He can be clingy when he first wakes up, but after a few more softly spoken words and some bribery in the form of a banana, he relents.

Handing him to her, I grab a *pão de queijo*—a baked cheese roll, just as a honk outside alerts me that my ride is here.

"There's breastmilk in the freezer and I have my phone on me. If he gets too fussy. I can always—"

"Go, Bibiana. We'll be fine," my mom tells me. I hesitate for a moment before the sound of the horn again jerks me into motion. I give Luis a kiss on the cheek, grab my breakfast, and head for the door. "Call me if—"

"Yes. I know, *minha filha*. I raised you, and you turned out fine. Stop worrying. Go. Have fun."

Fun isn't the word I would use to describe high school, but I keep my feelings to myself and hurry outside.

Jaejun Yu—Jae for short—is standing in my driveway beside a sleek, cherry red Acura TLX. He grins when he looks up from his phone and realizes I'm there before he rushes around to the passenger side to open my door.

"Thanks." I offer him a tight smile and slide into the passenger seat, tucking my backpack between my legs on the floor as he jogs around the car to get back in. I hate when he does that. I know he's being chivalrous or whatever, but it still feels weird. Like it means something more than it should.

"You all set?" he asks, a smile on his too-handsome face. He leans forward and tucks a strand of my curly black hair behind my ear, lingering a second longer than he should before settling back in his seat. "You look beautiful, Bibi."

I fight my grimace and mutter out a thank you as I buckle my seat belt.

Don't get me wrong, Jae is great. He's kind and handsome and he's always there to lend a helping hand like right now, taking me to school when he doesn't even go to Sun Valley High. He isn't even in high school. He graduated two years ago, so why he insists on driving me and wasting his time when I know he has classes at Suncrest U that he'll be late for baffles me.

I sound ungrateful. I should probably work on that. It's just that Jae tries really hard. All the time. We met at one of my mom's boyfriend's—Miguel's—work events and we sort of hit it off. But in the let's be best friend's way, not the I want to date you way. I thought we were on the same page, but the more and more we're around one another, I get the feeling that we're not.

I have no idea why he's even remotely interested in me. He's interning with Miguel's security firm while he finishes his degree, and he has his entire life laid out in front of him. Everything meticulously planned to ensure success.

He even has his own townhouse at twenty. He bought it when he was eighteen as an investment property shortly after graduation. Even as a teenager he had a plan. He's smart. Responsible. Has a good head on his shoulders and probably has health insurance.

Meanwhile, I'm an eighteen-year-old single mom with zero plans for my future beyond making it to graduation. I want to do something with my life, sure. But I'm still very much in survival mode here. I don't have the mental capacity to focus on anything or anyone beyond school and Luis and, let's be honest, he could do so much better than me.

Mom likes to nudge me in his direction every chance she gets, but...I sigh. I'm not ready for that.

Jae's an exotic kind of good-looking. Half Korean and half Italian, he has hazel eyes and dark brown hair worn long on top in a bun and shaved on the sides. He turns more than a few heads when he enters a room, and there is zero question as to why. His cheekbones are high and sharp, his jawline angular, and there's just something striking about him that makes it hard to look away.

But I don't have time for a relationship. And even if I did, I'm not sure I want one. No matter how much my mother pushes or how much I try to convince myself that I should give him a chance, I'm not ready to jump back on that particular horse. With my luck, the next person I sleep with will get me pregnant too. I snort. Okay, probably not thanks to the wonderful IUD I got after Luis was born, but still. Accidents happen and while I wouldn't trade Luis for anything in the world, my days of being reckless are over. No more unplanned pregnancies for me, thank you very much.

I haven't been with anyone since Luis's father. Pathetic, I know. I get one night of incredibly reckless sex only to become a spinster afterward. It's unfair. I grit my teeth and silently curse him. Thinking back on that night all this time later, my skin still prickles with heat, my body still desperate and longing for him. It's naive of me to think one day our paths will cross again. I know that. But it doesn't stop me from looking. The little girl inside of me still believes in fairy tales regardless of how stupid it sounds. I think a teeny, tiny piece of me will always wonder what would happen if I saw him again? If he knew about Luis?

It's not like I owe him my fidelity or anything but ... I don't know. A part of me feels like the idea of pursuing something with anyone else would be a betrayal.

It's been eighteen months since Monique and I crashed a Sun Valley Party, and unless he was a lot older than he looked and already graduated, there is a chance he still goes to Sun Valley High.

If he does, I'm going to find him. And if he doesn't, maybe I'll finally be able to put that night behind me.

Continue Reading and grab your copy of *Savage Devil*!
https://hi.switchy.io/SavageUS

And if you're curious about Allie's friends from Richland, be sure to check out The Savage, Book 1 in the Boys of Richland series. https://amzn.to/3AV8ijI

Wicked Devil Playlist

Miedo by Leroy Sanchez
The End if Where we Begin by Thousand Foot Krutch
I Hate This by Tenille Arts
Grey by Grey Area ft Sofia Carson
There's No Way by Lauv ft. Julia Michaels
Without You by Breaking Benjamin
Now or Never by Halsey
Here Tonight by Brett Young
Let Me Go by April Lavigne featuring Chad Kroeger
I Love You by Billie Eilish
Despues que te perdi by Jon Z and Enrique Iglesias
Hold me while you wait by Lewis Capaldi
Perfect by Hedley
Issues by Julia Michaels
Lovely by Billie Eilish and Khalid
The part that hurts the most by Thousand Foot Krutch
Your Guardian Angel by The Red Jumpsuit Apparatus
Till it happens to you by Lady Gaga

Only you by Zara Larsson
In my blood by Shawn Mendes
Lento by Lauren Jauregui
Falta amor by Sebastian Yatra and Ricky Martin
Little Do you know by Alex & Sierra

About the Author

Daniela Romero is a USA Today and Wall Street Journal bestselling author. She enjoys writing steamy, new-adult and paranormal romance that delivers an emotional roller coaster sure to take your breath away.

Her books feature a diverse cast of characters with rich and vibrant cultures in an effort to effectively portray the world we all live in. One that is so beautifully colorful.

Daniela is a Bay Area native though she currently lives in Washington State with her sarcastic husband and their three tiny terrors.

In her free time, Daniela enjoys frequent naps, binge reading her favorite romance books, and is known to crochet while watching television because her ADHD brain can never do just one thing at a time.

Stop by her website to find all the fun and unique ways you can stalk her. And while you're there you can check out some free bonus scenes from your favorite books, learn about her Patreon, order signed copies of her books, and swoon over her gorgeous alternative cover editions.

www.daniela-romero.com

You can join my newsletter by visiting
https://hi.switchy.io/VIP

A Glimpse inside my Head

This book is probably the single book I am most proud of and these characters will always hold a special place in my heart. For those unaware, prior to the release of Wicked Devil, I exclusively wrote Urban Fantasy. But, at the time of writing this, I was struggling with this feeling of helplessness, while our country and much of the world were rife with turmoil. It went beyond politics. There is a period in our history, within my lifetime, where I can confidently say that our administration made it okay to hate again, and I experienced what I can only assume was a deep sense of depression and hopelessness for the first time in my life.

I was being bombarded with that hatred as a Mexican-American every single day. It was on social media. It was in the news. It was in the streets of my conservative town where because you can speak more than one language, people tell you to "go back where you came from," when I was born right here in the US. Where I was being told that "we" were all drug dealers and criminals and that the US needed a wall to stay safe.

Relationships I once thought were unbreakable were crumbling because people couldn't view life through the lens of those around them. So many fiends and family didn't understand why Black Lives Matter as a movement didn't mean all lives didn't matter. Or that black lives mattered more. It simply meant Black Lives Matter too.

Many of my white friends and family saw movements like this as personal attacks, while my brown and black friends and family couldn't wrap their heads around the lack of understanding and the unwillingness from so many to even try to see things as they were. To recognize white privilege for what it is, and to separate that from socio-economic privilege. That having white-privilege didn't make you a bad person. Or a good person. It was just an acknowledgment that because of the color of your skin, you do not face the same struggles.

Then Blue Lives Matter became a thing. And don't even get me started on that because while I have the utmost respect for our men and women in blue, at the end of the day, it's a t-shirt. They can put it on and take it off. A black or brown person does not have that luxury and even that fact is still difficult for some people to wrap their heads around.

So, through all this, the idea for Wicked Devil, my very first contemporary romance book, was born. Dominique's scene with Allie is actually where it all started. I saw that scene so clearly in my head. I wanted it to be the scene where people who could never before relate to racism could feel, even if only for a moment, what that fear and anger and devastation is like. When you're faced with racial profiling. When you aren't doing anything wrong. When someone who doesn't know anything about you has decided who and what you are, and how much your life is worth. And worse, when that individual is tasked with keeping the public, which includes people like you... safe. And they are, instead, the monster under your bed. The monster in your story who makes you nervous every time you hear their sirens. Not because you have done anything wrong, but because you already know it doesn't matter.

A friend of mine called me one day after reading Wicked Devil to tell me her entire body hurt. I smiled and said, "Good,"

I hope you felt something when reading this book. If you have experienced sexual assault, I hope reading beside Allie showed you how strong you are. That you are not simply a victim. And that it is okay to be broken. You just have to recognize that you won't be broken forever.

I know in books there is a level of fantasy where we always get the bad guy. But, in reality, we often don't. And I didn't want to sugar-coat that reality when it came to Allie. I wanted people to see how strong she is. I wanted her to realize that even without getting the bad guy, that she was going to be okay. That she could move on with her life. And that it's okay to lean on the people around you. To find comfort in your friends. And to know that there is always another tomorrow, and that if you allow them to, the cracks in your exterior will eventual mend.

Now, because this is fiction, we will in fact eventually get the bad guy. But you'll have to keep reading to see how it all unfolds.

Thank you again, from the bottom of my heart, for reading my story. I would be incredibly grateful if you took a moment to leave an honest review for the book, and I hope you have a terrific day and an even brighter tomorrow.

xoxo

Daniela Romero